IN THE DARK OF THE NIGHT

IN THE DARK OF THE NIGHT

AMANDA ASHLEY

In the Dark of the Night

Cover design by Cynthia Lucas

ISBN: 978-1-68068-230-4

This book is published on behalf of the author by the Ethan Ellenberg Literary Agency.

You can reach the author at:
Email: darkwritr@aol.com
Website: www.amandaashley.net OR www.madelinebaker.net

In the Dark of the Night

In a time of desperation, Lorena Halliday's father sold her into service to wealthy Lord Fairfield. After years of servitude and unwanted sexual advances, Lorena finds the courage to run away, only to be accosted by a man with a knife.

Standing on the roof of his home, Demetri witnesses the attack and goes to the young woman's rescue. After dispatching her assailant, Demetri takes the unconscious woman to an inn and procures a room for her, tucking her into bed. She is young and beautiful and her blood calls to him like no other.

Needing to see her again, Demetri returns to the inn and offers the lovely redhead a position in his home as his housekeeper. Desperate and with nowhere else to go, Lorena accepts. She soon discovers that her mysterious benefactor hides many secrets. Nevertheless, Lorena finds herself falling in love with a man who lives In the Dark of the Night.

DEDICATION

*Dedicated to all my readers
who are fascinated by dark, dangerous heroes.
I hope you'll love Demetri as much as I do.*

TABLE OF CONTENTS

CHAPTER ONE

Demetri stood atop the roof of the old manor house he
called home. Located in the small village of Woodridge
Township, it stood at the peak of a high plateau overlook-
ing the small seaside town below. All looked peaceful in
the light of the midnight moon, but with his preternatural
vision, he could see the footpads haunting the dark streets,
the night guards patrolling the wealthier part of town, the
drunks huddled in the alleys, bottles clutched like lovers to
their chests, the light skirts plying their age-old trade along
the wharf.

He frowned when he saw a young woman creeping down
one of the back streets. She stopped frequently to glance
over her shoulder. Even from a distance, he could see the
fear in her eyes. He rarely involved himself in mortal affairs,
but he found himself wondering who she was running from,
and why.

He leaned forward as a man wearing a black mask
stepped out of the shadows and trailed the woman. The
stalker caught up with the woman a block later. Catching
her around the throat, he slammed her up against the side
of a building.

Moonlight glinted off the knife in his hand.

Lorena let out a strangled cry as she tried to fight off her attacker, but to no avail. She couldn't stop staring at the knife in his hand, knew she was moments from death.

And then, from out of nowhere, another man appeared. At first, she feared he was in league with the first, until he jerked the knife from her assailant's hand and drove it deep into his chest.

Lorena stared at the second man, but it was too dark to see him clearly. Nor did it help that he was dressed in black from head to foot. All she saw before she fainted dead away was a pair of glittering red eyes.

Demetri caught the woman before she hit the garbage-littered street. Cradling her in his arms, he carried her swiftly to the nearest decent inn where he procured a room for her. He paid for a week in advance, then carried her up the stairs and put her to bed. She was a pretty thing. Her hair, dark red and curly, fell to her waist. Earlier, he had noticed that her eyes were gray, her lashes long and thick, her skin unblemished. He wondered again what she had been doing skulking through the dead of night.

The scent of her hair, her skin, the whisper of the rich, red blood flowing through her veins stirred his senses. Did she taste as good as he imagined? Bending down, he brushed her hair aside and gently sank his fangs into the slender curve of her throat, satisfying both his thirst and his curiosity.

Lorena came awake with a start, the remnants of last night's nightmare still fresh in her mind. She had been accosted in the street by a stranger wielding a knife, and then another man had appeared, seemingly out of nowhere and killed the first. She must have fainted then, because she didn't remember anything after that.

Sitting up, she glanced around. She was fully dressed, in an unfamiliar bed, in an unfamiliar room with no recollection of how she had gotten there.

Rising, she tiptoed to the door and opened it. A glance left and right showed a carpeted corridor with rooms on either side. An inn, she thought, someone had brought her to an inn. But who? And when? And why?

Brow furrowed, she made her way down the stairs, then stopped at the desk.

"Good morning, miss," the clerk said with a cheerful smile. "I'm glad to see you looking better this morning. How may I help you?"

"This may sound a little strange, but do you know who brought me here?"

"Why, no, miss. The gentleman didn't leave his name. I assumed…" He cleared his throat, his cheeks suddenly flushed. "That is, I, ah, assumed he was your husband."

"No. How much do I owe you for the room? I'm afraid I can't pay you right now but—"

"No need. The gentleman paid for a week's rent."

"He did?" Lorena shook her head. Why would a stranger do that?

"Yes, miss."

Nodding, she turned away from the desk. She had no money to pay for a room or for anything else. Not even a cup of tea, she thought, as her stomach rumbled in a most unladylike way.

Feet dragging, she returned to her room. Better to go hungry than go back to Fairfield Manor, she thought glumly.

She was trying to think of a way to earn enough money to pay for transportation out of town when there was a knock at the door. Frowning, she called, "Who is it?"

"Robert Carstairs. I'm the desk clerk."

Wondering what he could want, she opened the door.

"I … uh … thought you might like something to eat," he said, thrusting a cloth-covered tray into her hands.

Lorena stared at him.

"You don't have to pay me back," he said, the words coming out in a rush.

"I don't know what to say."

"No need to say anything. I've got to get back to the desk." And so saying, he turned and practically ran down the hall.

Lorena kicked the door closed with her heel, then carried the tray to the small table in the corner. Sitting down, she lifted the cloth, revealing two poached eggs, a thick slice of ham, toast and marmalade, as well as a cup of tea. Bless the boy!

She hadn't eaten since yesterday and it took all her self-control not to gobble her food like some hungry street urchin.

When she was finished, she sat back, wondering how long she would be able to hide from the monster who owned her body and soul. Lord Fairfield was a powerful man. A wealthy man. Sooner or later, he would find her and drag her back to Fairfield manor.

Blinking back her tears, she crawled into bed and sought forgetfulness in blessed sleep.

Demetri rose with the setting of the sun. He washed quickly, combed his hair, and dressed, strangely eager to see the woman he had rescued last night. She didn't look like a harlot, she hadn't been wearing a wedding ring. Yet it was obvious she wasn't from the gentry, since he had found her creeping along a back alley. A thief, perhaps? Or a runaway?

No matter. He wanted to see her again.

He quickened his steps. If she had left the inn, it would take but little effort to track her down.

Lorena looked up when there was a knock at the door. Hand pressed to her heart, she took a deep breath, wondering who it could be. No one knew she was here, she thought. Perhaps it was Carstairs, kindly bringing her another meal. Her stomach growled as she padded to the door. It had been several hours since breakfast.

She was reaching for the latch when the door swung open. Her heart threatened to leap out of her chest when it wasn't Carstairs standing in the hallway, but a tall, broad-shouldered stranger with hair as black as the devil's breath and eyes as blue and dark as a midnight sky. "Who...who are you?" she squeaked. "What do you want?"

Uninvited, he stepped into the room and closed the door behind him. "I merely wished to see how you were faring this evening."

Taking a wary step backward, she stared at him. His voice was like dark velvet, tinged with an accent she didn't recognize.

"I see you do not remember me. I came to your rescue last night."

"Oh. I...thank you. If you've come to collect for the room, I'm afraid I can't repay you."

Smiling wryly, he shook his head. "I am not in need of your money."

Lorena took another step back, her arms crossing protectively over her breasts. "What do you want?"

"Not what you are thinking."

"What, then?"

Demetri lifted one shoulder and let it fall. "I have not yet decided." He glanced around the room. It was small and clean. The table in the corner held the remains of a morning meal. He wrinkled his nose against the lingering stink of cooked meat and eggs. "What are you running from?"

"I'm not running from anything," she exclaimed with a defiant tilt of her chin.

"You are a poor liar."

She puffed up like a ruffled hen. "How dare you!"

He shook his head. "I can smell a lie at a hundred paces."

She glared at him. Then, shoulders slumped, she sat on the edge of the bed, hands tightly folded in her lap. "I ran away from the man who owns me."

"Owns you?"

"Some years ago, my father lost a great deal of money on several bad investments. When he couldn't pay his debts, he sold me to one of his creditors to pay the mortgage on our home and keep food on the table." Even though she understood her father's reasoning, she had never got over the hurt. Never seen her mother or her sisters since that awful night.

Demetri swore under his breath. Selling a child wasn't an unusual occurrence. He knew it happened all the time. Why it bothered him now was beyond his comprehension. "Shall I kill him for you?"

"What? No! Of course not!"

He shrugged. "How are you called?"

"Lorena."

His assessing gaze moved over her from head to heel. "And your surname?"

"Halliday."

"Come along, Miss Halliday," he said, reaching for her hand. "I have need of a housekeeper."

"But... I don't know anything about you. Not even your name."

"I am Demetri. That is all you need to know."

She stared up at him. He was an austere man. Judging by the cut of his clothes and his imperious manner, he was obviously a man of good breeding and accustomed to giving orders. Some might call him handsome, with his clean-cut features but she found him quite frightening. Still, she shuddered at the thought of going back to Lord Fairfield's estate and fighting off his unwanted advances—advances that had grown more frequent and increasingly more intimate since his wife's passing a few months ago.

"Shall we?"

She stared at Lord Demetri's outstretched hand. Some said better the devil you know, but she didn't agree. Hoping she wasn't making a dangerous, perhaps fatal, mistake, she put her hand in his and let her new employer pull her to her feet. For better or worse, her fate was now in his hands.

CHAPTER TWO

Lorena stared at her new home as she stepped from the carriage. Lord Demetri's house, built of gray stone, sat on the top of the hill that overlooked the town. It was a magnificent old place, even more impressive than that of Lord Fairfield.

Following Demetri inside, she glanced around the front parlor. Lord Fairfield's house was large, filled with costly items, but they paled in significance when compared to that of Lord Demetri. The furniture, upholstered in muted tones of gold, white, and sage green was exquisite, the carpets the most beautiful she had ever seen. Having lived in Lord Fairfield's house, she knew that the half-dozen pictures on the wall had been painted by some of the Old Masters. A curio cabinet filled with an assortment of ebony and jade figurines stood alongside the fireplace. All were lovely, though she found it odd that they all depicted creatures of myth and legend—trolls and mermaids, angels and demons, and what she guessed was a werewolf.

Drawing her attention from the cabinet, she risked a look in her new master's direction. What did he expect of her?

As if reading her mind, he said, "I need a housekeeper. The last one left…abruptly. You may have full run of the house. I will provide you with clothing and nourishment and a generous allowance, in exchange for which you will look after the house and do whatever else I require. Are we agreed?"

"Yes, my lord."

"The bedrooms are upstairs. Mine is at the end of the hall on the right. You may take whichever of the others you prefer."

"What time do you wish to take your meals?"

"I dine out."

"So, you don't require me to cook for you?"

"No. And I am rarely in residence during the day. However, I shall expect you to be at my disposal in the evening."

She nodded. He was an odd duck. Never home during the day. Taking all his meals out. She couldn't fathom why he needed a full-time housekeeper when he could easily hire someone to come in once or twice a week to clean. But she wasn't about to argue. It would be wonderful to have this magnificent house all to herself until nightfall, with no one to order her about, or make demands on her person that she found abhorrent and degrading.

"Do you have need of anything?" he asked.

Lorena glanced down at her attire. Lord Fairfield had provided her with three dresses—one brown, one dark green, one a hideous shade of yellow. All were made of cheap cotton. Finding her voice, she said, "I should like a new frock if you have no objection."

He grunted softly as his gaze moved over her. "At the moment, business calls me away. Make yourself at home. I will take you to the dressmaker tomorrow night."

A low bow in her direction and he left the house.

Lorena stared after him, her brow furrowed, confused by the way he treated her. Not as a friend, certainly, but not as a servant, either.

Feeling a chill in the room, she scrubbed her hands up and down her arms. There was wood laid in the fireplace, matches on the mantel. She quickly lit a fire, then warmed herself in front of hearth for several minutes before she decided to go exploring. In addition to the front parlor, where guests were received, there was a back parlor for the family, a kitchen and a scullery.

A closed door adjacent to the parlor drew her curiosity and when she opened it, she discovered a large library. Floor-to-ceiling bookshelves flanked a large desk. A pair of comfortable-looking chairs covered in a dark blue-and gray stripe stood in front of the fireplace. A large, leaded window with damask draperies looked out on the side yard.

She found four bedrooms upstairs. The first three were sparsely furnished. None of them held any clothing or personal items. She picked the second one on the left simply because she liked the rose-flowered paper on the walls. A three-drawer chest, a bed with a mahogany head-and-foot-board, a small side table, and a padded rocking chair were the room's only furnishings.

Curious, she opened the door to the last room on the right. His room. Heavy drapes hung at the windows. Thick carpets covered the floor. The furniture—wardrobe, chest of drawers and nightstand—were oak. A dark spread covered the bed. The room was neat and clean but contained nothing of a personal nature—nothing that hinted at his likes or dislikes. The walls were bare. The top of the dresser held only a plain white bowl and pitcher.

The third floor held rooms for the servants. Between two of the rooms she saw a set of stairs she assumed led down to the kitchen. She was surprised he hadn't insisted she sleep up there.

Lorena frowned as she returned to the back parlor. The furniture here was less formal than that in the front parlor—a large sofa and two overstuffed chairs faced each other in front of a stone fireplace. A large painting of a windswept desert hung over the hearth. Silver candlesticks stood at either end of the mantel. A large Oriental carpet covered most of the floor.

For a man who lived in such a large house in the wealthier part of the town, he certainly lived frugally, she thought. It was none of her business, of course, but she couldn't help wondering where he spent his days and why his last housekeeper had quit.

Padding into the kitchen, she searched the larder and the cupboards, which were mostly bare, save for a set of inexpensive dishes and silverware, crockery, glassware, and a couple of pots. She counted herself lucky when she found half a loaf of bread on a shelf, as well as a pot of strawberry jam and a tin filled with tea. Another shelf held salt, pepper, and a few other spices.

With food and drink in hand, she headed up to the bedroom she had chosen. Sitting on the bed, she nibbled on the sandwich, praying that she hadn't made a mistake in coming here, that she hadn't traded one lecher for another.

It was after midnight when Demetri returned home. Lights shone through the front windows, both upstairs and down.

His nostrils filled with the woman's scent as soon as he entered the house. For a moment, he stood in the center of the floor drinking it in—the fragrance of her hair and skin, the heady temptation of her life's blood, the scent of the jam she had eaten before she'd gone to bed. An odd sensation stirred within him as he listened to the soft, even sound of her breathing.

As if drawn by an invisible string, he took the stairs two at a time, following her scent to one of the bedrooms.

She lay on her side, fully clothed. Her hair spread across the pillow like a splash of red ink. He stared at her for several moments. He had no idea why he had brought her home. There were scores of abused young women in the city. Had he been so inclined, he could have filled his home with dozens of them. Odd, he mused, that Lorena was the only one he had felt impressed to rescue.

Unable to resist the temptation, he moved closer to the bed, ran his knuckles over her cheek. Her skin was as smooth and soft as it looked.

Desire stirred deep within him and with it a yearning to taste her again. He fought it for a moment, but the need was too strong.

Like the shadow of death, he bent over her neck and took that which he could not live without.

CHAPTER THREE

Lorena woke feeling sluggish. Her dreams the night before had taken place in an odd world of shifting shadows where horned, red-eyed demons lurked around every bend in the road. There had been no hint of light or salvation, only endless darkness. Lord Demetri had not been there, but she had sensed him at every turn, waiting to pounce and devour her like a rabid, hungry wolf.

Tossing the covers aside, she padded into the water closet, then made her way down the stairs to the kitchen. A cup of tea and two slices of toast slathered with strawberry jam served as breakfast. If he took her shopping for a new wardrobe, as he had promised, would he also let her buy a few groceries? Or would he expect to use her allowance for food and drink?

What was she to do with the rest of her day? Wandering into the library, she perused the bookshelves. *David Copperfield, The Scarlet Letter, Moby Dick, Walden, Uncle Tom's Cabin, North and South, The House of Seven Gables,* and *Frankenstein* among dozens of others. Mixed in with the novels were numerous books on history and geography, philosophy, science and religion.

She finally decided on *The Man in the Iron Mask*. Settling in a corner of the sofa, she turned to page one and lost herself in the story of the rightful heir to the throne of England.

She woke to the sound of someone knocking on the back door. Laying the book aside, she made her way into the kitchen. "Who's there?"

"I have a grocery delivery for a Miss Halliday."

Curious, she opened the door a crack and peered outside.

A young man with shaggy brown hair stood there. Two large boxes were stacked beside him. "Miss Halliday?"

"Yes."

"Shall I carry these inside for you?"

Lorena bit down on her lower lip before she stepped back to allow him inside.

She stayed by the open door while he carried the groceries into the kitchen, breathed a sigh of relief, when, with a tip of his cap, he left the house.

After locking the door, Lorena opened the first box. She smiled in delight as she unwrapped one package after another, revealing, among other things, a freshly baked loaf of bread, a container of rich, creamery butter, a pot of marmalade, a dozen eggs, and a side of bacon. The second box held a round of cheese, a small bag of potatoes, as well as small sacks of corn, sugar and flour. More than enough food to fill the empty larder. More than enough to make up for her scant breakfast.

As the sun set, Lorena found herself constantly glancing at the clock on the mantel. Would her mysterious new employer be home that evening? He had said he would take her shopping for a new dress. To that end, she had bathed and washed her hair, reluctantly put on the well-worn frock that was her only garment. She wished she had thought to launder it earlier, but it was too late now. At least she was clean.

She had just finished supper when she heard the front door open. A moment later, Demetri strode into the back parlor. He loomed tall and dark and forbidding in the doorway. His very presence seemed to dwarf the room.

"I made an appointment for you at the dressmakers," he said. "Are you ready to go?"

Nodding, she followed him outside to where an elegant carriage awaited them.

To her mortification, Lord Demetri took her to visit the most exclusive dressmaker in town. She flushed under the knowing gaze of the proprietor, who obviously thought she was his mistress.

"I am Miss Tomlinson," the woman said, speaking to Lord Demetri. "How may I serve you?"

"This young lady requires a new wardrobe—a dozen dresses for every day, several gowns for evening, as well as undergarments, night wear, and whatever else she needs or wants."

"Yes, my Lord. Miss, if you will follow me, I'll take your measurements."

Lorena stared at Lord Demetri, who dismissed her with a wave of his hand.

Feeling ill at ease, she followed the other woman into the back of the shop.

Demetri paced the floor, a slow anger rising within him when he heard the derogatory way Miss Tomlinson spoke to Lorena.

When the two women emerged from the back some forty minutes later, Lorena's cheeks were flushed, her eyes cast down.

"Miss Tomlinson," he said, curtly. "May I have a word?"

"Of course, my Lord."

"If you speak to my charge in that tone of voice again, I will assume you no longer desire my business and I will take it elsewhere."

The tone of his voice, the look on his face, sent a shiver down Lorena's spine.

"I sincerely apologize for my lack of manners and for anything I might have said that offended her," the woman said tremulously. "Please, forgive me."

"Tell Miss Halliday," he said, his voice sharp. "Not me."

Red-faced, her hands clenched at her sides, the dress-maker repeated her apology.

Uncertain of how to respond, Lorena inclined her head.

"I should like two of the day dresses, night clothes, and a gown suitable for evening by tomorrow night," Demetri said. "Along with a hat and gloves and anything else a young lady requires."

"Yes, my lord."

"Do you have anything she can take now?" he asked. "What she's wearing is hardly suitable."

"Well…" Miss Tomlinson frowned. "I do have a rather lovely dress that would suit, but it was made for Lady Wallington."

"Make her another one."

Something in his tone drained the color from the woman's face. "Yes, my lord. Miss Lorena, please come with me."

Feeling chilled to the bone, Lorena followed the proprietor into the back room. When she emerged some fifteen minutes later, she was clad in a sky-blue day dress trimmed in antique lace. A matching hat sporting a jaunty feather perched atop her head.

"I hope this will do," Miss Tomlinson said, not meeting Demetri's eyes. "It's the only item I have in her size."

"It will do nicely. Come along, Lorena."

She followed him out of the shop and into the carriage that waited at the curb.

"Is there any place you would like to go?" Demetri asked as he handed her into the coach.

Lorena blinked at him. She was accustomed to taking orders. No one, including her own father, had ever asked—or cared—about what she wanted to do.

"I am talking to you, girl."

"I should like to have a cup of tea."

Demetri stared at her in disbelief. Woodridge, though small when compared to London, had a number of shops and entertainments and all she wanted was a cup of tea? After instructing the driver to take them to the best shop in the city, he joined her in the coach.

Lorena slid a sideways glance at Lord Demetri. He was a strange and frightening man. She wondered if anyone had ever dared to deny him anything he desired.

A short time later, the carriage pulled up in front of Miss Mavis' Tea Room. The driver opened the door, lowered the steps, and then backed away as Demetri descended. Turning, he offered Lorena his hand.

Feeling like a real lady in her new finery, Lorena placed her hand in his and alighted from the carriage. She had once overheard Lady Fairfield talking about this place. Never had she expected to see it for herself.

Lord Demetri held the door open before following her inside. It was a lovely room, all done in pink and white.

Beautiful women clad in beautiful clothes were accompanied by equally beautiful men.

Glancing around, Lorena noticed that several of the tables were occupied by two or three women. She had also overheard Lady Fairfield remark that a tea room was one of the few places a lady could go unchaperoned.

A hostess seated them at a small table laid with fine linen and silver and then handed them each a menu. Demetri set his aside.

Lorena looked at the choices, wondering how she would ever decide.

"Order anything you wish," he said.

"Anything?"

At his nod, she said, "I should like a custard tart and a cup of Earl Grey, please."

"Anything else?" he asked.

It was so very tempting, but she shook her head, afraid to ask for too much.

"Very well." Demetri relayed her order then sat back in his chair, regarding her through narrowed eyes.

She wondered why he didn't request anything for himself but lacked the courage to ask.

"How old were you when your father sold you?"

"Fourteen, my lord."

"And how old are you now?"

"Almost nineteen."

Naught but a child, he thought. "Who bought you?"

She bit down on her lower lip, afraid of repercussions if Lord Fairfield discovered she had betrayed him. He had warned her on numerous occasions that discussing how she came to be in his household would have serious consequences.

Demetri's gaze burned into hers. "You will tell me what I want to know."

"Lord Fairfield," she murmured, unable to resist the mesmerizing power in his eyes.

Demetri grunted softly. The man had a reputation as a notorious lecher. "Did he mistreat you?"

She stared at him, her cheeks flushed, her expression stricken.

"Tell me."

"I'd rather not."

"Tell me," he said again, though his voice was gentle now.

"He said things, made lewd suggestions. He touched me inappropriately when no one was looking. Then one night when Lady Fairfield was away, he took me to his room and tried to … to …" She couldn't say the words. "If one of the maids hadn't announced a late-night visitor, I don't know what he might have done. He was more careful after that. But then, three weeks ago, Lady Fairfield passed away." Uncomfortable under his regard, she stared at her hands. "The very next night, he tried to get me alone again. I told him I would scream if he laid a hand on me. I ran away the next night while he was at his club."

Lorena slid a sideways glance at Lord Demetri. Dressed all in black, his linen snowy-white, he was more handsome than any other man in the room, she thought, only then noticing the admiring glances he received from the three middle-aged women at a nearby table.

She felt a wave of relief when her tea and custard arrived. It gave her something to focus on besides the enigmatic man sitting across from her. Not knowing if or when he would bring her here again, she savored every bite.

Demetri watched her, intrigued by the girl in spite of himself. Young and vulnerable. And still untouched in spite of Fairfield's no doubt clumsy attempts to deflower her.

With some reluctance, Lorena finished her tea, wiped her mouth with her napkin, then folded it neatly and set it beside her plate.

"Are you ready to go?" Demetri asked. "Or would you like something else?"

Although she very much wanted another custard, she lacked the courage to ask for one.

Reading her thoughts, Demetri asked the waitress to wrap four to go.

After paying the check, and with the second order of tarts in hand, Demetri ushered her out of the shop, only to come to an abrupt halt when he saw Fairfield striding toward them.

Lorena saw him, too. With a gasp, she glanced around, searching for a place to hide.

But it was too late. Fairfield had seen her.

"There you are, you ungrateful chit," he growled as he grabbed her roughly by the arm and yanked her toward him. "Wait until I get you..."

"Take your hands off her," Demetri said, his voice quietly menacing.

"See here!" Fairfield exclaimed. "The chit belongs to me."

"Not anymore. She is mine now."

"How dare you defy me!"

Eyes narrowed, Demetri said, "I dare anything I wish."

Fairfield glanced around, aware that they were drawing the attention of passersby. Had it been anyone but Demetri, he would have argued, but he knew all too well the kind of man he was dealing with. There were any number of rumors about Demetri. None of them were flattering. All of them were true. "Very well," he blustered with as much dignity as he could muster. "Take her. She was scarcely worth the cost of her upkeep."

"A wise decision," Demetri said with a sneer. "Come along, my dear, our carriage awaits."

Heart pounding, Lorena hurried into the coach. Hunched in a corner, she tried to understand the odd tremor she had felt in the air when the two men confronted each other. It had obviously come from Demetri, judging by Lord Fairfield's reaction. Whatever it was, it had raised the hair on her arms and made her stomach clench. She knew Lord Fairfield had felt it, too, because she had never known him to back down in front of anyone. As a peer of the realm, he wielded his wealth and his title like a sword.

So, what had that mysterious, seemingly otherworldly, power been?

Whatever it was, she hoped never to experience it again.

She flinched when Lord Demetri stepped into the carriage and took the seat across from hers.

"Did he hurt you?" he asked, glancing at her arm.

"No."

Demetri grunted softly as he rapped on the roof of the carriage. A moment later, the coach lurched forward.

When they returned home, Lorena murmured a hasty good night and hurried up to her room, all too aware of Lord Demetri's gaze on her back. She was grateful that he had taken her in, grateful that he hadn't let Lord Fairfield take her away with him, and yet she couldn't help wondering if she might have been safer with Lord Fairfield. The mysterious power Demetri had exerted frightened her on some deep primal level she didn't understand. Was he some sort of warlock or magician that he could conjure such a thing?

She might have thought she had imagined it, but she had seen its effect, not only on Lord Fairfield but also on Miss Tomlinson, the dressmaker. She had no doubt it was real. Had Demetri's previous housekeeper experienced it, as well? Was that why she had abruptly resigned such a plum position?

With trembling hands, Lorena removed her shoes and undressed. She ran her hand over the blue gown before carefully hanging it in the wardrobe. Clad in her undergarments—and feeling vulnerable—she locked her door and then slid under the covers, only to lie awake, staring at the ceiling.

And wondering what manner of man was now her master.

Standing in front of the hearth, one hand braced against the mantel, Demetri followed his new housekeeper's movements in the room above. He sensed her confusion, the fear she tried to hide, her feelings of vulnerability at being alone in the house with a man who was, for all intents and purposes, not a man at all, though she did not yet realize it.

He supposed he could pretend to be a magician. No doubt the thought that his preternatural powers were merely magic tricks would put her mind at ease. In centuries past he had often presented himself as a mage, or a warlock. Both guises had served him well, since it was considerably easier—and safer—to live a lie rather than let the truth be known.

He drew a deep breath, inhaling the sweet fragrance of her skin and hair, the tantalizing scent of her life's blood. Young. Innocent. Vulnerable. Tempting to a man such as he on so many levels, he mused.

And his for the taking.

CHAPTER FOUR

She was walking through a long, twisting path in a dark forest. Tall, black trees rose on all sides, their branches entwined overhead, blocking out both moon and stars. An eerie silence rose from the silver-gray mist that swirled around her. She froze when she heard a low growl, took a hasty step back when a figure clad in an ebony cloak stepped into her path. Terror held her frozen in its grip as the creature closed the distance between them, its eyes glowing red in the darkness.

Unable to move, she could only stand there, her breath coming in harsh gasps, as the creature's lips peeled back, revealing fangs as white as new-fallen snow.

Galvanized by fear, she let out a shriek when the creature sank those sharp teeth into her throat…

Lorena woke with the sound of her own terrified cry ringing in her ears.

Clutching the blankets to her chest, she cast a frantic glance around the room.

Dark, so dark.

With hands that trembled, she found the matches and lit the oil lamp on the bedside table.

"Just a nightmare," she gasped, as pale-yellow light filled the room. "A nightmare, nothing more."

But it had seemed so real.

❧ ❧ ❧

Lorena's bad dream faded in the light of day. After breakfast, she found an apron and set to work doing what she had been hired to do—clean the house. She didn't know how long ago Lord Demetri's last housekeeper had left, but except for a fine layer of dust on the furniture, the rooms were reasonably clean. Still, for lack of anything better to do, she dusted upstairs and down and mopped the floors in the kitchen and the scullery. When that was done, she filled a large pot with water and put it on the stove. While waiting for it to heat, she washed the windows in the front parlor.

When the water was hot, she poured it into a large tub she found in the backyard, then stripped the sheets from her bed and carried them outside.

By the time they were clean and hanging to dry, it was time for supper. With one hand pressed to her aching back, she trudged into the parlor and sank down on the sofa. More tired than hungry, she closed her eyes and drifted off to sleep.

She woke to someone knocking on the door. Rubbing the sleep from her eyes, Lorena padded to the foyer. "Who's there?"

"Delivery for Miss Halliday from Madame Tomlinson."

"Oh!" Her dresses were here. She could hardly wait to see them. She quickly unlocked the door. A young man stood on the porch balancing five large, flat boxes. Two round hat boxes dangled by silken cords from his wrists.

"Miss Halliday?"

"Yes."

With a nod, he thrust the boxes into her arms, dropped the hat boxes on the floor and quickly retreated down the path toward a small horse-drawn wagon.

Lorena stared after him. What was the lad so afraid of, she wondered. Surely not her, and yet it had been blatantly obvious he had wanted to finish his business and be gone as soon as possible.

Still puzzled by his strange behavior, Lorena closed the door. Sitting on the floor, with boxes scattered around her, she forgot all about the boy as she opened them one by one. She had picked out the colors and fabrics for the new frocks but she'd no idea how they would look when made.

The first box yielded a mauve-and-white striped day dress with puffed sleeves, a V-neck, and a flared skirt. The second was of a similar cut of pale green with a white collar and cuffs and a dark green sash.

She pressed a hand to her heart when the third box revealed a shockingly low-cut evening gown of pale-blue silk. Almost reluctantly, she ran her fingertips over the material, unable to believe it was hers.

The fourth box contained a long, white sleeping gown of fine lawn and several pairs of convent-made drawers, some trimmed with lace, some with ruffles.

The last box contained a corset, three petticoats, a chemise, gloves, and stockings. Frowning, Lorena held up the corset. She had never worn one, never needed one under the shapeless dresses Lord Fairfield had given her. She shook her head as she dropped the corset into the box. Even if she wanted to wear the uncomfortable-looking thing, she had no one to lace her into it.

The other two boxes contained hats trimmed and decorated to match the dresses.

She sat there for a long while, running her fingertips over the bounty spread before her. Never in her life had she expected to have so many lovely things.

Suddenly eager to try on her new clothes, she heated another pot of water, took a quick sponge bath when it was hot, then piled the boxes one on top of the other and hurried upstairs.

The new underwear felt wonderful against her skin, the dresses were beautiful, although she felt she might need the corset for the silk gown. The hats were precious.

She put on the mauve dress, then carefully hung the other clothes in the wardrobe, placed the hats in their boxes on the shelf, folded the underwear and stockings and put them in the chest of drawers, along with the gloves. The only things missing were shoes.

For a moment, she pondered what her next task should be. Scrubbing the kitchen sink in her new dress was out of the question. And since she wasn't yet ready to take it off, she decided her other chores could wait until tomorrow. Gathering her old dress, underwear, and apron, she dropped them in the hamper and made her way downstairs.

In the kitchen, she fixed herself a cup of tea, collected her book from the library and padded into the front parlor. For the rest of the afternoon, she would pretend she was the lady of the manor instead of merely the hired help.

Demetri rose with the setting of the sun. Though he spent his waking hours in the manor house, he kept his lair in a room below the basement. Until Lorena came to live in the house, the only thing in his lair had been a large brass bed. Now, he kept several changes of clothes, a bowl and pitcher, and a barrel of water for emergencies. In actual fact, he had no need for any of the creature comforts that mortals could not live without. His only needs were the human blood necessary for his survival and a safe, secure place to pass the daylight hours.

Transporting himself to his rooms in the manor, he bathed and donned clean clothes. And all the while, he was aware of the tantalizing sound of the woman's heartbeat, the velvet whisper of the warm, crimson river flowing through her veins, and the arousing scent of the woman herself.

His desire for her grew stronger as he descended the stairs to the front parlor. He paused in the doorway. She had fallen asleep on the sofa, her lips slightly parted. The book she had been reading had tumbled to the floor.

She looked like a storybook princess lying there. His gaze moved over her, resting on the swell of her breasts, the curve of her neck, the pulse throbbing in the hollow of her throat. Candlelight spilled softly over her cheeks and cast gold highlights in the rich, red fall of her hair. He noted she was wearing a new dress. It had been money well-spent, he thought.

He had not yet fed and as he listened to the slow, steady beat of her heart, his hunger grew stronger. As his need intensified, the sound of her beating heart seemed to grow louder and louder, until it was all he could hear.

His fangs brushed his tongue as he took a step toward her.

He stopped abruptly when she woke with a start. Eyes wide, she bolted upright. "Was there something you required, my lord?"

Looking away from her, Demetri took a deep breath, blew it out in a long, shuddering sigh. In control again, he shook his head. "Forgive me for disturbing you."

"Are you sure I can't get you anything? A glass of wine, perhaps?"

He nodded, though it wasn't wine he craved, but the warm, scarlet nectar that flowed beneath her skin.

Scrambling to her feet, Lorena hurried into the kitchen. She stood there a moment, blinking rapidly, telling herself she had imagined that faint red glow in his eyes.

When she returned to the parlor, he was gone.

Demetri paced the floor in Sir Everleigh's library, damning the woman, damning his own infernal hunger.

"Please, my friend, slow down before you wear a hole in my lovely new Turkish carpet."

Huffing a sigh, Demetri slumped into the chair across from the only man in the city he trusted. Everleigh was a tall, spare man with brown eyes, a shock of iron-gray hair and a bushy mustache. A widower, he shared his lavish estate with his older sister, Beatrice, who was confined to a wheelchair, and a small household staff.

"I'm sorry, Everleigh," Demetri muttered, "but the woman in my house is slowly driving me insane."

Everleigh laughed softly. "I have never seen you so hopelessly entranced by a woman. Why not have your way with her and be done with it?"

"She is too young. Too innocent. Too…" Demetri shook his head. "I want her as I have wanted no other woman in my life. And yet she frightens me."

"You? Afraid?" Everleigh scoffed. "I do not believe it. You are the most powerful being in the country. What have you to be afraid of?"

Lowering his gaze, Demetri murmured, "Only myself."

"Ah, my old friend," Everleigh said sympathetically. "Now I understand."

It had been a mistake to bring Lorena into his home, Demetri thought. It had taken him centuries to learn to control his hunger and now it was about to be undone by one young female with the soul of an angel and the body of a temptress. He should send her away as soon as he returned home. Keeping her with him would likely be his undoing. Or hers.

And even as he contemplated sending her away, he knew he lacked the will to do so.

"Can I offer you a glass of port?" Everleigh asked.

"Yes, thank you."

Reaching for the decanter on the ebony table beside him, Everleigh filled two crystal goblets and passed one to Demetri.

"Wine and women," his host said with a crooked smile. "Both are hard to live without."

Nodding in agreement, Demetri stared at the wine in his glass. A rich, sweet, ruby red, it reminded him of blood, something else he couldn't live without. He wondered what Lorena had thought when she returned with his drink and found him gone.

"I'm having a birthday ball for Beatrice tomorrow night," Everleigh said. "I know it's short notice, but why don't you come? I would love to meet the young woman who has you tied in knots. Besides, it will do you good to get out."

"You think so?"

"I know so. I shall expect you tomorrow night," Everleigh said with a grin. "Just promise me you won't dine on any of my guests."

Demetri took his leave a short time later. He had expected to find that Lorena had gone to bed in his absence. Instead, she was in the back parlor doing a bit of needlework. He shrugged out of his coat and removed his gloves. He had no need for either and wore them only for appearance's sake. Tossing them onto a chair, he poured himself a glass of wine.

"How was your day?" he asked, taking the chair across from the sofa.

"Uneventful, my lord. How was yours?"

"Quiet. Are you pleased with your new wardrobe?"

"Oh, yes," she murmured.

"We have been invited to a birthday celebration tomorrow night," he said. "It will give you an opportunity to wear another of your new gowns."

Lorena stared at him. "A celebration?" What was he thinking? She was his servant, not a highborn lady of the realm.

He didn't ask if she wanted to go, merely said, "Be ready at eight. And don't tell me you have nothing to wear."

It wasn't an invitation, she thought, but a command. She knew a moment of excitement followed by a wave of apprehension. Clothing was the least of her worries. She didn't know how to dance, or how to engage in light conversation with strangers, or how to comport herself in the company of highborn men and women.

"I'll be ready, my lord," she said reluctantly. "Now, if you don't need me for anything, I should like to retire."

Demetri waved his hand in dismissal, one brow raised in amusement as she practically bolted from the room.

Foolish child, to run away, he mused. It was all he could do not to pursue her.

CHAPTER FIVE

In the morning, Lorena was still fretting over Lord Demetri's invitation when someone knocked at the door. She opened it to find Madame Tomlinson's delivery boy standing on the porch, his arms again laden with boxes.

"Bring them inside, please," Lorena said.

"No, ma'am, not on yer life," he exclaimed. With alacrity, he dropped the boxes in the entry hall, paused briefly to take a quick into the parlor beyond, then turned and raced down the stairs.

What on earth was he so afraid of? With a shake of her head, Lorena closed the door.

Thinking it was getting to be a pleasant past time, she sat on the floor in the middle of the floor, once again surrounded by boxes. It was better than Christmas, she thought, as she opened box after box. Never in her life had she expected to own so many wonderful clothes, and not just dresses, hats, and gloves, but another exquisite gown, this one of pale green silk with a high waist, fitted sleeves and a slim skirt. There was also another sleeping gown, robe, and slippers, as well as enough underwear for two changes a day. The last three boxes held two pairs of shoes and a pair of kid half-boots. Odd, she didn't remember trying on shoes, though she recalled thinking that footwear was the only thing they had neglected to order. More surprising was the fact that they fit perfectly.

She might be a servant, Lorena thought, trailing her fingers over the fashionable bounty spread before her, but thanks to Lord Demetri's generosity, her attire tonight was likely to be as fine as any worn by the richest ladies of the town.

The day passed all too quickly. Lorena was all aflutter by the time she bathed and dressed for the party. She wished she knew how to arrange her hair in one of the styles so popular with the upper class, but she had to no one to help her and no mirror in the house by which to judge the results, so she simply pulled it back into a chignon. She had to make do with peering at her reflection in a window to see how she looked before leaving her room.

Lord Demetri was waiting for her at the foot of the stairs. His gaze swept over her from head to heel, so intense it was almost palpable. Was he pleased? Disappointed?

She had hoped for a compliment, but he merely gestured for her to precede him to the front door. She was all too aware of him at her back as he reached around her to unlatch it. A carriage and driver awaited them.

The coachman hopped off the box and opened the door. Demetri handed her into the coach, then followed her inside.

Lorena settled herself in the luxuriously padded seat, smiled tentatively as Lord Demetri took his place across from her. He looked devastatingly handsome in evening clothes. His linen was impeccable, his face inscrutable.

Silence hung heavy between them. When it became unbearable, she blurted, "I've never been to a ball before. I hope I don't embarrass you, my lord."

"The women will be quite jealous when they see you. No doubt the men will flock to your side."

She stared at him. Was he making a jest? Why would anyone be jealous of her? She was the lowborn daughter of a man who had sold her into servitude. If the ladies discovered she was nothing more than Lord Demetri's house-keeper, they would shun her company. And the men … no doubt they would try to take liberties with her that they would never attempt with a real lady.

"Put your mind at ease," Demetri said quietly. "No one will dare be rude to you."

"How can you be so sure?" she asked. *And how did he know what she was thinking?*

"Because you are with me."

Moments later, the carriage halted in front of a large house fronted by an acre of lawn bordered by primroses. Lights blazed in every window. Colorful lanterns lit the long, flagstone pathway that led up to the massive entrance. It put Lord Fairfield's manor to shame, she thought, as Demetri handed her out of the carriage.

Lorena took a deep breath as he escorted her along the winding path to the front door. Music and laughter spilled from inside the house.

"Relax," he said, giving her hand a squeeze. "They are just people."

Hoping to calm her nerves, Lorena took several more deep breaths as they crossed the threshold into a world she had never seen before. Lamplight made the interior as bright as day. Dozens and dozens of elegantly dressed men and women gathered in small groups, laughing and talking as servants moved silently through the room, offering drinks and *hors d'oervres*. In the adjoining ballroom, she caught a glimpse of couples dancing while others looked on.

Demetri smiled as a tall man with gray hair and a bushy mustache strode toward them.

"Good of you to come," the man said, shaking Demetri's hand. "This must be the lovely young lady you were telling me about."

"Indeed. Sir Everleigh, may I present my ward, Miss Lorena Halliday. Lorena, this is my oldest friend, Sir Everleigh."

"So pleased to meet you, my dear," Everleigh said, as he bowed over her hand. "This young fellow has been alone far too long."

Lorena bit down on her lower lip, uncertain of how to respond.

"Don't be shy, my dear," Everleigh chided with a smile. He released her hand, his smile broadening as he said, "We have no secrets, Demetri and I."

Lorena smiled in return, though she had no idea what secrets he meant.

"Dinner will be served as soon as Beatrice comes down," Everleigh said.

"Beatrice is Sir Everleigh's sister," Demetri explained. "The party is in her honor."

"Yes, indeed," Everleigh said jovially. "The old girl turned sixty today, but don't tell her I told you so." He gestured toward the ballroom. "Go enjoy yourselves, you two. I must go and greet Lord and Lady Fitzroy."

"He seems like a nice man," Lorena remarked.

"He is a true gentleman," Demetri said. "Would you care to dance?"

She blinked up at him, hesitant yet strangely excited at the thought of being held in his arms.

"Lorena?"

"I...I don't know how."

"Then allow me to teach you." Taking her hand, he escorted her into the ballroom. He waited until the orchestra began to play a slow waltz, then he led her onto the floor and took her in his arms.

At first, Lorena was self-conscious, fearful of making a fool of herself in front of the other couples. But in moments, she was following his lead as if they had danced together countless times before. Although she wore gloves, she was acutely aware of his hand holding hers, of the undeniable force of his presence.

Demetri drew her closer as his mind brushed hers, guiding her feet in the steps. She looked incredibly beautiful, her eyes sparkling with excitement, her cheeks flushed, as he twirled her around the floor. He sensed the envy of the young men, especially that of Lord Ainsley's son, Oliver.

As soon as the waltz ended, Oliver was at their side. "Lord Demetri, please introduce me to your partner."

"Lorena, this is Oliver Ainsley. Oliver, my charge, Miss Lorena Halliday."

"I'm delighted to meet you, Miss Halliday," the young man gushed. "Might I have the pleasure of the next dance?"

Lorena smiled uncertainly. Oliver was very handsome, with pale blue eyes and hair the color of ripe wheat. Should she accept or refuse? She sent a hasty glance in Demetri's direction, wondering what her answer should be.

"I shall collect you later," Demetri said. With a curt nod at Ainsley, he quit the floor.

"Shall we?" Oliver asked.

Lorena nodded as he took her hand. "I really don't know how," she murmured, as the music began.

"We don't have to dance," he said. "I merely wished for a chance to introduce myself. We can go out on the balcony and talk, if you would rather."

"Yes, I believe I would," she replied, thinking that polite conversation would be far less intimate than dancing.

Oliver plucked two glasses of wine from a passing servant, then escorted her out onto a covered balcony that offered a view of the gardens below. Gesturing for her to take a seat on a bench, he offered her one of the glasses before taking the place beside her.

"I don't recall seeing you before," Ainsley said. "Have you just arrived in our city?"

"Yes, recently."

"I thought so. I'm sure I would have remembered you had we met before. How long will you be staying with Lord Demetri?"

"I'm not sure." She sipped her wine, wondering if she should tell him the truth, that she wasn't Demetri's ward merely his housekeeper. It didn't seem right to deceive him. But if she told the truth, she would be making a liar of Lord Demetri, since he had introduced her as his ward.

"Would you care to go out for a buggy ride tomorrow afternoon?" Oliver asked.

"I...I don't know."

"You don't know?"

"I mean...I don't know if I can."

Ainsley frowned at her.

"I would need to ask Lord Demetri's permission."

"He is coming this way. We can ask him now."

Lorena's stomach clenched as Lord Demetri strolled toward them, his face impassive.

"Lord Demetri," Ainsley said, his voice cool. "I was just asking this lovely young lady if she would care to accompany me on a buggy ride tomorrow afternoon."

"And what did she say?"

"Some nonsense about needing your permission."

Lorena frowned as something unspoken passed between the two me.

"I trust you have no problem with my taking her out?" Ainsley said.

A muscle twitched in Demetri's jaw. "It is entirely up to the lady."

Lorena stared at Demetri in surprise. She had been so certain he would refuse.

"Good!" Oliver beamed at her, a look of triumphant in his eyes. "I shall call for you at one-thirty."

Lorena nodded, confused by the dark undercurrent between the two men.

Oliver smiled at her. "Would you care to give dancing a try?"

"I am afraid this waltz is mine," Demetri said, capturing her hand with his.

Taken aback, Ainsley stammered, "Of course. No problem. Until tomorrow, Miss Halliday."

Lorena's heart skipped a beat at the idea of dancing with Lord Demetri again. Unfortunately, Everleigh's butler chose that moment to announce that dinner was being served.

Lorena and Demetri joined the couples wending their way toward the dining room. She could only gaze in amazement at the long tables covered in crisp white linen, the sparkling crystal glassware, gleaming silverware, and flowered china. When everyone was seated, Everleigh's sister arrived, her wheelchair pushed by a footman, who positioned her chair at the foot of the table. Sir Everleigh reigned at the head. Beatrice Everleigh was a tiny thing, her gray hair upswept in a most becoming style studded with brilliants. She wore a simple yet elegant velvet gown of jade green that matched her eyes.

Servants poured into the room, carrying enormous platters and gleaming silver trays. Lorena gaped at the assortment of knives, forks, and spoons beside her plate. However was she to know which one to use?

Leaning toward her, Demetri whispered, "Just watch me and do as I do."

Lorena thought supper would never end as course after course—including a number of foreign dishes—were elegantly presented in a seemingly endless array. She had never seen so many varieties of meats, cheese, and bread. Wine flowed like water. Everything was excellent. And just when she thought the meal was over, dessert arrived. Mince pies and sticky toffee puddings and a wide variety of tarts, from raspberry to custard.

When the meal was finally over, there were numerous toasts to Sir Everleigh's sister, congratulating Beatrice on her birthday, wishing her health and happiness and many more years ahead.

Following dinner, the guests returned to the ballroom, where Demetri claimed her for another dance.

"Are you angry with me?" she asked. "For accepting Mr. Ainsley's invitation?"

"You are not my prisoner, Lorena. You may come and go as you please."

His words should have made her feel better, so why did they leave her feeling so disappointed? But she soon forgot it as he twirled her around the room. The people, the music, all seemed to fade into the distance when she was in his arms, and there was only Lord Demetri, his eyes dark with an intensity she didn't understand. She shivered when he bent his head to her neck, his breath cool against her skin as he whispered her name.

She blinked up at him when he led her toward a pair of velvet-covered chairs. She sat down, suddenly light-headed. She didn't remember the music ending, didn't remember anything but the intensity of his gaze while they danced. It was most peculiar. And a little unsettling.

The rest of the evening passed in a blur. She was glad when he suggested they go home.

She fell asleep in the carriage with her head on his shoulder.

Demetri scrubbed a hand over his jaw as he listened to Lorena's quiet breathing. He hadn't meant to take quite so much, but holding her so close, hearing the enticing beat of her heart, drinking in the tantalizing scent of her life's blood, had been a temptation he couldn't resist. He had worked a little vampire magic so that anyone watching would assume he was merely whispering in her ear.

He slipped his arm around her shoulders. He had been a fool to agree to let her go out with Ainsley. Few young ladies could resist young Oliver's ready smile. The man was of good stock and well-to-do. Many of the unmarried females had their caps set for him.

At home, Demetri carried Lorena up the stairs to her bedchamber. After removing her shoes and gown, he tucked her under the covers. He stood there a long time, just watching her sleep, listening to the rhythmic sound of her breathing, inhaling her sweet womanly scent.

He had rarely denied himself anything he set his mind to. He was a powerful being, accustomed to taking whatever he wanted, and he saw no reason to stop now. And he wanted her. Desperately. The little he had taken on the dance floor had only whet his appetite for more. She was here. She was his. He saw no reason why he should not take it all.

He bent over her neck, his desire for her sweet blood growing almost unbearable—until she sighed softly in her sleep and whispered his name.

Cursing under his breath, Demetri jerked upright and stalked out of the room, damning himself for bringing such a tempting morsel into his home in the first place.

CHAPTER SIX

Lorena woke late the next morning. For a time, she lay there, staring at the ceiling as she pondered her uncertain feelings for Lord Demetri, and her upcoming rendezvous with Oliver Ainsley. She had never been out with a young man, had no idea how to make small talk with someone who was little more than a stranger.

Heaving a sigh, she swung her legs over the edge of the bed, wondering what she would do until Ainsley arrived. She paused as her bare feet hit the floor. She was in her underwear, yet she had no recollection of going to bed last night. Heat flooded her cheeks as she realized that Lord Demetri must have carried her to bed and undressed her. Such a thing was unthinkable, yet no one else could have done it.

He had seen her in her undergarments! How was she ever going to face him again? Cheeks still burning with embarrassment, she made her bed, pulled on her robe, stepped into her slippers, and shuffled down the stairs.

Feeling suddenly famished, she heated a pan of water for tea while she prepared breakfast. Lord Demetri had undressed her. Why didn't she remember?

She had no trouble remembering she had agreed to go for an afternoon buggy ride with Oliver Ainsley. She was sorry now that she had said yes.

She dawdled over breakfast as she searched her mind for some plausible reason to avoid going out with Mr. Ainsley.

Sadly, other than pleading a headache, nothing came to mind, and that seemed like a weak excuse at best.

Resigned to her fate, she washed and dried her dishes, then reluctantly made her way up to her room get ready.

Oliver arrived promptly at one-thirty.

Settling her bonnet on her head, Lorena pulled on her gloves, then took a deep breath before she went downstairs to greet him.

He smiled warmly when she opened the door. "I've been looking forward to this since last night," he said as he escorted her down the porch steps toward a handsome cabriolet. A beautiful white horse stood in the traces.

Lorena forced a smile as he handed her into the conveyance. He looked quite dapper in a pair of fawn-colored trousers, a short, black jacket, and a pair of Wellington's polished to a high shine.

"We've a lovely day for an outing," he remarked as he settled onto the seat beside her. Taking the reins in hand, he clucked to the horse. "Did you have a good time at the party last night?"

"Yes, indeed," she said, remembering her dances with Lord Demetri. "It was quite nice."

"I'm not sure how to say this, but, well, you seemed a little ill at ease last night. Is anything amiss at Demetri's?"

"What? No, of course not."

"Are you two related?"

Lorena twisted her fingers together, uncertain how to answer. Single women didn't share a house with single men unless they were kinfolk.

"Miss Halliday?"

"It's hard to explain."

"I'm sorry," he murmured. "I didn't mean to pry."

But she heard the questions he didn't ask, saw the suspicion in his eyes. Did he think her a kept woman? In spite of that disconcerting thought, she enjoyed the ride into the county. It was late spring and everything was in bloom.

Lorena knew a moment of trepidation when he reined the horse to a halt in the midst of a patch of green grass.

Oliver flashed a reassuring smile as he handed her out of the cabriolet, then reached under the seat and withdrew a small basket.

He indicated she should sit down before he dropped down beside her. Opening the basket, he withdrew a variety of sweet cakes and a small bottle of wine. "Tell me about yourself," he said as he filled two glasses and offered her one.

"I'd rather hear about you," she countered.

"Well, I'm the oldest of three sons. One of my brothers is a soldier. He's married with two children. The other is a priest."

"And you're still unwed. Isn't that odd?"

His gaze met hers. "Maybe I've just been waiting for the right woman."

"I'm sure there are many who would like to be Lady Ainsley," she said quickly.

"Are you one of them?"

Lorena stared at him. "We've just met!"

"I know what I want when I see it." He lifted a hand to stay the protest he saw rising in her eyes. "I'm not suggesting we marry right away, Miss Halliday. I can be a very patient man."

Something in the way he said it gave her pause. Telling herself she should be flattered by his interest, she brushed her uneasiness aside as a case of nerves.

❦   ❦   ❦

"I should love to see you again," Oliver said when he reined the horse to a halt in front of Lord Demetri's home an hour later. "May I?"

"I guess so, as long as Lord Demetri has no objections."

Giving her hand a squeeze, Ainsley stepped down from the cabriolet. After helping her from the carriage, he walked her to the door. Taking her hand in his, he lifted it to his lips and kissed her palm. "Until next time, I bid you good day."

Sighing, Lorena watched him drive away. To her surprise, it had been rather pleasant, spending time with Oliver, she mused, as she stepped inside.

She hummed softly as she made her way up the stairs to her room. Removing her hat and gloves, she took the pins from her hair. And forgot all about Oliver Ainsley as her thoughts turned to Lord Demetri. Where did he spend his days? Even the busiest of men must take a day off now and then. At least a Sunday afternoon from time to time.

She changed out of her day dress and into a skirt and shirtwaist and padded downstairs, her thoughts still on her mysterious employer as she dusted the furniture, straightened a pillow here and there, shook out the rugs, and then prepared something to eat.

Later, bored, she wandered through the house again. To her surprise, she came upon a room she hadn't noticed before. She found it quite by accident, hidden behind a heavy drapery in one of the third-floor storage rooms.

It opened with a squeal of hinges.

Lorena stared into the blackness. She hesitated a moment, then hurried back to her room where she lit her bedside lamp and returned to the hidden room. Holding the lamp high, she took a deep breath and stepped inside.

Odds and ends of furniture were mixed among the myriad boxes and trunks that lined the walls. Several large paintings were covered by dust cloths. Chewing on the inside corner of her lower lip, she tried to ignore the rush of curiosity that swept through her, but to no avail. Setting the lamp on a small antique desk, she dropped down on her knees and opened the nearest trunk, revealing an assortment of men's attire that appeared to be from former times. She lifted the items out one by one. Lord Demetri didn't seem like the sentimental type, yet the clothing must have belonged to people from a bygone era, people he cared about, or why keep them? His ancestors, perhaps?

She opened one of the other trunks, revealing hats and gloves, ornate walking sticks, old-fashion shoes and boots, long cloaks and short capes. All for men. Odd, she thought, that there were no clothes for women or children.

She sat there for a while, thinking about Demetri, wondering about his childhood. Had it been happy? Did he have brothers and sisters? Were his parents still alive? She had dreamed of him last night, though she couldn't now remember what it had been about. Only that he had been in it—tall, dark, and imposing. An indominable presence not to be taken lightly.

With a shake of her head, she lifted the lids on the last three boxes, which sat side by side.

They all held stacks of old books, the pages faded and yellowed with age, and what appeared to be diaries written in a bold hand in a foreign language. She picked one up and thumbed through the pages, wishing she could read the entries. Had Demetri written them? Or had the journals belonged to an ancestor who had passed away decades ago?

With a huff of exasperation, she returned the diary to the box. Standing, she dusted off her skirts. A last look around, and she made her way downstairs, the rumble in her stomach reminding her that it was time for evening tea.

From his lair under the house, Demetri listened to Lorena as she wandered through his home, then stumbled onto the hidden room that housed his past. He wondered what he would do if she discovered his lair, unlikely as that might be. Tell her the truth? Bestow the Dark Gift on her? Or wipe the memory and the location from her mind?

He had never turned anyone. What would it be like to bring Lorena across? To sire one as lovely and desirable as she? Would she hate him for all eternity? His lips twisted in a smile. It might be worth it. Perhaps, in a century or two, she might even thank him.

His smile faded. He had not thanked the one who had turned him, nor had he any wish to do so now. He thrust the memory of his sire aside. Why contemplate the past when Lorena awaited him upstairs?

He dressed quickly, ran a comb through his hair, and entered the house through the front door.

Lorena smiled an uncertain smile when she saw him. "Good evening, my lord."

He inclined his head in acknowledgement. "Lorena. I have made arrangements for us to attend the opera tonight if you have no objection."

"The opera!" She clapped her hands, her eyes child-bright with excitement. "I should love to go."

Lorena could hardly sit still in the carriage. Her anticipation was palpable. Demetri smiled inwardly. It had been centuries since anything had excited him. He watched her through heavy-lidded eyes. She had blossomed in the short time she had lived under his roof. Amazing what good food, a comfortable bed, and the opportunity to bathe frequently could do for one, he thought. Tonight, she looked radiant.

Lorena's eyes widened when she saw the theater. It was a grand old place, with spires and domes that reminded her of some ancient palace. Demetri handed her out of the carriage, but she was scarcely aware of him beside her, she was so busy looking at the ornate facade and the well-dressed and perfectly coifed men and women preceding them up the stairs.

Demetri led her to a private box. She leaned forward, mesmerized by the opulence of the interior, the painting on the ceiling, the chandeliers that sparkled like diamonds. She sat transfixed as the curtain parted.

Demetri paid scant attention to what was happening on stage. He had eyes only for Lorena. He watched the play of emotions on her face as the story unfolded. He had known many women, been fond of a few, but none had captured his heart or his attention quite like this one.

Lorena sighed as the notes of the last aria died away. She couldn't believe it was over. Time had ceased to matter as she had lost herself in the beauty of the music. Never had she heard anything so lovely. She hummed softly as they left the theater, wondering what it would be like to perform on stage in front of hundreds of people, to hear their applause.

"You enjoyed yourself?" Demetri asked as they settled in the carriage.

"Oh, yes! It was wonderful. Thank you so much."

"I shall take you again, if you like."

"Oh, I would, very much."

"Then I shall arrange it."

At home, he dismissed the driver, then followed Lorena into the house.

"Thank you again for a wonderful evening," she said as she removed her hat and gloves. "I don't know how I can ever repay you. Or why you're so good to me."

His gaze caressed her face, lingering on her lips.

Heat shot through her as he took a step toward her. He was going to kiss her. Should she let him? Did she dare refuse? Did she want to?

He drew her slowly into his arms. "Just one kiss, freely given, would be payment enough."

She couldn't think when he was so near, could scarcely breathe as he lowered his head to hers. Her eyelids fluttered down as his mouth covered hers. It was a gentle kiss, little more than the brush of his lips over hers, yet she felt it burn through every nerve and fiber of her being.

"Sweet." He traced her lower lip with his fingers. "So sweet," he murmured. "I fear one taste will not be enough."

A million butterflies took wing in the pit of Lorena's stomach as he claimed her lips a second time.

This kiss was not so brief. Or so gentle.

He ended it abruptly and stepped away from her. "It's late," he said, his voice thick. "Go to bed."

It never occurred to her to argue. Turning on her heel, she hurried up the stairs, though she had no idea what she was running from.

Demetri stared after her, hunger and desire warring within him. Silly child, to run from a hungry predator. But then, she didn't know what manner of man he was.

What would she do, he wondered, if she found out?

Demetri waited until the soft sound of her breathing told him she was asleep, then he left the house. He felt the darkness welcome him as he strolled down the deserted streets. It was a sensation he had never quite been able to put into words, that sense of belonging, the oneness that he felt with the night, the darkness itself. A cat hissed at him, its back arched, as he passed by. He smiled faintly as one predator recognized another.

Hunger drove him toward the dilapidated part of the neighboring city that was inhabited by footpads and streetwalkers, cut-purses and ragamuffin gangs.

He found his prey emerging from a tavern at the end of a dark street. She was young in the trade, he thought. She didn't yet wear the worn-out expression of her more experienced sisters. Her skin and eyes were still clear, her steps light.

He ghosted up beside her.

Had she been sober, she would likely have been afraid. Instead, she sent him a crooked smile. "Sorry, guv'nor," she mumbled, "but sure and I'm done for the night."

Draping his arm around her shoulders, he murmured, "Just one more trick."

When she started to protest, he captured her gaze with his. "I will pay you well for your trouble."

Interest sparked in her eyes. Then, as he wrapped her in his thrall, her gaze went blank.

Pushing her hair aside, he sank his fangs into the tender place just beneath her ear. And all the while, he wished it was Lorena in his arms, her sweet blood filling him with warmth and life.

After easing his thirst, he slipped a few pounds into the woman's bodice, released her from his thrall, and melted into the darkness, leaving her none the wiser.

Lorena. She was ever in his thoughts. Her scent intoxicated him, her smile filled him with a measure of contentment he hadn't known in centuries. Why? She was just a woman he had met by accident. Why was he so smitten with her? He had known hundreds of women. Preyed on them and forgotten them. Made love to many but loved none.

Lorena. Desire fanned to life as he imagined carrying her to his bed and making love to her all through the night.

A thought took him to her bedside.

Sweet Lorena. Beautiful. Innocent. Vulnerable. His for the taking. He clenched his hands to keep from reaching for her. He was no fit companion for one such as she.

Filled with self-loathing, he fled the room.

Chapter Seven

L orena was in the midst of scrubbing the kitchen floor when someone rang the bell. Wondering who would come calling in the middle of the day, she removed her apron and hurried to answer the door.

A young man dressed in livery stood on the porch, cap in hand. "Miss Halliday?"

"Yes."

He handed her an ivory-colored envelope. "I'm to wait for a reply."

Nodding in acknowledgement, and more than a little curious, she opened the flap and removed a sheet of vellum.

My dear Miss Halliday ~
It would be my pleasure if you would
accompany me to Lady Hazelton's soiree
Saturday next at nine o'clock in the evening.
Please send your
reply via my footman.
Respectfully, Oliver Ainsley.

Lorena read the note again, and yet again. Should she accept? Lord Demetri had assured her that she was not his prisoner and that she could come and go as she pleased. Still …

"Miss?"

"I…um…" She bit down on her lower lip. "Please tell Mr. Ainsley that I should be honored to accompany him."

"Very good, miss." He touched a finger to his forehead and then turned and ran down the stairs to the waiting carriage.

Beleaguered by second thoughts, Lorena stared after him.

❖ ❖ ❖

Demetri sensed Lorena's distress the moment he entered the house. She was obviously upset about something. After a few moments of small talk, he said, "You are fluttering around like a moth trapped inside a jar. Do you want to tell me what has you so upset?"

Lorena clasped her hands to still their trembling. "I…I accepted an invitation to accompany Mr. Ainsley to a party at Lady Hazelton's Saturday next."

Demetri raised one brow. "And?"

"I…I wasn't sure I should accept. I know you said I could come and go as I please, but…"

He held up one hand. "I said it and I meant it." Although, at this moment, he was lying. The last thing he wanted was for Lorena to spend the evening with Ainsley. Or any other man, for that matter.

She blew out a sigh of relief.

"Have you plans for this evening?" he asked.

"No."

"Would you like to go for a buggy ride?"

She glanced out the window. "In the dark?"

"Are you afraid?"

She shook her head vigorously.

Now *she* was lying, he thought. "Fetch your hat and coat while I bring the buggy around."

It really was a lovely night for a drive, Lorena thought as Demetri clucked to the mare. The sky was clear, dotted with stars and a bright yellow moon. As always when she was beside him, words failed her. He intimidated her, though she wasn't sure why. He had been more than kind to her, generous, and yet there was something about him, an aura of power that frightened her on some primal level she didn't understand—a power that alarmed and attracted her at the same time. Oliver Ainsley was a nice man, a gentleman. Lord Demetri also seemed nice, a gentleman, and yet she knew instinctively that in Demetri's case, it was only a thin veneer. She slid a sideways glance at him, wondering what he was hiding beneath that mask of civility, only to find him looking back at her.

For a moment, she forgot how to breathe. She was alone with him, far from home, far from town. If she cried out, no one would hear her.

Muttering an oath, Demetri reined the mare to a halt. "Lorena, I am not going to hurt you."

She stared at him, her heart in her throat.

"Please believe me, you have no need to fear me. I mean you no harm."

She swallowed hard, wondering if he could hear the pounding of her heart.

"Why are you so afraid of me?"

She shook her head. "I ... I'm not."

He stared at her, one dark brow arched in wry amusement. "You are not a very accomplished liar."

"All right, I am afraid!" she exclaimed, pressing her hands to her heated cheeks. "I don't know why."

He knew why. Almost, he was tempted to tell her the truth of what he was.

Almost.

Refusing to meet his gaze, she said, "Can we please go back to your house?"

"I was hoping you might come to think of it as your home."

"Why would I do that?" she asked, still not meeting his eyes. "I'm not a relative. I'm not a guest or a friend. Merely your housekeeper."

"Have I ever treated you like a servant?"

"No."

"It could be your house," he said slowly. "If you marry me." He didn't know where the words came from. A wife was the last thing he wanted. Or needed.

Lorena's gaze flew to his. Was he seriously proposing marriage? She scarcely knew the man. She had no idea of his likes or dislikes, knew nothing of his past, or how he earned his living, if he had brothers or sisters, if his parents were still living. He was little more than an enigmatic stranger.

"Marrying me would give you security, a home, wealth and position," he said quietly.

"But not love," she murmured, then clapped her hand over her mouth, horrified that she had spoken the words out loud.

"It might come, in time. Until then, we could be wed in name only." He smiled ruefully. "You would have all the advantages of being my wife with none of the intimacy."

She stared at him. Marry Lord Demetri merely to have the security of his name? It was unthinkable. Absurd. She would be bound to a man she didn't love for the rest of her life—wed to a man who didn't love her. She thought briefly of Oliver Ainsley and then shook her head. If she told Oliver that she was merely a servant in Demetri's house, she was certain he would no longer wish to court her.

"You need not decide now." Demetri clucked to the mare and she moved out at a brisk trot.

Lorena slumped in her seat, hands tightly clasped in her lap, while his words replayed themselves in her mind over and over again as she weighed the pros and cons of matrimony.

We can be wed in name only. You will have all the advantages of being my wife with none of the intimacy.

But could she trust a man like Lord Demetri—or any man—to keep such a bargain? Once they were wed, she would be his property, his to do with as he wished.

It was a sobering thought.

Lorena changed into her nightgown with no memory of the ride home. She could think of nothing but Lord Demetri's unexpected proposal. She still couldn't believe he had meant it. Why would he want to marry her, a woman he hardly knew and didn't love? He had nothing to gain from such a match. She had no wealth, no property, no dowry. Perhaps it was just some kind of sick jest and if she accepted his proposal, he would laugh in her face for thinking he had been sincere.

Crawling under the covers, she blew out the bedside candle, only to lie there staring up at the ceiling.

Being married to Lord Demetri would give her a lifetime of security, a home of her own. A kind of respect she had never known before. What would it be like, to be his wife? Would he expect to share her bed even if they were wed in name only?

The thought wasn't nearly as unpleasant as it should have been. He was, after all, a remarkably attractive man, though there was no denying the aura of danger that clung to him like a second skin.

Demetri paced the parlor floor, wondering what had possessed him to propose to Lorena. He had made love to many women through the centuries. Most had been courtesans or actresses, a few had been highborn ladies looking for a brief, discreet affair. Lady or whore, he had treated them all the same.

None had been like Lorena. He didn't quite know what to make of her. Sold into household servitude by her father, abused by Fairfield, she still maintained an air of innocence that he found appealing.

What would he do if she accepted his proposal?

What would he do if she refused?

Swearing under his breath, he left the house.

A thought took him to a tavern located on the waterfront. It was one of his favorite haunts, populated by pirates and prostitutes and other, equally unsavory characters, none of whom would hesitate to plunge a knife into a man's back, or steal his purse.

None of whom would be missed.

Standing inside the entryway, he glanced around the room. His gaze settled on a young streetwalker. She looked reasonably clean, unmarked by the pox. He detected no disease, not that it would affect him, but illness of any kind made the blood taste bitter.

Taking the seat beside her at the rough plank bar, he ordered a glass of red wine. He gestured at her empty glass. "May I buy you another?"

"That would be lovely," she said, smiling. "I don't think I've seen you in here before."

"No? I have seen you."

"Truly?"

He nodded.

"You should have made your presence known," she said, her voice suddenly husky. "Think of the time we've wasted."

"The lady will have another," Demetri told the bartender when he passed by.

"My name's Delilah," the woman said.

"Demetri."

She dropped her hand to his thigh and gave it a squeeze. "So nice to meet you, milord. Would you like to come to my place?"

"It would be my pleasure."

"Hopefully mine, too." She drained her glass and then reached for his hand. "Let's go, then."

Demetri let her lead him down the street until they came to an alley. Tugging on her hand, he pulled her into the shadows and took her in his arms.

"Impatient, are you?" she asked with a throaty laugh.

"You have no idea." His gaze burned into hers, stealing her will, and then he sank his fangs into the soft skin of her throat.

He took what he needed, what he couldn't live without. A flick of his tongue sealed the wounds, a word released her from his thrall. "Go home," he said. She stared at him blankly for a moment, then turned and walked away, her steps unsteady.

Demetri stared after her, his brow furrowed. He rarely gave any thought to those he preyed upon. It was a necessity and he pursued it with single-minded purpose. But he couldn't help wondering what had happened in her life that she had ended up selling her favors.

Leaving the alley, he strolled down the street, his thoughts turning again to Lorena. How had she become so important in such a short time? He was still thinking of the enchanting woman in his house—the woman he had asked to marry him—when two men dressed in black stepped out of a doorway.

Hunters!

Lost in thoughts of Lorena, he hadn't sensed their presence in time.

One flung the contents of a bottle in his face, temporarily blinding him even as it burned his skin. The second man drove a thick wooden stake into his chest, missing his heart by scant inches.

Unable to see clearly enough to fight back, Demetri ripped the stake from his chest. Calling on the last of his waning strength, he willed himself home.

After tossing and turning for over an hour, Lorena lit a candle and tiptoed barefooted to the kitchen where she fixed a cup of tea. Drink in one hand and candle in the other, she padded into the back parlor. After setting the candle in the sconce on the wall, she made herself comfortable in the big, old, overstuffed chair by the fireplace.

Sitting in the near-dark, she found herself thinking, as always, about Demetri. She had just taken a sip of tea when he entered the room. Startled, she practically choked in mid-swallow as she stared at him. The skin of his face was red and blistered, his shirtfront torn and blood-stained.

Eyes wide with shock, she stammered, "What…what's happened…to you?"

He swore softly. What the hell was she doing up at this time of night? "I was attacked by robbers."

She quickly put her cup aside. "I should send for a doctor."

"No need."

"But…your face…and…" Her words trailed off. Hardly aware of what she was doing, she stood and moved toward him. He had been stabbed. She could see the wound through the ragged hole in his shirt. The material was still wet with blood, but the bleeding had stopped. Even as she watched, the wound grew smaller and disappeared. And his face…the redness was fading, the blisters less angry-looking.

She had to be dreaming. That was the only explanation. Because what she was seeing was impossible.

"Lorena, look at me."

Lifting her chin, she met his gaze.

"Nothing unusual happened here tonight. You had a cup of tea before going back to bed. You did not see me or talk to me. Do you understand?"

"I didn't see you tonight," she murmured tonelessly. "I didn't talk to you."

"That is right. You will forget all this happened. You will go up to bed and go to sleep and have no memory of any of this when you wake in the morning."

"No memory."

"Goodnight, Lorena."

"Goodnight."

He watched as she moved like a sleepwalker toward the stairway, listened as she climbed the stairs and scuffed down the hall to her room. He heard the door close, a faint squeak as she settled into bed, the whisper of linen as she pulled the blankets over her. In moments, he heard the soft, steady sound of her breathing.

Going down to his lair, he stripped off his bloody shirt and tossed it in the trash, then ran his hand over his face. Holy water. It burned like the flames of the fiery hell that surely awaited him, he thought as he settled down for what remained of the night, but by tomorrow, his skin would be healed, the pain would be gone.

He clung to that thought as the dark sleep engulfed him and carried him away into oblivion.

Lorena was surprised to find Oliver Ainsley at her door early the following afternoon.

"Mr. Ainsley!" she exclaimed. "This is a surprise."

"I couldn't wait until Saturday next," he said. "I was hoping you would come out with me today."

"Now?"

"I'm sorry for my impertinence. I…"

"Actually, I'm glad you're here," Lorena said. "I'm afraid I won't be able to accompany you on Saturday evening."

"Oh." His disappointment was obvious and more than a little flattering.

"Lord Demetri has asked me to marry him."

"What!" He couldn't have looked more surprised if she had answered the door in her undergarments. "You can't seriously be considering his proposal?"

"Well, I…"

"You cannot marry that man!" Oliver said vehemently. "I'm not even sure he is a man."

"What are you talking about?"

"Surely you've heard the rumors."

Lorena's hand tightened on the edge of the door until her knuckles went white. "What... what rumors?"

Oliver took a step forward. "They say there's something unnatural about him," he confided, his voice little more than a whisper. "There are stories about his... habits."

"What habits?" She glanced over her shoulder, wondering if she should invite him in. Surely this wasn't a conversation to be had on the front porch. And yet, it wasn't seemly for her to entertain him in the house when she was alone.

He ticked them off on his fingers. "He is never seen in public during the day. He generally arrives at parties after supper. He never eats anything. He never drinks anything but a glass of red wine. Have you not noticed?"

Lorena bit down on her lip. Of course, she had noticed, but she had attributed it to some minor eccentricity. It had never occurred to her that it might be anything more ominous.

"So, you have noticed? But then, how could you not?"

She could only stare at him, her heart pounding with trepidation.

"Come away with me, Miss Halliday. I fear you're not safe here." When she didn't answer, he whispered, "There are stories of women who have come here and were never seen or heard from again."

Lorena's gaze slid away from his. What to do, what to do? Was she seriously in danger if she stayed? Was Lord Demetri truly some kind of Bluebeard?

"I know this comes as a shock," Oliver said.

"Yes," she murmured, stunned. "Yes, it does."

"I beg you to think it over today." Taking her hand in his, he said, "I can give you shelter in my home until you can make other arrangements. Please, for your own safety, think it over. I'll send my man around before dark for your answer."

Lorena nodded, her mind whirling as she watched him descend the porch steps to his phaeton.

When he was out of sight, she slowly closed the door. What to do, what to do? The words played over and over in her mind as the hours passed. Was Oliver telling the truth or merely trying to dissuade her from marrying a rival for her affections? She scarcely knew either man. She wished she had friends in town that she could talk to, a woman she could confide in.

She dropped into one of the chairs in the parlor. How was she to decide? Dared she repeat Oliver's suspicions to Demetri? If he was innocent, would he explain? Or would he find a way to silence her, perhaps for good? And maybe Oliver, as well? Of course, there could be logical explanations for Oliver's accusations, but there was no doubt that there was something different about Demetri.

Needing something else to think about, she picked up her book, hoping to lose herself in the pages of *The Man in the Iron Mask,* but to no avail. She couldn't concentrate on the story, couldn't think of anything but what Oliver had said.

He is never seen in public during the day. She didn't know if that was true, but she had certainly never seen him when the sun was up.

He generally arrives at parties after supper. She didn't know if that was true, either.

He never eats anything. He never drinks anything but a glass of red wine. There again, what Oliver had said was true. She had never seen Demetri sit down to a meal, but that proved nothing. She had no idea what he did during the day.

Laying the book aside, she leaned back in the chair and closed her eyes.

When she opened them again, Lord Demetri stood before her.

CHAPTER EIGHT

Lorena stared up at Lord Demetri, her heart drumming in her ears like thunder. She told herself to calm down, that he couldn't possibly know Oliver had been there earlier in the day or what he had told her.

Clasping her hands in her lap, she took a deep breath and gained her feet. "Is there something I can do for you, my lord?"

Demetri's gaze searched hers. Should he ask about Ainsley's visit? Would she admit the man had been there—or deny it? It was obvious that whatever message Ainsley had delivered had frightened her. Curious, he let his mind brush hers. His hands clenched at his sides as he determined the source of her agitation. He had known there were rumors about his odd behavior. Most had been started by Ainsley, but he had never dreamed the man would relate them to Lorena. Not that it surprised him. Ainsley was also smitten with her, willing to do or say anything to make his rival look bad in her eyes.

Lorena shifted from one foot to the other, uncomfortable by the intensity of his gaze. "My lord?"

"I require nothing," he replied, "although I would very much like it if you would ride with me this evening."

She blinked up at him.

"Do you ride?" he asked.

"No, my lord." She had always loved horses, had dreamed of one day owning one. But that dream, like all her others, had died when her father sold her. As a servant in Lord Fairfield's house, she had rarely been given the freedom to go outside, let alone take up horseback riding for pleasure.

"Would you care to learn?"

All thought of Oliver's warnings fled her mind as she exclaimed, "Oh, yes!"

Filled with excitement, Lorena followed Demetri out the back door and then down a slight incline to the barn. She'd had no idea that he owned horses, but then, she had never ventured out into the barn yard.

"Wait here," he said.

Murmuring, "Yes, my lord," she watched as he entered the dark stable. How did he find his way, she wondered, with no light to guide him?

A short time later, he emerged leading a pair of the most beautiful horses Lorena had ever seen. One was sleek and as black as the night, the other a beautiful dapple gray with ebony mane and tail. Only the stallion was saddled. Surely he didn't intend for her to ride that black beast?

Demetri dropped the reins of the black over the top of the corral fence. "Lady Gray is for you," he said. "She is quite gentle."

"She's lovely, but, you don't expect me to ride bareback, do you?"

He laughed softly. "No." He walked back into the barn, returning with a blanket and saddle. "Forgive me, but you will have to learn to ride astride as I have no side-saddle."

Lorena nodded. Close up, the horse looked much bigger. And taller.

"First, you must to learn to saddle her before you can ride."

Lorena spent the next thirty minutes learning how to properly saddle and bridle the mare, how to check the cinch, and to be sure the blanket was smooth so it didn't cause the horse discomfort.

"All right," he said. "I think you're ready."

She was looking around for a box to climb on so she could reach the stirrup when Demetri put his hands on her waist and lifted her effortlessly onto the mare's back. Taking the reins, he led her into the corral and closed the gate. Still holding the reins, he walked the mare around the enclosure.

She was riding! Excitement fluttered in Lorena's stomach as she leaned forward to stroke the mare's neck.

Five times around the pen and Demetri handed her the reins. "She's quite gentle. The perfect horse for a beginning rider. Just take it slow." Walking beside her, he explained how to turn the mare left and right, how to make her stop, then start again. "Keep your hands light on the reins," he instructed.

Moving to the side of the corral, he watched Lorena put his instructions into play. She had a natural seat, gentle hands. He felt a rush of pride. She rode as if she had been born to it.

When he suggested they stop for the night, she begged for just a little more time. Eager to please her, he perched on the top rail, content to let her ride for as long as she wished.

"How do I make her go faster?" Lorena called.

"Gently press your legs to her sides."

She let out a squeal of delight as the mare broke into a trot.

It was almost an hour later when she drew the mare to a halt beside him. "This is wonderful. Thank you so much!"

"The mare is yours."

"Mine? Do you mean it? She's truly mine?"

"Yes, truly yours."

"I don't know what to say."

"Your smile says it all. Are you tired of riding in circles?" She nodded vigorously.

After opening the gate, Demetri took up the black stallion's reins and swung effortlessly into the saddle.

An iron gate at the rear of the yard led to a wide trail that meandered through the wooded area behind the estate. Excitement gradually turned to trepidation as she followed Demetri deeper into the woods. The night was eerily quiet, with only the muffled sounds of the horses' hooves to break the stillness and the light of the moon to show the way. She let out a sharp cry of alarm as an owl swooped past her on silent wings. The mare darted sideways and sent Lorena tumbling from the saddle.

Demetri was beside her in an instant, his arms lifting her, cradling her to his chest. "Are you hurt?"

"I … I don't think so."

His gaze moved over her face. His voice was tight when he said, "Your head is bleeding."

She felt it then, a warm trickle sliding down the side of her cheek. "Is it … is it bad?"

"No. Just a shallow cut on your temple." Demetri wiped the blood away with his fingertips. Then, turning away so she couldn't see, he licked it off. Rising, he took her hands and pulled her to her feet. "Are you up to riding back? If not, you can ride with me."

She started to say she was fine, but he was so close, his eyes so intense, she couldn't find the words. He was going to kiss her. The thought sent a shiver down her spine followed by a sudden rush of heat as his lips claimed hers. She swayed against him, wanting, needing, to be closer. She moaned softly as his arms wrapped around her, drawing her body closer to his. So close. His mouth moved seductively over hers until she was mindless, breathless.

She felt bereft when he suddenly released her and took a step back.

"It grows late," he said. "And your head is bleeding again."

She lifted a hand to her temple. Feeling the warmth of her blood, she pulled a handkerchief from her pocket and pressed it to the wound. "Does the sight of blood distress you, my lord?" she asked, as he turned away.

"No," he said, his voice thick. In one swift movement, he lifted her onto the mare's back and thrust the reins into her hand.

He quickly mounted his own horse, his gaze never meeting hers.

Bewildered, she followed him home.

When they reached the barn, he lifted her from the saddle. "Go back to the house, Lorena."

Something in his tone sent her scurrying up the path, through the back door, and up to her room. As soon as she was inside, she locked the door. The cut had stopped bleeding. She filled the bowl on her dresser with water from the pitcher and used her handkerchief to wash away the dried blood. She stared at the bloody cloth a moment, then threw it into the trash basket.

Only when she was safely in bed did she remember what Oliver had told her earlier that day. He had hinted that she might be in danger. She wasn't sure what had happened between herself and Lord Demetri out there in the woods after she fell, but she couldn't escape the feeling that she was lucky to have made it back to the manor with nothing worse than a little cut on her forehead.

After unsaddling the horses and locking them in the barn, Demetri left the estate. Tension roiled deep inside him. He was becoming obsessed with Lorena. He wanted her as a man wants a woman, warm and willing beneath him, her hands eagerly caressing him. He wanted her body in his bed, her blood on his tongue.

Her blood. It was driving him crazy. Until he'd tasted Lorena, he had believed that all blood was the same—warm and red and life-giving. Differences in taste and texture were minor and of no consequence. It was something he could not exist without. He no longer felt the need to kill his prey, but the desire to hunt, to feed, had been the main focus of his life for over three hundred and fifty years.

Blood.

Why was hers so much more desirable? So much more satisfying? Was it simply that he cared for her as he had never cared for another woman that made him crave it? Vampire or not, he was still a man, with a man's wants. A man's needs. He had known countless women in the course of his existence, but none compared with Lorena. He wanted to know everything about her, explore every inch of her sweet flesh, carry her to his bed and make love to her until the sun drove the moon from the sky.

He could compel her to marry him, or just to share his bed, to obey his every command, fulfil his every desire, but he didn't want a zombie in his bed. He wanted a woman, one who wanted him in return.

Just thinking about it aroused his lust.

A thought took him to the city's most respectable brothel.

The madam welcomed him with a smile. He was, after all, her best-paying customer. She showed him to the best room in the house, brought him a bottle of her finest red wine, and sent Fleur, her most highly priced whore, to serve him.

Ordinarily, Demetri found pleasure and release in her arms, but tonight he could summon no enthusiasm for the woman in his embrace.

He drank a glass of wine, paid her extra for her time, and stalked out of the room.

Lorena had retired for the evening by the time he returned home. Unable to help himself, he took the stairs to her room two at a time. Standing at her bedside, he gazed down at her, his whole body thrumming with desire.

Finally, unable to resist the siren call of her blood, he bent down and took what he so desperately craved.

Lorena had an overpowering thirst when she woke in the morning. Donning her robe, she padded into the kitchen where she drank three cups of tea heavily laced with milk and sugar while she prepared eggs, sausage, and toast for breakfast. And drank yet another cup of tea.

And all the while, she wondered what answer she would give Demetri should he ask for her decision. To wed or not to wed, that was the question. After last night, she was inclined to refuse him. Something strange had happened between them, out there in the dark. Something for which she had no logical explanation. She lifted a hand to her lips. He had kissed her. She imagined she could still feel his lips moving over hers. She should have been outraged at such a liberty. Why wasn't she?

She had just finished dressing for the day when someone rang the bell. She could only think of one person who would come calling—Oliver Ainsley.

She ran her hand over her hair as she made her way downstairs. Took a deep breath. And opened the door.

"Miss Halliday! I'm so relieved to see you. I stopped by last night...I know I should not have come this morning without an invitation, but I was worried about you and I had to make sure you were well," he said, breathlessly. "When you weren't home when I came to call, I naturally feared the worst."

"The worst?" she asked, frowning. Whatever was he talking about?

"I was afraid that Lord Demetri had...that is...that he...I was concerned for your safety."

"I assure you I'm quite all right." She bit down on her lower lip, debating whether to invite him in when she was unchaperoned. And then she shrugged. Who would know? Or care? She gestured for him to enter the front parlor. "Please, have a seat."

He sat on the edge of the sofa, his hands resting on his knees. "Have you accepted his suit?"

"No, not yet."

"Does that mean you intend to?"

"No. It means I haven't yet made up my mind."

His relief was evident. "I am on my way to town. Would you care to accompany me? I had thought to stop for Apple Charlotte at Miss Mavis' tea room."

Lorena hesitated, certain she should say no. But she suddenly felt the need to get out of the house, to be around other people. "That would be lovely. Just let me get my wrap."

"This isn't the tea room," Lorena remarked as Oliver parked his phaeton in front of a lovely, three-story brick home surrounded by trees and an expanse of green lawn. Primroses grew along the walkway. She could see a portion of a sparkling blue lake in the back.

A groom hurried forward to take the reins as Oliver alighted from the phaeton.

"What are we doing here?" Lorena asked, feeling slightly alarmed as he lifted her from the conveyance.

"This is my home."

"It's very nice. But what are we doing here?" she asked again.

"I wanted to show you my family estate and speak with you alone."

"We were alone at Lord Demetri's," Lorena reminded him, her irritation rising. "You lied to me."

"It was for your own good."

"Please take me home."

"You needed to get away from Demetri's influence so you could think clearly."

When he reached for her hand, she folded her arms over her chest and backed away. "Miss Halliday... Lorena, you must listen to what I have to say."

"Mr. Ainsley, I insist that you take me home this instant!"

"This could be your home. Look around. It's beautiful, light and airy, not like that dark dungeon where Demetri lives."

Lorena glared at him. "I've been quite comfortable there. Now take me back."

"No. Not until you listen to what I have to say. I fear the man has bewitched you."

She huffed a sigh, turned on her heel, and walked briskly down the tree-lined drive toward the road, only to be brought up short when he ran up behind her and grabbed her arm.

"You're not going back there," he said.

Exclaiming, "Let me go!" she raked her nails down his cheek.

He cursed, but didn't release her. Taking a firmer grasp on her arm, he dragging her toward the front stairs. "You're not going anywhere. Not until you've heard the truth about that devil, and when you do, you'll thank me."

Try as she might, Lorena couldn't break his grip on her arm. Once inside the house, he pushed her ahead of him, then turned and locked the door. "All the other doors are also locked," he said when she hurried across the room.

She whirled around to face him, hands tightly clenched at her sides. "All right, tell me your truth and then let me go."

"You might want to sit down."

Mouth set in a firm line, she shook her head.

"Doesn't he seem strange to you?"

Lorena shrugged but said nothing.

"Think about it. Why doesn't he eat? Why is he never seen during the day? As far as anyone knows, he has no source of income, yet he lives in a grand house and is accepted by society."

"So, he's a bit eccentric. That doesn't prove anything."

"Do I have to spell it out for you? The man is not human. He is Nosferatu. A vampire."

A vampire? Lorena stared at Oliver in astonishment. "Do you seriously expect me to believe such an outlandish accusation?"

"It's the truth."

A trickle of unease crept down her spine. Oliver looked quite sane, but it was obvious he was delusional. A vampire, indeed. She had never heard of anything so ridiculous in her life. And yet...she had never seen Demetri during the day. True, he never dined at home, but that didn't mean he didn't take his meals elsewhere. As for his means of support, she had never given it any thought. An inheritance, perhaps? Wise investments?

"You've warned me," she said, careful to keep her tone reasonable. "I should like to leave now."

"I don't think so. You're not safe with that creature."

"I've been with Lord Demetri for some time now," she said with asperity. "And nothing untoward has happened." She thought briefly of his kisses, and brushed it aside.

"How do you know?"

"What do you mean?" Lorena asked, frowning.

"He could have mesmerized you. Hypnotized you so that you wouldn't remember whatever atrocities he might have inflicted upon you. His last housekeeper left, apparently in the middle of the night. No one's ever seen or heard from her since."

Feeling a little light-headed, Lorena sank down on the nearest chair. She didn't believe a single word Oliver had said—but what if it was true? If Lord Demetri could truly erase events from her mind, how was she to know?

Chilled by his words, she wrapped her arms around her waist. Could Demetri be a vampire? She told herself it was preposterous, but what if it wasn't? Demetri had taken her in—a complete stranger. He had fed her and clothed her. Had he done so for his own selfish interests, whatever they might be? Was he merely lulling her into a false sense of security before he pounced? Once the seeds of doubt had been planted, she couldn't root them out.

"I know this is hard to believe, but perhaps this will help," Oliver said quietly, and laid a book bound in black leather in her lap.

Lorena stared at the title. *The Secret Life of Vampires. Everything You Need to Know About the Undead.* Her hand trembled slightly as she opened the thin volume. She read quickly, her gaze skimming the pages.

Vampires existed in every civilization. Some survived on the energy of others, some on blood. They were able to move quicker than the human eye could follow. Alter their appearance.

When injured, they healed almost instantly. The majority preyed on humans for their blood, often killing their victims.

They did not consume mortal food or drink. They were compelled to return to their lairs before sunrise, where they lay helpless until sundown.

They cast no reflection.

They were able to divine, control and manipulate human minds. Lord, what if Oliver was right? Demetri could have ravished her dozens of times and wiped the memory from her mind. But, oh, that was ridiculous. Surely, if Demetri had violated her, she would know it, feel it.

Vampires were extremely hard to kill. The best way to destroy them was to cut off the head and burn the body. A wooden stake through the heart was also deemed effective, but, again, it was recommended to burn the remains.

Lorena shuddered at the grisly images the last few sentences conjured up.

Could it be true?

Was Lord Demetri a vampire? What had happened to his last housekeeper?

"Here, drink this," Oliver said, thrusting a goblet into her hand. "You look a trifle pale."

She took a swallow, eyes widening as the liquid burned her throat. "What...what was that?"

"Brandy."

It warmed her immediately and she took another sip. She had never had anything stronger than an occasional glass of wine.

He jerked his chin toward the book in her lap. "Now do you believe me?"

An hour later, Lorena paced the floor in one of the guest-rooms in Oliver's home. It disturbed her that he had locked her inside. She had gone to the window as soon as he locked the door, intending to climb out, but the ground was a considerable ways down, with nothing to hold onto along the way. And even if she'd found the nerve to jump, she would have landed in the midst of a thorn bush at the bottom, resulting in numerous cuts and scratches at best, and broken bones at worst.

She didn't want to believe what Oliver had told her. He had no physical proof, only his accusations and some words in a book. But...what if Oliver was right? If there was even the slightest chance it was true, did she want to go back to Lord Demetri's house and put herself at his mercy?

She lifted a hand to her neck. What if he *was* a vampire? What if he had already bitten her?

Hurrying to the mirror over the dressing table in the corner, she stared at her reflection, and as she did so, she suddenly realized there were no mirrors in Demetri's house.

Vampires cast no reflection.

Turning her head from side to side, she looked for any telltale bite marks, but there was nothing there.

Sighing with relief, she began to pace again. How long did Oliver intend to keep her here? She pounded on the door, but no one responded.

Feeling a headache coming on, she sank down on the bed. Pressing a hand to her brow, she fell back on the mattress and closed her eyes, while a little voice of doubt played over and over in her mind.

What if it was true?

CHAPTER NINE

Demetri rose with the setting of the sun. He knew immediately that Lorena was not in the house. Dressing quickly, he materialized inside her room. A quick search showed that she had taken nothing with her, leading him to believe she intended to return. But where was she?

Descending the stairs, he moved through the house. Her scent was freshest in the front parlor, and it was there that he found his answer. Ainsley had been here a few hours ago and taken her away with him.

He swore softly as he saddled the black and followed the link between himself and Lorena to Ainsley's house in the country. Lights blazed in the front window.

Dismounting, he ground-tied the stallion, his senses probing the house's interior. Save for a handful of servants, she was alone with Oliver.

Tamping down his rage and his jealousy, he rapped on the door.

Several moments passed before the butler answered it.

Without waiting for an invitation, Demetri strode past the servant. He found Ainsley in the library. "Where is Lorena?"

All the blood drained from Oliver's face. "What ... how ... how dare you come in here uninvited!"

"How dare you take my woman," Demetri retorted. Pivoting on his heel, he stalked out of the library and up the stairs. Her scent guided him to the room where she was being held. A wave of his hand unlocked the door.

At the sound of the door opening, Lorena glanced over her shoulder, her eyes widening when she saw Demetri, dressed, as always, in ubiquitous black.

"Lord Demetri," she exclaimed. "What are you doing here?"

"I have come to take you home. If you wish to go."

"How did you know I was here?"

"To my knowledge, there is no one else you associate with. Shall we?"

What to do, what to do? She worried her lower lip between her teeth. What if Ainsley was right? *Vampire.* Demetri certainly looked the part standing there, all in black, his jaw clenched, his dark-eyed gaze burning into hers.

"Lorena?"

"I..."

Curious to know the reason for her hesitation, he let his mind brush hers, swore under his breath as he realized the cause of her unease. Damn Ainsley for filling her mind with stories of vampires, planting the seeds of suspicion and doubt. He could take her home by force, or bend her will to his, but he didn't find either option appealing. He didn't want a slave. "I shall send your things over tomorrow," he said quietly.

He was leaving. She watched him stride out the door, felt a peculiar ache in her heart at the thought of perhaps never seeing him again. He had taken her in, been kind to her and asked nothing in return save her companionship. Why had she listened to Oliver? Vampires were myths, nothing more. "Lord Demetri! Wait."

He paused at the head of the stairs but didn't turn around.

"I … I … I'm coming with you."

Demetri closed his eyes as a wave of sweet relief swept through him.

Ainsley was waiting for them at the foot of the stairs, backed by the butler and two other male servants. All were armed.

"She is not going with you," Oliver said adamantly.

Demetri raised one brow. "You think not?"

"At least tell her the truth of what you are."

Demetri's eyes narrowed ominously. "And what am I?"

"Tell her why you never eat. Why you are never seen when the sun is up."

"I prefer to dine in private. It is a peculiar habit of mine. As for being out during the day, I have business in the city that takes me away. Business that is none of your concern." His gaze settled on the faces of Ainsley's servants. One by one, they sidled out of the room.

Oliver swallowed hard when he realized he was alone. But he stood his ground.

"Come along, Lorena," Demetri said, confidently descending the stairs.

She trailed behind him, wondering if the two men would come to blows. But when Demetri reached the next-to-last step, Oliver lowered his gaze and backed away.

She glanced over her shoulder as she followed Demetri out the front door, but Oliver hadn't moved.

Demetri's stallion whinnied softly as Demetri lifted her into the saddle, then took up the reins and swung up behind her.

Lorena was acutely conscious of the iron-hard arm around her waist as they made their way home. She searched for something to say to break the taut silence between them, but nothing came to mind. She could feel the tension emanating from him, the barely suppressed fury. Was it aimed at her? Or Oliver Ainsley?

At home, Lorena hurried up to her room while Demetri went to look after the stallion. She stood in the middle of the floor, wondering what to do, what to believe. Had she just made a horrible mistake in coming home with Demetri? Or had she been in more danger with Oliver?

What if Demetri really was a vampire? She shook the thought away. Surely, if such things existed, people would know about it. And if the townspeople believed it was true, surely men like Sir Everleigh wouldn't invite him into their homes.

And yet, a little seed of doubt refused to die. What if it was true? She had never seen him eat, never seen him in the light of day. There were no mirrors anywhere in the house.

If she asked him if what Ainsley claimed was true, would he tell her? Did she really want to know?

"Lorena?"

She flinched at the sound of his voice.

"May I come in?"

She glanced at the bed. It wasn't seemly for him to be in her room, but she lacked the nerve to tell him so. "Y…yes."

She backed up a few steps as the door swung open. Her mouth went dry as she stared at him. He was tall and broad-shouldered, his arms muscular. If he chose to attack her, she would be helpless to fight him off.

"Have you changed your mind?"

"What?"

"Are you sorry you came home with me?"

"I don't know."

"You do not believe all that nonsense about vampires, do you?"

How should she answer? If she said yes, would he silence her forever? If she said no, would be believe her?

"Lorena?"

"I don't know what to believe."

His gaze met and held hers. "Then will you believe that I care for you deeply and would never do anything to bring you harm?"

"Yes, my lord."

"Then shall we go on as before?"

"Yes, my lord, if you wish."

At her words, he visibly relaxed. "Until tomorrow night, then."

"My lord?"

"Yes?"

Summoning her nerve, she asked, "Would you ... could we go into town tomorrow afternoon?"

He lifted one brow. "Is this a test?"

The guilt in her eyes was answer enough.

"Be ready at one o'clock," he said. "Goodnight."

She breathed a sigh of relief as he closed the door behind him.

Demetri prowled the rooms downstairs, quietly cursing Ainsley for filling Lorena's mind with doubts and suspicion. There had been a time when he would have killed the boy out of hand, but he had mellowed since those days. He hadn't taken a human life except to save his own in centuries. He had spent the last twenty years in this small town, rarely drawing attention to himself, slowly gaining the trust of the population. He had kept a low profile, rarely hunting where he lived. What had happened to arouse suspicion in Ainsley? Had he voiced them to others?

He wondered suddenly if the hunters he had encountered had been hired by Ainsley. And then found himself considering the very real possibility that Ainsley was one of them. He grunted softly. Perhaps he would have to get rid of the boy after all.

Feeling the house closing in on him, he transported himself to the city. It was easy to lose himself on the busy streets. Though it was after ten, shops were still open. Men and women milled around, enjoying the balmy night air. A pair of drunks staggered across the road, barely avoiding being struck by a coach and four.

Demetri lifted his head as a cool breeze wafted down the street. There would be a change in the weather by morning. The gods must have taken pity on him, he thought with a faint grin. A layer of dark clouds were gathering in the distance. By the morrow, they would block the sun, allowing him to be out and about without pain.

A woman sitting by herself on a park bench was a temptation he couldn't refuse. A few quick sips took the edge off his thirst.

Whistling softly, he headed home.

After tossing his cloak over the back of the sofa, he glided up the stairs to Lorena's room. She had locked her door, but no mere lock could keep him out. A wave of his hand and the door swung open on silent hinges. He moved to her bedside, his gaze caressing her as he inhaled her scent. She was like a peach, he thought, warm and ripe for the taking.

Bending down, he brushed a kiss across her lips. With a fervent, "Forgive me," he bit her gently. One taste, two, and his hellish thirst was satisfied as never before.

It was amazing, he thought as he licked the twin puncture wounds in her throat to seal them. If only he could bottle that warm, red elixir, he would never have to hunt again.

"Sweet dreams, my sweet Lorena," he murmured. One last look, and he left her room, quietly closing the door behind him. A wave of his hand engaged the lock.

She was here.

She was his.

And he would never willingly let her go.

CHAPTER TEN

The next morning, Lorena counted the hours until one o'clock. Would Demetri really take her to town? If he backed out, what would his excuse be? *Sorry, my dear, I'm a vampire?*

She shook her head in annoyance. Why had she let Oliver poison her mind? She didn't believe in vampires. The man who had written the book about them never even claimed to have seen one, so what made him an authority on the subject? There had been no personal accounts, no hard facts, just supposition and innuendo.

She busied herself with mundane tasks. Now that Demetri had agreed to take her to town, what would her reason be? She had no need of anything. Still, if he was willing to indulge her, she would love to buy a new hat. She didn't think she would ever get used to having more than three dresses, or being allowed to pick and choose her own wardrobe, or spend her days as she saw fit, with no one to order her around during the day and few demands on her time at night.

He hadn't mentioned marriage again. Had he changed his mind? If not, what would her answer be?

She wandered through the house, thinking of the changes she would make if she were the lady of the manor. Some bright colors here and there, she thought. Maybe a new sofa. A new quilt for her bed, something in green, or maybe pink, to match the flowers in the wallpaper.

A new set of dishes.

New curtains for the back parlor.

The chiming of the mantel clock sent her scurrying up to her room. She had less than an hour to get ready.

Demetri paced the parlor floor as he waited for Lorena. As predicted, the weather had changed. Gray clouds hung low in the sky, a light rain pattered on the roof.

He looked toward the stairs at the sound of footsteps, felt a rush of pleasure as Lorena descended the staircase. She was the loveliest, most desirable creature he had ever seen.

She smiled when she saw him. "Good afternoon, my lord."

"Lorena."

She glanced at the front window. "I didn't realize it was raining."

"We shall have to buy you a warm coat while we are in town. Until then, you can wear this," he said, as he draped a long, black cloak around her shoulders, then lifted the hood to cover her hair. "Are you ready?"

She nodded, her nostrils filling with his scent as she drew the cloak around her.

Hand in hand, they hurried down the porch steps to where an elegant coach awaited. He held the door for her, then ducked in after her.

There was always a coach or a carriage waiting for them when he needed one, she thought. How was that possible?

But she had no time to wonder about it because he was speaking to her.

"So, what errand takes us to town today?" he asked.

"I thought it would be nice to go out for tea and maybe, if you don't mind, I could buy a new hat?"

"Tea and a hat?" He lifted one brow. "I think we can manage that. Anything else?"

"I should like a new set of dishes. The ones you have are chipped and cracked."

"Anything else?"

She shook her head, hesitant to ask for more.

They arrived at the Miss Mavis' Tea Room a short time later. Due to the weather, there were few customers. They took a table by the window so Lorena could watch the rain. She ordered tea and a custard tart, then looked expectantly at Demetri.

"Just tea," he told the waitress. Forestalling the question he saw in Lorena's eyes, he said, "I have no liking for sweets."

Lorena searched her mind for some topic of conversation to break the silence between them, but nothing came to mind.

When their order arrived, she added cream and sugar to her tea. Demetri took his black with no sugar.

Conscious of Lorena watching him, he lifted his cup and took a drink. One taste and he wished he had hypnotized her to think he had shared a cup of tea with her. It was bitter beyond belief and hit his stomach like acid. It took all his self-control to keep it down, though he knew that, sooner or later, it would come back up.

The rain had let up a little by the time they left the tea shop, though there were few people on the streets.

Lorena was ever conscious of Demetri beside her as they strolled toward the millinery shop on the corner. She paused at the window, perusing the array of hats on display.

"Which shall it be?" he asked.

"I can't decide. They're all so lovely."

"I shall wait out here while you make your choice," Demetri said.

"I won't be long."

"Take your time," he said with an indulgent smile. As soon as she was out of sight, he ducked into the alley between the millinery and the shop beside it and expelled the vile contents of his stomach.

Lorena chattered happily on the way home, thanking him for being so generous, so patient. He had waited for half an hour while she was inside the milliners, trying to decide between a blue hat with a lovely peacock feather, or a white one adorned with lavender flowers and pink ribbons. Finally, he had come inside and told the proprietor to wrap them both.

He had also insisted on buying her a wool coat and a pair of fur-lined gloves. Before leaving for home, he had also purchased a set of delicate china dinnerware, as well as a lovely set of silver.

Demetri sat back, charmed by her laughter, her smile, her enthusiasm for something as trivial as a couple of hats. He would have bought her a dozen more just to see the sparkle in her eyes.

The rain had stopped altogether by the time they reached home. As they removed their damp outer clothing, Demetri said, "How would you like to go for a ride?"

"Isn't it awfully wet for that?" she asked, hanging his cloak on the hat rack and running her fingers through her hair.

"Not at all. What do you say?"

"I say, let's go. Just let me change my clothes."

With a nod, he followed her up the stairs.

She was in her room, in the midst of unfastening her dress, when the door opened. Alarmed, she took a step back. Did he intend to come in while she changed?

"Lorena," he said, sliding a package wrapped in brown paper and a box through the opening. "These are for you. I bought them the other day."

"What is it?"

"Open the package and see. I will meet you downstairs."

She waited until he closed the door before picking up the mysterious package. Inside, she found a black riding habit. Eager to try it on, she quickly removed her dress and tossed it on the bed. The jacket had long sleeves and flared at the waist. The skirt was divided, something she had never seen before. She frowned at it a moment, then realized it had been cut that way so she didn't have yards of material to contend with the way she would have with a regular skirt and petticoats. There was even a jaunty black hat with a matching feather.

The box held a pair of black riding boots. Like the jacket and skirt, the boots fit perfectly.

As she tugged them on, she found herself again wondering how he knew her size.

Demetri was waiting for her at the foot of the stairs when she left her room. He smiled when he saw her.

"Do I look all right?" she asked.

"Perfect."

"When did you buy these?"

"Soon after I took you riding the first time."

"It was very thoughtful," she said, following him out the kitchen door. "Thank you."

"You like it, then?"

"Yes, very much."

When they reached the barn, the horses were saddled and waiting. Lorena felt a rush of excitement as Demetri lifted her into the saddle. She loved riding. It gave her a sense of freedom, a kind of peace she had never experienced before.

"Ready?" Demetri asked, swinging effortlessly onto the stallion's back. At her nod, he headed for the trail behind the house.

Lorena clucked to the mare, then reached forward to pat her neck. Of all the things Demetri had given her, she loved Lady Gray the most.

It was near dusk. The clouds had fled, and the sun was setting in a blaze of bright pink and orange and ochre. As they rode along the narrow trail, birds flitted through the treetops, their chirps and tweets like music. Gradually, the path widened and became a meadow.

Demetri glanced at her over his shoulder. "Are you ready to try a canter?"

Taking a firmer grip on the reins, Lorena nodded enthusiastically. Even though she had only spent a few hours in the saddle, she wasn't afraid. Lady Gray was just as gentle as Demetri had promised. And she had faith in both man and beast, as well as her own ability. Heart pounding with excitement, she lightly touched her heels to the mare's flanks, let out an exultant shout as the horse broke into a canter. The stallion raced ahead.

After a mile or so, Demetri slowed the stallion to a trot until Lorena caught up with him. "Are you doing all right?" he asked.

"Yes! It's wonderful. How do I make her gallop?"

"Perhaps we should save that for next time."

"Why not now?"

"I think you need a little more experience." His gaze moved over her face. "I should hate for anything to happen to you."

"Please?"

"Just a short one," he said as he touched his heels to the stallion's sides.

Lorena grinned at him, then gasped as the mare surged forward. It was like flying, she thought as she urged Lady Gray to go faster still. Nothing had ever been so exhilarating, or so much fun. She would have been happy to run forever, but, all too soon, Demetri slowed the stallion to a canter and then to a walk.

"You were born to ride," he remarked as they neared a narrow stream bordered by trees and shrubs. "Let us rest the horses for a while."

When they stopped, Lorena slid from the saddle, then looped the mare's reins over a bush.

Demetri ground-reined the stud.

"Aren't you afraid he'll stray away?" she asked.

"No. He is well-trained. Let us sit, shall we?"

She sank down on a patch of damp grass, felt a flutter of excitement as Demetri dropped down beside her, close enough to touch. As always, she was overwhelmed by the sense of strength he exuded. Even motionless, there was an aura of power and authority about him that excited her even as it gave her pause. She had never known anyone like him, not that she had known that many men.

Unbidden, a little voice in the back of her mind whispered, *vampire,* but she quickly shut it out. He had taken her shopping in the afternoon, taken tea with her, both of which proved he was just a man, albeit a most peculiar one.

"Lorena."

His voice moved over her like a velvet caress. She looked at him, suddenly speechless, as he took her hand in his, his thumb lightly stroking her palm. Just a light touch, yet it sent frissons of heat pulsing through her. She swallowed hard as he leaned toward her, her heart racing as he cupped the back of her head in his hand and kissed her. It was like nothing she had ever known before. He had kissed her a few times, but this was different somehow, as if he was claiming her for his own. She told herself that was foolish, but then, as he deepened the kiss, she didn't care. All she wanted was his mouth on hers, his tongue teasing her own in a most inappropriate manner, his arm sliding around her waist to draw her closer, pulling her down on the grass so that she felt the length of his body pressed intimately against her own.

It was madness.

It was heaven.

He groaned deep in his throat and then, abruptly, he rose to his feet and turned his back to her.

She stared at him, her body on fire, her lips bruised from his kisses.

"We should go," he said, his voice ragged.

Go? She stood, her legs wobbly, her head spinning with confusion.

Avoiding her gaze, he lifted her into the saddle and thrust the reins into her hands. "Give the mare her head," he said, his voice tight. "She will take you safely home."

"Where are you …?"

But she was talking to empty air as he swung onto the stallion's back and raced away.

Frowning, Lorena stared after him, then touched her heels to the mare's side and followed him down the trail, wondering all the while what had just happened.

CHAPTER ELEVEN

Oliver Ainsley paced back and forth in front of the hearth, his brow furrowed, his thoughts troubled. He hadn't had a good night's sleep since Demetri spirited Lorena away. He hated to think of her in the evil clutches of that monster. How could she not see Demetri for what he was? Couldn't she sense the darkness that clung to him, feel the otherworldly power that radiated from him like the devil's own breath? He had to get her away from Demetri, help her to see him for the disgusting, blood-sucking creature he was. Once she realized the horrible fate she had escaped, she would thank him for not giving up.

But how? That was the question that kept him up nights. How was he to prove it? His words and the book he had shown her had meant nothing. Perhaps she was under some kind of hypnotic spell, he thought, some wicked enchantment that blocked her from seeing the truth.

He paused to stare into the cold ashes in the hearth. There had to be a way to make the fair Lorena see the light.

Chapter Twelve

During the next two weeks, Lorena saw Lord Demetri far more frequently than she had in the past, though rarely when the sun was up. He had explained his absence during the day, informing her that he rose early in the morning to take care of business in the neighboring city where he owned several properties and had an interest in the bank. Once he explained it to her, it all made sense. Of course he would dine in the opulent restaurants in the city rather than travel back home for his meals. It also explained his wealth.

To pass the time, she tried her hand at embroidery, needlepoint, and painting.

She rearranged the furniture in both parlors, cleaned the cupboards in the kitchen, ordered new draperies for the back parlor from a mail order catalog.

Each day, she spent hours down at the barn, brushing Lady Gray's velvety coat, turning her out in the corral, or just riding around the yard. She had been tempted several times to leave the property and explore the winding, tree-lined trails behind the house but never quite found the courage to do so on her own.

She bought a rooster and a few hens from a traveling peddler and housed them in the small coop beside the barn.

She had never been happier or more carefree, she mused, as she knelt in the gardens late one afternoon, pulling weeds and dead flowers from the beds. Next time Demetri took her to town, she would see about buying some new plants. Demetri...

Lorena traced her lips with her fingertips, remembering the taste of his kisses, the way his caresses made her whole body tingle in a most pleasurable way. Odd, that his touches didn't repel her the way Lord Fairfield's had. Her cheeks grew warm as she wondered what it would be like to be intimate with Demetri, to feel the long, muscular length of his body against hers, with nothing between them.

Embarrassed to be having such erotic thoughts in broad daylight about a man she hardly knew, she shook the images from her mind. Reluctantly, she admitted she would love to know more about him, to know him better. He never mentioned his parents or talked about his past. Was he an orphan? But that hardly seemed likely, given the clothes and books in the attic. Perhaps he'd had a falling out with his family.

Shaking the dust from her skirts, Lorena went into the house for a cold drink, determined to learn more about the fascinating man who filled her thoughts by day and her dreams by night.

⚜ ⚜ ⚜

Lorena had just washed the dirt from her hands when she heard a knock at the door.

Thinking maybe her new drapes had arrived, she hurried to answer it. But it wasn't a delivery. It was Oliver Ainsley.

"Oliver!" she exclaimed. "What are you doing here?"

"I came to apologize in hopes that we might still be friends."

"Do you think that's wise, considering our last encounter?"

"Perhaps not, but I care a great deal about you. With Demetri away during the day, I thought you might enjoy some company."

"No more talk of vampires?"

"No."

"You were wrong anyway," she said. "He took me out for tea just the other afternoon, and shopping later in the day."

Ainsley made a vague gesture with his hand. "I shall beg his pardon when next I see him. So, what do you say, Miss Halliday? Friends, again?"

"I guess so."

His smile spread ear to ear. "I look forward to renewing our friendship." He bowed from the waist, then sauntered down the porch stairs, whistling softly as he swung onto the back of his horse.

Lorena stared after him, her brow furrowed thoughtfully while she watched him ride away.

Had she made the right decision? He had kidnapped her, though he had claimed it was for her own protection. She would be friendly and polite, she decided as she closed the door, but she would never again be alone with him.

Lorena had just finished cleaning up after dinner when Demetri entered the kitchen. One look at his face and she knew something was wrong. She had a terrible feeling she knew what it was, and his first words proved her right.

"What was Ainsley doing here?"

She wondered how he could possibly have known even as she searched for an answer. Arms folded across her chest, she stammered, "I...he came to...to apologize for his foolish accusations...and he...he asked if we couldn't be friends again."

"And what did you say?"

She swallowed the lump of fear rising in her throat. "I...I said I thought it would be all right, but—"

"Did you?" His gaze speared hers. "Is that what you want?"

She stared at him, chilled by the anger she sensed boiling just under the surface.

Demetri inhaled deeply and let it out in a long, slow sigh. "I told you once before you are not a prisoner here," he said, clenching his hands at his sides. "If you feel the need to socialize with him..." A muscle twitched in his jaw. "The decision is yours."

"But you would rather I didn't."

"I think I have made that perfectly clear."

Relief washed through her and yet she felt a horrible sense of guilt for disappointing him when he had been so kind to her. Had she just ruined their relationship? Perhaps if she explained her decision. "Lord Demetri, I—"

"Sir Everleigh has invited us to a card party tomorrow night," he said, cutting off her explanation. "If you wish to go, be ready at nine. I am sure Ainsley will be there, as well."

Before she could think of a reply, he pivoted on his heel and stalked out of the house.

Outside, Demetri unleashed a torrent of profanity. Damn Ainsley! The man was handsome and charming and a complete pain in the ass. All that talk of apologizing and wanting to be Lorena's friend was an outright lie. Ainsley had been trying to destroy him in one way or another for years.

He paced the yard, his anger growing with every step. He paused when he heard the front door open, followed by Lorena's tentative footsteps coming up behind him.

"My lord?"

He did not look at her. "What is it?"

"I didn't mean to upset you, nor do I intend to let Lord Ainsley call on me in the future. My offer was of friendship, nothing more than that."

Demetri slowly turned to face her. "Forgive me," he said. "I frightened you and I did not mean to. I have no excuse except that I cannot abide the thought of you with another man."

He was jealous, she thought, pleased and surprised.

He closed the distance between them until they were only a breath apart. "Lorena?"

"Yes, my lord?"

He cupped her face in his hands, his gaze searching hers, and then he kissed her.

Going up on her tiptoes, Lorena slipped her arms around his neck as she pressed her lips to his. Why was it that all her doubts vanished when she was in his arms? She thought of him by day, dreamed of him by night. Could she be falling in love with him?

Demetri groaned softly, pleasure and pain ripping through him as he lifted his head, torn between need and desire.

Lorena darted backward as two dark shadows rose up behind him. Moonlight glinted on the blade of a knife.

Demetri swore a vile oath as he whirled around to face his attackers.

She watched in silent horror as he battled two men clad in long black cloaks. Men armed with daggers and what looked like thick wooden stakes. She watched in mute horror as they came together. Locked in a deadly ballet, they struggled, two against one. Blood. So much blood. It gleamed wetly on Demetri's back, high up, near his shoulder, and from a wicked gash along one arm. Bile rose in her throat as, with a quick twist, he broke the neck of the assailant closest to him and tossed the body aside like kindling.

The second man let out a cry as he lunged forward, driving the stake in his hand into Demetri's back.

Lorena closed her eyes for a moment, her stomach roiling with nausea and fear.

When she opened them again, Demetri was still standing.

The second man lay at his feet, the wooden stake piercing his heart.

"Lorena," Demetri hissed, his voice tight with pain. "Go to your room and lock the door."

She shook her head and took a step toward him, her hand outstretched. "You're hurt. You need help."

"You cannot give me the help I need," he growled. "Go into the house!"

Something in his tone warned her not to argue. And not to run. Confused and suddenly afraid, she walked quickly up the stairs, into the house and closed the door, then ran up to her room and locked herself in.

She stood there a moment, shivering uncontrollably, and then hurried toward the window and drew back the drapes.

Demetri was gone.

And so were the bodies.

CHAPTER THIRTEEN

Demetri carried the bodies of the hunters deep into the woods. It took all his remaining strength to bury them. Then, weak from the blood he had lost, his back and arm on fire from the wounds the hunters had inflicted, he dropped to his knees and waited for the worst of the pain to pass. He needed to feed. Fresh blood would ease the pain and heal his wounds more quickly.

Closing his eyes, he filled his mind with thoughts of Lorena—her scent, the silk of her hair against his skin, the warmth of her smile, the comfort of her touch. The sweet taste of her lips. She might not love him. She might be afraid of him from time to time. But he knew she craved his kisses almost as much as he longed for hers.

The pain lessened as one hour slipped into the next. Sometimes it surprised him that he possessed the strength and power of twenty men, that most injuries healed instantly and yet he was not immune to pain.

Shortly before dawn, he made his way to the city in search of prey

In the morning, the events of the night before seemed like a bad dream. Peering out the window of the front parlor,

Lorena saw no telltale signs of the battle that had taken place. Nothing at all. Maybe it really had been a nightmare. If so, it had been the most realistic and terrifying one she'd ever had.

Smiling faintly, she lifted her hand to her lips. She hadn't imagined Demetri's kisses, though. They had been all too intoxicating, all too real. Where was he now? If it hadn't been a dream, then he had been badly hurt last night. Had he gone to the hospital? Sought medical aid from a friend? Why hadn't he asked her for help? Why had he sent her into the house?

So many questions with no way to get answers until she saw him again.

If she saw him again.

Lorena paced the parlor floor. Never had the hours passed so slowly. She had tried to read, tried to paint, had gone outside and pulled weeds, but she couldn't concentrate on anything. All she could think about was Demetri. Where could he be? She had peeked into his bedroom earlier but it had been empty. Had he come in last night while she slept and left before she rose this morning?

As the sun began its slow descent, she looked out the window every few minutes, peering into the dusk, hoping to see him striding up the path toward the door.

At full dark, she pulled a chair up to the window, her fear that something terrible had happened to him growing stronger with every passing moment. He had always come home by now.

Where could he be?

❧ ❧ ❧

Demetri lifted his head from his prey's neck, his brow furrowing as Lorena's troubled thoughts flitted across his mind. She was worried about him. The thought made him smile. How long had it been since anyone worried about his safety?

He released the woman in his arms, sealed the tiny punctures in her throat, wiped his memory from her mind, and sent her on her way.

Transporting himself to his lair, he stripped off his torn and bloody cloak and shirt. He had been too weak, in too much pain, to clean up last night. Now, wishing he dared go upstairs and soak in a hot bath, he filled a large bowl with water, heated it with a glance, and washed up as best he could. Drying off, he dressed quickly and combed his hair.

Unable to will himself into the house without causing alarm or raising questions he didn't want to answer, he willed himself to the head of the road that led up to the manor.

As he neared the house, he caught sight of Lorena at the front window. She was waiting for him, her expression anxious. How long had it been since anyone cared if he lived or died? It was a good feeling.

As he approached the front steps, the door flew open and Lorena ran out of the house and down the stairs.

"My lord?" Lorena's gaze ran over him from head to foot. He looked perfectly fine, not a hair out of place. There was no sign of his injuries from the night before. "You're all right?"

"Of course."

"But…last night…those men…they…they stabbed you. With a knife. And a wooden stake."

"Merely flesh wounds," he assured her with a smile. "They did more damage to my best cloak than my flesh."

She shook her head in disbelief. And then frowned. "You killed them."

"No," he lied. "Merely rendered them unconscious."

Seconds ticked into eternity as she stared at him, weighing his words against what she had seen with her own eyes—or thought she had seen—the night before. And what she saw now. Had the fight been less deadly that it appeared? Had her imagination made it seem worse than it was?

"Sir Everleigh's card party starts within the hour," he reminded her. "Were you planning to accompany me?"

"What? Oh, yes, the party." She glanced down at her day dress. "I need to change."

"Take your time. Everleigh will forgive us if we arrive late."

With a nod, she hurried up the stairs.

Lights blazed from the windows of Sir Everleigh's home. They were obviously late, as several fancy carriages already lined the drive, including one she recognized as Oliver Ainsley's.

Demetri handed her from the coach, took her arm as they made their way up the steps. A butler met them at the door to take her wrap.

Several round tables had been set up in the ballroom. A small orchestra played quietly in one corner. Servants meandered through the maze of tables, offering *hors d'ourves*, wine, and brandy. Merry laughter and the slap of cards punctuated the air.

Demetri led her to Sir Everleigh's table, where there were two vacant chairs.

"I had about given you up," Everleigh said, smiling a welcome.

"Women," Demetri said with a grin. "Are they ever ready on time?"

"Well, this one is certainly worth waiting for," Everleigh replied with a twinkle in his eyes. "We hadn't yet started to play, so you're not really late."

"I'm so glad the two of you could make it," Beatrice said, beaming at Demetri. "It wouldn't be any fun without you."

"You're the reason I came," Demetri said gallantly. Bending down, he kissed her cheek, then held a chair for Lorena before taking his own seat.

In spite of her years, Beatrice blushed like a young girl.

Lorena tapped Demetri on the shoulder, then leaned over to whisper, "I don't know how to play cards."

"Then it's time you learned," he whispered back as Sir Everleigh's sister dealt the cards—thirteen to each player.

Demetri taught her the rules of play as they went along, occasionally looking at her hand to advise her. To Lorena's surprise, she won the first hand.

"Beginner's luck," Everleigh said, with a wink.

At the end of the first round, the players changed tables. Lorena was dismayed to find herself in the company of Oliver Ainsley and a man and a woman she didn't know.

"Miss Halliday," Oliver said, beaming at her, "what a nice surprise. I don't believe you know Lady Margaret or Viscount Davenport."

Feeling ill-at-ease, Lorena nodded to each in turn. What was she doing here? She didn't belong with these people. They had been born to wealth and privilege, their manners were impeccable. She had been raised on a farm and sold into servitude.

She wasn't sure how she got through the hour, but when the players rose to change tables again, she slipped out of the room and hurried toward the balcony. It was cool and quiet there, with a magnificent view of Sir Everleigh's rose garden. A majestic fountain sat in the center of the garden.

She whirled around at the sound of footsteps. Expecting to see Demetri, she let out a gasp of dismay when she saw Oliver Ainsley striding purposefully toward her.

"Alone at last," he murmured with a sly grin.

"Hardly," Lorena retorted, glancing through the open doorway to the crowded room beyond.

He chuckled. "Don't be alarmed. I don't intend to seduce you. I merely wished to ask if all is well."

"Of course it is. Why wouldn't it be?"

"Why do you not let me put you up in my home? It isn't seemly for you to share a house with Demetri, especially when there are no servants in attendance. I would provide you with a maid and a chaperone, so that your reputation remains pure and intact. And a carriage and driver of your own, if you wish."

"That's very generous," Lorena said. "But I'm quite content where I am. And I fear any *damage* to my reputation has already been done."

He took a step toward her, a glint in his eye. "Let me take care of you, Lorena."

"She has no need of your help."

Ainsley paused in mid-stride to glance behind him at the sound of Demetri's voice. "I was merely offering her a choice," he said smoothly.

"I believe she has already made it."

Ainsley looked at Lorena. "The offer still stands." Bowing over her hand, he kissed it, then returned to the card room.

"Are you still happy with your decision to stay with me?" Demetri asked when they were alone.

"Yes, my lord."

"And are you still considering my offer of marriage?"

The thought stirred a flutter of excitement in the pit of her stomach. "Yes, my lord."

His look of relief touched her heart. As did his smile. "Shall we return to the games?"

"If you wish."

"What do you wish, Lorena?"

She wished he would take her in his arms, that she had been born to the nobility so that she felt like she belonged in his world, with his friends. "I wish," she said, her voice little more than a whisper. "I wish you would kiss me."

For a moment, Demetri simply stared at her, unable to believe his ears. And then, feeling as if he had been given a rare and precious gift, he took her into his arms and kissed her ever so tenderly. "Lorena, my love, let us go home."

From his place in the middle of the card room, Oliver Ainsley's gut twisted with hatred and jealousy as he watched the two of them bid goodnight to Sir Everleigh and collect their coats.

Someday, he vowed, someday Lorena would look at him like that.

My love. Demetri's words echoed in Lorena's mind on the carriage ride home. Her nerves were all aflutter when they reached the house. *My love.* No one had ever called her that before.

Inside, he locked the door, lit the lamps, and then drew her into his arms once again. He caressed her cheek with his knuckles. "What are your feelings for me, Lorena? I need to know."

"I'm not sure. I care for you. I'm grateful for all you've done for me, for getting me out of Lord Fairfield's home…but…I don't know if it's love." She made a vague gesture with her hand. "I've never been in love before."

He smiled down at her. "It is enough to know you care, my sweet Lorena. Dare I hope you will soon be my bride?"

Her gaze slid away from his. "I don't think I'm ready for intimacy yet," she murmured, and felt her cheeks flame with embarrassment.

"As I said before, I will not demand that you fulfill your wifely duties unless and until you feel comfortable doing so."

"May I give you my answer next week?"

"As you wish. May I kiss you goodnight?"

Her cheeks grew hotter as she whispered, "You never have to ask me that."

Her reply filled him with hope.

Lorena's eyelids fluttered down as he lowered his head and covered her mouth with his in a long, slow kiss that made her knees go weak and her heart beat double-time.

"Until tomorrow night, my love," he said.

"Tomorrow," she murmured, and smiled inside, her lips still tingling from his kisses.

CHAPTER FOURTEEN

Things were different between them after that, Lorena mused a few nights later. The tension that had always been between them had disappeared. Demetri seemed less stern, less reserved. He smiled more often. He took her for long walks in the countryside, horseback riding in the moonlight, dancing under the stars in the backyard. They attended the opera and the theater. They played whist with Sir Everleigh and his sister.

As time passed, Demetri's kisses came more often, grew deeper and more intense, his hands bolder when he caressed her. She knew she should object when he took such liberties, but she craved the press of his hard, muscular body against hers, his hands stroking where they had no right to touch. She knew if she asked, he would stop, but to her shame, she remained silent. Being in his arms was more intoxicating than the finest wine. She loved being near him, gloried in his touch, loved his strong, masculine scent, the deep, throaty sound of his voice that did funny things in the pit of her stomach.

In two days, he would expect an answer to his proposal. She still hadn't made up her mind, but how could she refuse when she wanted him so badly?

Now, they were in a carriage on their way home from the opera. His arm was around her and he was kissing her as if he would never stop. She tilted her head back as he rained kisses along the side of her neck. His touch made her whole body tingle with anticipation. She was on fire for him, ready to give him whatever he asked, when there was a shout from outside, the harsh report of gunfire as the carriage came to an abrupt stop and both doors flew open.

Lorena let out a shriek as rough hands grabbed her and yanked her out of the carriage. She caught a brief glimpse of Demetri as three men dressed in black and wearing masks leaped into the coach. She cried his name as her captor dragged her away, fought and scratched like a woman possessed as he held her down, then pressed a smelly cloth over her nose and mouth. She screamed as the world spun out of focus and disappeared into nothingness.

Frantic for Lorena's safety, Demetri fought back against the hunters. They had come well-prepared. One of them managed to wrap a thick silver chain around his neck, quashing his attempt to dissolve into mist and escape, while the other two stabbed him repeatedly with silver-bladed knives. Only the fact that they were young and scared saved him from certain death.

Driven by fear and excitement, thwarted by his efforts to resist, they continually missed the mark.

Wracked with pain, Demetri called on every ounce of his remaining strength as he tossed one of his attackers through the window, broke the arm of the second. When he reached for the third, the man let out a yelp, jumped out of the coach and bolted down the road.

Bleeding from numerous wounds in his chest, back, and shoulders, his teeth clenched against the pain, Demetri fell out of the carriage.

Using one of the coach wheels, he pulled himself to his feet and staggered toward Lorena, who lay sprawled on her back in the dirt a few feet away. He feared she was dead, she lay so still. But no, her heart was still beating, slow and steady. She was merely unconscious.

Whispering, "Forgive me, my love," he knelt beside her. Too desperate for relief to be gentle, he sank his fangs into her throat.

Lorena woke with a start. Something was eating her! Was she dead? She tried to roll away, but the same something was holding her down, something that growled when she tried to push it away. She lashed out with her fist and the pain stopped.

Scrambling to her feet, she felt momentarily dizzy. Where was Demetri? A glance around showed the driver lying face down in the dirt. A dagger protruded from his back. There was no sign of the other three men.

She gasped when she saw Demetri lying on the ground at her feet, covered in blood. A crimson stain was smeared across his mouth. "Demetri?"

He groaned low in his throat as he sat up. "Lorena," he said hoarsely. Come to me."

Wanting to help, she knelt beside him.

"I need more of your blood."

More? She frowned at him. What was he talking about? "My lord?"

"Your blood. I need it." Grasping her shoulders, he pulled her closer. And bit her.

She knelt there, frozen, unable to believe what was happening. She had hit her head earlier. Perhaps she was hallucinating. But it felt so real. There was no pain, only a rush of sweet, sensual pleasure as he drank from her. She felt light-headed when he stopped.

"Lorena," he murmured. "Go to sleep."

Her eyelids immediately fluttered down, her head drooping.

Demetri rose to his feet, lifted her in his arms and transported her home, where he settled her on the sofa. Her blood had eased the pain somewhat, but he needed more. Much more than she could spare. A last look to make sure she was sleeping peacefully, and he left the house, everything else forgotten but the relentless need that pounded through him.

In the morning, Lorena woke with a start, one hand pressed to her neck. She glanced wildly around, relaxing only when she recognized her surroundings. She was home. But what was she doing on the sofa, still fully clothed?

Fragmented images of the night past paraded through her mind—men in black attacking them ... pulling her from the carriage ... the driver of the coach lying dead in the road, a dagger in his back ... Demetri biting her ... Biting her!

Scrambling to her feet, she ran up the stairs. Unbeknownst to Demetri, she had bought a small hand mirror on their last trip to town. In her room, she opened the top dresser drawer and retrieved it from its hiding place beneath a pile of gloves. Holding it up, she turned her head to the right. Nothing there. But on the left side of her throat she saw two tiny red marks. A cold chill raced down her spine. *Bite marks.* She dropped the mirror and grabbed the sides of the dresser to steady herself.

It hadn't been a hallucination. It hadn't been a dream. It had been all too real. She rubbed her fingertips over the tiny bit of dried blood below her ear.

Oliver had been right all along.

Demetri was a vampire. There was no other logical explanation.

For a moment, she stood there, faint with shock and dismay.

Vampire, vampire, vampire!

It couldn't be true. There were no such things.

But he had bitten her. She hadn't imagined it. The proof was right there before her eyes.

Driven by a primal fear of the unknown, she ran down the stairs and out the back door.

At the barn, she saddled the gray mare with hands that trembled uncontrollably. Standing on a bale of hay, she climbed into the saddle and rode out of the yard. She had no destination in mind save a desperate need to get as far away from Demetri as she could before nightfall.

Where to go, where to go? Returning to Lord Fairfield was out of the question.

She had no friends, other than Oliver Ainsley, but she shied away from the idea of going to him for help. She thought of Sir Everleigh, but he was Demetri's friend, not hers. Like it or not, her only choice was Oliver. She had nowhere else to go, no money for lodging... the memory of Mr. Carstairs, the kind desk clerk at the inn, swam to the surface of her mind. He had helped her once before. Perhaps he would again.

Lorena breathed a sigh of relief when she arrived at the inn. Sending a fervent hope toward heaven that he was still employed, she dismounted and tethered the mare to a post out front. She smoothed a hand over her hair as she stepped inside, thanked her lucky stars when she opened the door and saw Mr. Carstairs standing behind the desk.

He looked up and smiled when he saw her. "Miss Halliday, welcome back."

"Thank you."

"How many nights will you be staying?" he asked, somewhat eagerly, she thought.

"I'm not sure."

"No matter. You're welcome to stay for as long as you wish."

Lorena bit down on her lower lip, only then remembering that she had left the house in such a hurry she hadn't brought any money with her. If he would let her stay the night, she could return home in the morning for her reticule and a few changes of clothes.

"Is something wrong?" he asked.

"I desperately need a place to spend the night, but I can't pay you just now."

"We have several empty rooms," he said kindly. "You're welcome to stay in any one of them."

"I don't want you to get in trouble."

"No need to worry. My father owns this place. You're more than welcome to stay as long as you like."

"That's very kind of you. Rest assured, I'll pay you tomorrow."

Reaching behind him, he pulled a key from a hook on the wall and handed it to her. "Room 317," he said, with a wink. "It's our best one."

Lorena shook her head. "That's not necessary."

"Would you deny me the blessing of doing a good deed?" he asked with a twinkle in his eye.

"No, kind sir," she said gratefully. "I would not."

"Perhaps you would dine with me this evening?"

She hesitated a moment before nodding. "That would be lovely. Thank you."

"I shall call for you at eight."

Lorena smiled, then turned and made her way up the stairs, vowing that someday, somehow, she would repay him for his kindness and generosity.

As soon as he roused that evening, Demetri knew that Lorena was nowhere in the house.

He cursed long and loud as he realized that, lost in the pain of his wounds and the desperate need for blood, he had forgotten to erase the events of the night past from her mind, or seal the tiny wounds he had left in her throat.

And she had fled from the truth.

Lorena glanced around her room. It was larger than the one she had stayed in before, the furnishings of better quality, the bed larger. The single window looked out over the street below.

Earlier, Mr. Carstairs had brought her a pail of hot water. She had washed her hands and face, run her fingers through her hair and then sat in the chair by the window, wondering where she would go from here. At least this time, she didn't have to rely on his charity. She could pay her own way, at least for a little while. Perhaps she could find a position as a housekeeper or a governess at one of the manor houses.

It was a few minutes shy of eight o'clock when there was a light knock at the door. Mr. Carstairs was early, Lorena thought, smiling as she hurried to let him in.

She gasped when she opened the door and saw Demetri standing in the hallway, tall and forbidding. And looking every inch the vampire she now knew him to be.

She backed up, her heart pounding with fear. "What...what are you...doing here?"

"I have come to take you home."

"No." She shook her head vigorously. "No. I'm staying here."

She cringed when he stepped into the room, felt a brief surge of hope when Mr. Carstairs appeared behind him in the doorway.

Carstairs glanced from her to Demetri and back again.

Demetri did not turn around. "Get out of here, boy," he said, his voice quiet and laced with menace.

"See here, sir, how dare you...?" Carstairs fell silent when Demetri turned to look at him.

Lorena didn't know what Mr. Carstairs saw in Demetri's eyes, but he pivoted on his heels and ran down the corridor.

Demetri closed the door behind him. "Why did you run away?"

She clenched her hands to still their trembling. "You know why."

"Have I ever hurt you?"

She swallowed hard. "No."

"Have I ever threatened you?"

"No."

"I am the same man tonight as I was the night before. You were not afraid of me then. Why are you afraid of me now?"

"You bit me!" She lifted a hand to her throat. "You drank my blood!"

"For that, I am sorry. But I was badly hurt, and I needed it."

She stared at him, her brow furrowed, her eyes filled with confusion.

"Blood eases the pain and heals my wounds," he explained. "Had there been another choice, I would not have taken what I needed from you." It was mostly true. He could have fed from the dead coach driver, but that was repugnant in the extreme. "I never meant to frighten you. Do you believe me?"

She nodded slowly.

"I want you to come home."

"And if I refuse? Will you drag me there against my will?"

"Is that what you think?"

"I don't know." *Vampire.* He was a vampire. He had seemed frightening a moment ago. Now he was just Demetri, looking at her with hurt and hope in his fathomless eyes.

"I would never force you to do anything you did not wish to do."

"Then I wish to stay here tonight and think it over."

"Very well. I will return tomorrow night for your answer."

That wasn't the only answer she owed him, he thought. But she would never agree to marry him now. The best he could hope for was that she would return home with him. For a moment, he considered wiping the memory of what had happened from her mind, but perhaps it was better this way. She had been bound to discover the truth sooner or later, he mused, though he wished she had learned it in a less traumatic way.

Reaching into his pocket, he withdrew several banknotes and dropped them on the dresser. "Until tomorrow," he murmured as his gaze moved over her. Mouth set in a hard line, he turned and strode out the door.

Lorena stared after him, relieved that he had left without argument and yet, strangely hurt that he had not tried harder to convince her to go home with him.

Carstairs shrank back when the man who had been in Lorena's room descended the stairs. Never, in all his life, had he seen such a frightening character. He knew, somehow, that he was lucky to be alive. Knew, in the depths of his soul, that the stranger could have killed him with no more than a thought.

Fear for Lorena's life overcame the fear for his own and he ran up the stairs and pounded on her door. "Lorena!"

She opened the door before he could knock again. "Mr. Carstairs! What's wrong?"

He stared at her, wide-eyed. "You're all right?"

"Of course."

"But ... that man ..."

"Forget about him," Lorena said, and wished she could do the same. "Let us go to dinner, shall we?

Filled with bitterness and a hurt unlike anything he had ever known, Demetri stalked the night, his cloak fluttering behind him like the wings of death. He should have wiped the memory of what he was from her mind, he thought angrily. He should have dragged her home. But no, some long-forgotten sense of right and wrong, some lingering shred of humanity, had made him let her go. Stupid, he thought, already regretting his decision. Sheer stupidity to throw away the best thing that had ever happened to him.

He preyed on the first mortal he saw, drank his fill, and left the thief lying in the gutter, alive, but barely. And he didn't care.

The lights of a brothel appeared in the distance and he ducked inside. The whores were not particularly young, but they were clean and available. He chose one and followed her up the creaky stairs to her room. Inside, he pulled her into his arms.

"Easy, gov'nor," she murmured. "We've got all night."

"Shut up," he growled, and covered her mouth with his. One kiss, two, and he pushed her away.

"What's wrong?" she asked, a whine in her voice. "Don't I please you?"

Filled with self-loathing, hating the woman because she wasn't Lorena, he slammed out of the room and into the dark of the night, where he belonged.

CHAPTER FIFTEEN

Lorena groaned softly when she awoke in the morning. She felt as if she hadn't slept at all. Last night, she had enjoyed spending time with Mr. Carstairs. He was pleasant company, polite and witty. But all the while, she found herself comparing him to Demetri. Mr. Carstairs was and would always be a boy at heart, whereas she found it hard to imagine that Demetri had ever even been young. Had he ever laughed and joked and played pranks on his fellows? Or had he been solemn and reserved, even as a child? She wondered again if he had brothers and sisters, and if his parents were still living. She thought it odd that he never mentioned his family or made any reference to his past.

Last night, after returning to her room, she had paced the floor, torn between what she knew was the smart thing to do and the yearning of her own heart.

There was no way to have a normal, lasting relationship with Demetri. He was a vampire. He had bitten her, taken her blood, and likely killed many men. And women.

So why did her heart ache for him? Why did she feel sorry for him? Why did she long to take him in her arms and comfort him?

It made no sense.

Her indecision had kept her tossing and turning most of last night. She was no closer to a decision this morning than she had been when she finally fell asleep.

What was she going to say when Demetri came for her answer?

She washed her hands and face, then made her way downstairs. There was a new man at the desk. Mr. Carstairs' father, perhaps?

Leaving the inn, Lorena walked slowly down the street until she came to a bakery. Using some of the money Demetri had left her, she bought a loaf of bread and several muffins. Moving on down the street, she bought a bit of cheese from one vendor, a few apples from another.

Returning to her room, she breakfasted on apples and muffins, wishing, all the while, for a cup of tea to wash it down.

With her appetite appeased, her thoughts drifted back to Demetri. Sitting on the chair beside the window, she stared outside, recalling his kindnesses, his generosity, the sadness in the depths of his eyes when he bid her farewell the night before.

If he would agree never to bite her again, to reassure her that she could leave anytime she wished, perhaps she would return to his house. She had been happy there until she learned the truth—happier than she had ever been with anyone else. But he was a vampire. How was she ever to trust him again?

As the sun slid behind the horizon, her heart began to pound in anticipation.

He arrived a short time later, and even though she had been expecting him, she flinched when he rapped on the door.

Taking a deep breath, she called, "Come in."

Her gaze moved over him. Broad shoulders, long legs, muscular arms, fathomless dark eyes. He was dressed in black, as always, yet she couldn't imagine him in anything else.

"Lorena."

"My lord."

"Have you reached a decision?"

She swallowed hard. "I have, yes."

He felt as if all the air had left the room as he waited for her answer.

"I will return home with you on two conditions."

"Name them."

"You will never bite me or drink from me again."

A muscle twitched in his jaw, and then he nodded.

"And if the day comes that I wish to leave, you will let me go."

He nodded again, his expression inscrutable.

Feeling suddenly shy and uncertain, she said, "Lady Gray is in the stable behind the inn."

"Yes, I know. Shall we go?"

She glanced around the room, but she had brought nothing with her. Ever frugal, she did however pick up the small sack that held the remaining items she had purchased earlier in the day.

As they left the room, she was conscious of Demetri walking silently behind her. Seeing Mr. Carstairs at the desk again, she paused to thank him for his kindness. He refused to accept payment for her room.

"I hope everything works out for you," he said, keeping one wary eye on Demetri. "If you ever need anything..." He shrugged as his words trailed off.

"Thank you, Mr. Carstairs." Turning away from the desk, she left the inn.

At the stable, Demetri saddled the mare, lifted her onto the horse's back, and swung up behind her. She stiffened as he slipped his arm around her waist.

The move was not lost on Demetri. It cut him to the quick to know she was now afraid of his touch. As they rode out of the yard, he wondered if he would ever again have her trust.

Lorena's nerves were on edge as Demetri reined the mare to a halt at the foot of the front porch stairs. Dismounting, he lifted her from the saddle, then led the horse around the side of the house to the narrow path that led to the barn.

She stared after him a moment before going up the steps and into the house, praying that she had made the right decision. He had agreed to her stipulations, but she had no proof that he would keep his word. The stark reality was that she was putting her life in his hands. She told herself that, except for taking her blood, he had never hurt her, that he had treated her with nothing but kindness and respect.

She flinched when he entered the parlor.

Reaching into his pocket, he withdrew a folded sheet of paper. "This is the deed to the house. I have signed it over to you."

"Why would you do that?" Her gaze searched his as he thrust the document into her hand.

"If I ever do anything that frightens you, you have only to order me out of the house and I will be forced to leave."

"I don't understand."

"I don't know how it works. I only know that it does. I believe it is some kind of built-in protection against my kind. Vampires cannot enter a home uninvited, nor can they stay if that invitation is revoked. I want you to feel safe while you are here."

"You came into my hotel room without an invitation."

"It is not a home."

"What about Ainsley's home?"

"I had been invited there long ago. The invitation was never rescinded, although I rather think he will have done so now."

"May I ask you something?"

"Of course."

"Where do you spend the day?"

"I have a secure location where I rest during the daylight hours." He didn't tell her it was below the basement, or that, if she revoked his invitation, he would have to find a new place to hide from the world.

She nodded slowly. "I guess it's a secret."

"By necessity."

Taking a seat on the sofa, she looked up at him. "Tell me about vampires."

He propped his shoulder against the door jamb. "What do you wish to know?"

"Have you been what you are for a long time?"

"Depends on what you call long."

She lifted one brow, obviously not satisfied with his answer.

"I was turned three hundred and fifty-three years ago last Christmas."

She stared at him, wide-eyed. "I should call that very long, indeed."

"You have no idea." Three hundred years of hiding what he was, eluding hunters, learning to adapt to a completely foreign lifestyle. There had been times when he had been tempted to end it. He was glad now that he had not.

"How did it happen?"

"I had been on my way home from buying presents for my wife and family when a woman came running up to me. She grabbed my arm, said her child was sick, begged me to help her. I followed her to her house where I found a young man who appeared to be ill. I asked her what I could do to help, and she said he needed blood. I had no idea what she meant until he flung himself at me and buried his fangs in my throat. I remember nothing after that.

"When I came to myself, I learned that the woman was the vampire's mate. He had been wounded to the point of death by hunters. Ordinarily, I would have died from the amount of blood he took, but because I had saved her mate's life, she did me a favor and turned me instead." He laughed harshly, bitterly. "A favor. My maker told me how to survive and then she left me. Not knowing what else to do, I went home. My family and friends wanted nothing to do with me. I lost my wife and my family, friends I had known since childhood. They were all terrified of me, of what I'd become. Not that I could blame them. And yet I did."

"I'm so sorry." The words seemed totally inadequate, but she didn't know what else to say.

He shrugged. "I left our village, left Thrace, and came here. I learned the language and learned to survive."

It was a sad story. He had made no mention of anyone special in his life since that fateful night, although he seemed to get on well with Sir Everleigh.

"How is it done?" she asked. "How do you make a vampire?"

"Are you sure you want to know?"

She bit down on her lip, then nodded.

"If I were to turn you, I would drink from you until you were very near death, and then I would give you my blood."

"Give it to me? How?"

"I would bite my wrist and you would drink from me."

She stared at him, felt all the color draining from her face. "Have you turned others?"

"No."

"Why not?"

He laughed, but there was no humor in it. "No one has ever asked me for that particular gift. Is there anything else you would like to know?"

"Did you ever marry again?"

"No."

"So, you've lived alone all this time?"

"Yes. Anything else?"

"One more thing. Is the reason I've never seen you eat because you can't?"

"I find solid food abhorrent."

"Is sunlight abhorrent, too? Or do you really have business in the city during the day?"

"Sunlight is extremely painful on preternatural flesh. It can be deadly to very young vampires."

She frowned. "But you took me into town one afternoon. You drank a cup of tea."

"The sky was overcast that day. Remember? As for the tea…" He shrugged.

"So you can be awake during the day?"

"If I choose, as long as I avoid the sun's light."

She sat back, pondering everything he had said. And hadn't said.

Demetri watched the play of emotions on her face as she considered what he had told her. Would she now change her mind about staying? In spite of his promise, how could he bear to let her go? She had become his whole world, his reason for going on. Until Lorena moved into his house, he hadn't realized how lonely he had been.

How alone.

She looked up at him, her expression thoughtful. "The clothes in the attic, were they all yours?"

"Yes."

"And the books and the diaries?"

"Yes."

She blew out a sigh as she folded the deed in half and laid it on the table beside the sofa.

Demetri tensed. Was she rejecting his offer? He watched with trepidation as she stood and walked toward him.

"It's a lovely evening for a walk, my lord. Will you go with me?"

His relief was so intense it was almost painful. "I should like that very much."

It was a beautiful night, the sky clear, the air warm, fragrant with the scents of foliage and night-blooming flowers. They walked quietly side-by-side. Lorena wondered if he was as aware of her nearness as she was of his. He was a vampire. Tonight, she finally understood that odd, otherworldly sense of power that she had always felt in his presence. He had lived such a long time, she must seem like a child to him. But there was nothing fatherly in his glance when he looked at her, only a naked longing that frightened her even as it excited her.

He paused in a pool of moonlight, a tall, dark, enigmatic man. His isolation, his loneliness, called to the loneliness deep within her own soul. When he lowered his head, it seemed like the most natural thing in the world to go up on her tiptoes, wrap her arms around his neck, and close her eyes as his lips met hers. Warm, liquid heat spread to every nerve and fiber of her being, awakening sensations she had never known existed. She moaned softly as his hands cradled her hips, felt her knees go weak when he drew her body closer to his.

She wondered if he was feeling the same sense of wonder as he sank down to the ground, carrying her with him, his mouth never leaving hers. She didn't feel the cool grass beneath her, didn't feel anything but the heat of his kisses, the welcome weight of his body pressing intimately against hers. His tongue teased and tempted as his hands caressed her, until she was on fire, reaching for something she didn't fully understand but wanted desperately.

"Lorena." He groaned her name as he put her away from him and sat up.

"What's wrong?"

"Nothing," he said, his knuckles caressing her cheek. "Everything."

"I don't understand."

"I know, love." He took a deep, shuddering breath. "Vampires tend to be very sensual creatures," he remarked, searching for a way to explain it without frightening her. "Our need for blood is closely interwoven with our physical desire. Sometimes it is hard to separate the two." Especially when he was in love with the woman in his arms. He wanted to bury his fangs in her throat even as he yearned to sheath himself inside the velvet warmth of her body.

She blinked at him, then frowned. "So, you want to drink from me?"

"Yes."

"And make love to me at the same time?"

"Yes."

"And if I refuse?"

He rested his forehead against hers. "I shall abide by your decision."

"I've never been with a man that way," she said, her cheeks burning, her voice barely audible.

"I know."

She sat up, her cheeks growing even hotter. "What do you mean, you know? How could you?"

Demetri shook his head, sorry that he had ever started this conversation. "Your lack of experience is obvious." That was true, but it was more than that. He had no explanation for how he knew she was still a virgin. He just did. It was simply a part of being what he was. "I am not Fairfield," he said quietly. "I would never force you." Had Fairfield taken Lorena against her will, he would have killed the man without a second thought. "Come," he said, reaching for her hand. "We should go home."

Lorena sat on the sofa in front of the fireplace, her legs tucked beneath her. She gazed into the cold hearth, her thoughts chaotic as she tried to process all the things Demetri had told her. After they returned home, he had left "to go hunting." He said it so casually, yet the very words had chilled her.

Hunting. That was a concept she was trying to grasp. He hunted humans and drank their blood to survive. He only took a little, he had assured her, with no harm to his prey.

Prey. Hunting. He said the words so nonchalantly, but they conjured images of a hungry lion stalking a deer, its teeth savagely closing around the terrified animal's neck.

But the thing that troubled her the most was how much she craved his kisses, even now, when she knew what he was. Most disturbing of all was the fact that she couldn't decide if she was relieved he had stopped when he did, or sorry.

Her eyes widened with a new thought. Did vampires make love like ordinary mortals? How was she to know? She had little experience with men—save for the offensive pawing and clumsy kisses Lord Fairfield had inflicted on her—and the earth-shattering effect of Demetri's caresses.

She glanced at the Grant Deed on the table beside the sofa and felt her heart melt. Demetri had willingly given her his home, just to make her feel safe. She ran her fingertips over her lower lip, remembering the erotic heat of his kisses, the way his touch had moved through her like liquid fire.

Lorena shivered when she felt an odd shift in the air, let out a startled shriek when Demetri suddenly materialized before her.

"Sorry, love," he said. "I did not mean to frighten you."

"How...how did you do that?"

"Mind over matter, I suppose. Are you all right?"

She took a deep breath and let it out in a huff. "I may never be all right again."

"I guess I forgot to mention I can think myself wherever I wish to be."

"Yes," she agreed. "I guess you did. Do you have any other surprises I need to be aware of?"

"I can also move faster than the human eye can follow, so that, if I chose to leave somewhere in a hurry, it looks as if I have simply disappeared."

She pressed a hand to her heart. "Anything else?" she squeaked.

He hesitated a moment. "I can change shape."

She lifted one quizzical brow.

"I can alter my form."

"What do you change into?"

"Usually into large dogs. Sometimes a wolf. I have only done it a couple of times in an attempt to avoid hunters." He eyed her warily. "You look a little pale. You are not going to faint on me, are you?"

"I don't think so. It's just a lot to take in, what with everything else."

He gestured at the sofa. "May I join you?"

"Of course."

Not wanting to crowd her, he sat at the other end of the sofa. Noting that she was shivering, he focused on the fireplace. "There's one more thing I forgot to mention," he said as flames licked at the wood in the hearth. "I can summon fire."

Lorena stared at him, eyes wide. How was it possible for him to do all those frightening, amazing things? Thinking of the powers he had, abilities no mere mortal possessed, was mind-boggling. No wonder people were afraid of vampires. No wonder men hunted them. With their preternatural ability to destroy, to heal, to live for centuries, they could rule the world.

Demetri grinned inwardly as he watched the play of emotions chase themselves across her face. He had one more ability she wasn't aware of, Demetri mused. But perhaps now wasn't the time to let her know that he could also read her thoughts whenever he chose to do so.

CHAPTER SIXTEEN

Oliver Ainsley met with his companions in a small lake-side hunting lodge hidden behind a dense screen of trees and over-grown brush. There were nine of them gathered in the well-appointed parlor, all wealthy landowners. All vampire hunters, like their fathers and grandfathers before them. There had originally been more, but, over time, Demetri had decimated their number.

They met once a week to exchange information.

Oliver sat back in his chair, a glass of port in his hand, as Lord Fairfield gave the weekly report.

"To our knowledge, there are no vampires within the city, save Demetri. Three of our group endeavored to dispatch him recently but they failed. Any other creature would have been destroyed in the last attack, yet he continues to survive. And now he has an innocent woman in his house."

Oliver's jaw clenched at the mention of Lorena. It still stung that she had chosen that monster over him.

"We need to flush this danger from our midst," Lord Fairfield continued. "The woman in his household is my property, and I want her back."

Fairfield's property? Oliver bit back a gasp at this unexpected bit of news.

"I would welcome any suggestions about how to destroy Demetri once and for all," Fairfield went on, "without causing harm to my property, of course."

"We haven't tried burning him out since that one time five years ago," Lord Tinley remarked.

"And you know how that turned out," Oliver said dryly.

Fairfield grunted. They had lost two of their number that fateful night.

"I know this isn't a popular idea," Lord Stanton said, "but why not leave him alone? He doesn't hunt within the city. He causes us no trouble..."

"Are you mad?" Lord Minton exclaimed. "Just let that creature live among us?"

"He is already received in several homes, including Sir Everleigh's," Lord Whitfield muttered.

"Stanton has a point," Lord Dutton said calmly. "In addition to minding his own business, Demetri's presence has kept other vampires out of the city."

"Our members are killed or badly wounded every time we attack him," Lord Hamilton pointed out. "Perhaps Stanton and Whitfield are right. As long as Demetri continues to hunt elsewhere, perhaps we should just leave him alone."

"I say we take a vote," Lord Devereaux suggested.

"Very well," Fairfield said. "All those in favor of leaving the creature alone for the time being?"

Only Fairfield, Ainsley, and Tinley voted nay.

"Very well," Fairfield said gruffly. "For the time being, we will refrain from hunting Demetri. Given that decision, our meetings will be held monthly in the future."

A short time later, the members took their leave, save for Fairfield and Oliver who lingered over a glass of port.

"I was appalled by the vote," Fairfield remarked as he swirled the wine in his glass.

Oliver grimaced. "As was I."

"He may not be preying on our citizens," Fairfield said, "but he is holding one of them prisoner in his home. If he is bold enough to take one woman, why not two? Or three? Who knows what he's doing to that poor girl."

"Indeed. You said she belonged to you," Oliver said with a leer. "I take it she's not kin?"

"No. She was a servant in my household, one I paid a high price for." Fairfield smiled. "But she was well worth the cost, if you catch my meaning."

"I do, indeed," Oliver said, raising his glass. "Between us, we should be able to find a way to permanently dispose of the vampire and reclaim your property."

Property he intended to claim as his own, Ainsley vowed. One way or the other.

CHAPTER SEVENTEEN

Lorena spent the next day wandering through the house—a house that was now hers. In her whole life, she had never owned more than the clothes on her back, and after her father sold her, even her clothing had belonged to someone else.

And now she owned a large manor house on a lovely piece of property and enough dresses and shoes to clothe all of her sisters. Even though the deed was in her name, she couldn't help feeling that the house still belonged to Demetri. It had been a nice gesture on his part, but now that it was hers, would Demetri expect her to pay for needed repairs and new carpets, for hay and grain for Lady Gray?

She worried her lower lip as she headed into the kitchen to prepare afternoon tea. She would need to go to town for groceries soon. Would he expect her to pay for her own food and drink, as well?

Sitting at the kitchen table, she gazed out the window into the back yard, remembering what she had learned last night, the fears that had plagued her while she waited for sleep now that she knew she was living with a vampire.

A vampire who loves you.

She glanced over her shoulder, expecting to see Demetri standing behind her. But there was no one there. How could that be, when she had heard the words so clearly?

Troubled, she hurried up to her room and changed into her riding habit, then grabbed a carrot from the scullery, and ran out of the house and down the path to the stable. The gray mare whickered softly when she stepped into the barn.

"Hello, pretty girl," Lorena murmured as she offered the treat to the mare. "You'd like to give me a ride, wouldn't you?" After slipping a bridle over the horse's head, she led her into the corral, then climbed onto the top rail, and slid onto the horse's bare back. A touch of her heels, and the mare broke into a trot.

For a time, Lorena forgot everything but the warmth of the sun on her face, the joy of being alone with her horse, the sense of freedom that riding gave her, even in the confines of the corral. She put Lady Gray through her paces—walk, trot, lope. First one way, then the other.

Lorena rode for an hour before dismounting and leading Lady Gray back to the barn. She spent a few minutes currying the mare, scratching between her ears. She eyed the big black stallion warily, thinking it was the perfect mount for Demetri.

The sun was setting by the time she fed and watered the horses and walked back to the house. She knew, as soon as she stepped inside, that Demetri was there.

Taking a deep breath, she padded into the living room.

He turned at the sound of her footsteps. "Good evening, Lorena."

"My lord."

"Could you not call me Demetri?"

"If you wish."

Demetri swore under his breath, disliking the tension between them, the uncertainty in her eyes. Time to end it, he thought, one way or the other. Two long strides and he took her in his arms and kissed her.

For a moment, she stiffened in his embrace, and then she leaned into him, her breasts flattening against his chest, her slender arms sliding around his waist, creating a different kind of tension.

He murmured her name as he rained kisses along the length of her neck. "Do you know what holding you like this does to me?"

She did, indeed. It should have frightened her. Instead, it filled her with a kind of wild exhilaration. If only she had the nerve to follow the primal instinct that was urging her to throw caution to the wind and take him to her bed, to let go of her doubts and fears and surrender to the smoldering desire she read in his eyes. The same desire pounding through her. If only...

As if sensing her hesitation, he lifted his head, his gaze hot and hungry. "You want me," he said. "I want you. Why do you hesitate? Is it because you're afraid of me?"

"No. I mean, I confess I'm a little intimidated by what you are, but..."

"Go on."

"My mother took me and my sisters to church every Sunday. We were raised to believe that we should remain chaste until we were wed. She told us it was important to keep ourselves for our husbands, that our virginity was the best gift we had to offer. A gift that, once given, could never be given again." But, more than that, she was a little afraid of the act itself. She had heard things from the maids about what went on between a man and a woman while she was in Fairfield's house—things that frightened her.

Demetri nodded slowly. It had been centuries since he had given any thought to right or wrong. As a vampire, he had long ago stopped worrying about the laws of society that mortals adhered to. His only concern had been survival at any cost. He had taken what he wanted, what he needed, with no thought for the consequences because they no longer affected him.

Until Lorena entered his life.

Taking a deep breath, he kissed her lightly, and then released her. "Go change out of your riding habit and I will take you to town. I noticed the larder is getting low."

Lorena was acutely conscious of Demetri trailing behind her as she wandered from one vendor to the next. Nor did she miss the looks that were cast his way, everything from envy and admiration from the women to fear and trepidation from the men. For the first time, she wondered if anyone in town, other than Ainsley, knew—or suspected—what he was.

"Where would my lady like to go next?" he asked when she reached the last stall.

"Could we go for a cup of tea?" she asked as they walked back to the carriage.

He nodded as he stowed her parcels under the seat of the hackney then handed her onto the bench and swung up beside her. Lifting the reins, he clucked to the gray mare.

"Where did this come from?" she asked, indicating the two-seater conveyance. It wasn't as grand or as private as the carriages he usually rented.

"'Tis mine, though I rarely use it."

They reached Miss Mavis' Tea Room a few minutes later.

Lorena ordered a cup of green tea and a custard tart.

"Nothing for me," Demetri told the waitress, "but we would like half a dozen tarts to take with us."

Lorena smiled inwardly, knowing the extra tarts were for her. He spoiled her as no one else ever had.

"Tell me about your childhood," Demetri said when they were alone.

"There isn't much to tell. I was the oldest of five children, all girls. I helped in the fields as best I could. My father worked hard to take care of us and although we were never rich, we always had enough. Then, as I told you, a so-called friend of his talked him into making what turned out to be some very bad investments. I used to hear him pacing the floor late at night when he thought we were all asleep. There was always tension in the house. I often heard my mother crying at night after we had all gone to bed." Lorena paused when the waitress brought her order, along with the extra tarts.

"Go on," he said.

She waited until the waitress was out of hearing. "One night he came home late and told me to get dressed. He wouldn't tell me why, just took me into town and introduced me to Lord Fairfield. He said I would be staying at Fairfield Manor from then on. He kissed me on the forehead, told me to be a good girl, and left me there. I haven't seen him or my mother and sisters since that night."

It was a sad but familiar story, Demetri thought. He had never had a child. He never would, but he found it hard to sympathize with any man who would sell a child into servitude, whether it was his own flesh and blood or not. "You must have hated him for what he did."

"I did, at first. But I understand now why he did it. Lord Fairfield paid him a great sum of money. Enough to feed our family for a very long time."

"Lorena, my sweet, you have the heart of a saint."

She blushed at his words.

She was far too good for him, Demetri thought as they left the tea room. But as long as she was with him, she would never want for anything. "You must miss your family."

"Yes, very much."

"It is still early. Would you like to visit them this evening?"

Excitement sparkled in her eyes. "Do you mean it?"

He nodded as he lifted her into the hackney, thinking he would do anything she asked just to see that look in her eyes.

Her home was located an hour away from town. It was, Demetri thought, the saddest excuse for a house he had ever seen. He would not have stabled his horses there. The paint was peeling, the roof sagged, the front door was badly warped. The place was dark save for the flickering light of a candle in one of the front windows. Except for a few withered weeds and one scrawny tree, the yard was nothing but dirt and rocks. A slat-sided, brown-and-white dog crawled out from under the dilapidated front porch, a low growl rising in its throat.

When Demetri reined the gray mare to a halt, Lorena dropped lightly to the ground and threw her arms around the dog's neck. "Digger! I've missed you."

The dog whined, tail wagging, as it licked her face.

A moment later, the door opened and a man peered out. "Who's there?"

Rising, Lorena brushed the dirt from her skirt. "It's me, Papa. Lorena."

"Lorena?" He stepped outside. "Lorena, is it really you?"

"Yes."

Her father shambled towards her, his eyes damp with tears. "How did you get here?" he asked and then frowned when he saw Demetri standing beside the hackney. "Who's that with you?"

"This is Lord Demetri, Papa. I work for him."

"Did Fairfield sell you?" Halliday asked, looking confused.

"No, Papa. Lord Demetri saved me from Lord Fairfield and his . . . he saved me."

Her father's eyes narrowed. "Did Fairfield mistreat you, girl?"

"None of that matters now. Lord Demetri, this is my father, Morton Halliday."

Demetri stepped forward and offered his hand, although what he wanted to do was strangle the man for selling Lorena into Fairfield's household.

After a moment, Halliday shook Demetri's hand and quickly released it. Then, smiling at Lorena, he said, "Come inside, daughter. The girls will be glad to see you."

Demetri followed the two of them inside, his nose wrinkling against the smell of sickness and decay.

"Lorena!" The four girls gathered in front of a pitiful fire surged to their feet and threw their arms around her. They hugged for several minutes, laughing and crying.

"Where's Mama?" Lorena asked when the first burst of excitement had passed.

The four girls fell silent.

Demetri glanced around the room. A faint heartbeat came from somewhere down the narrow hallway, and with it the scent of impending death.

"Your Ma's been feeling poorly for a while now," Halliday said. "I reckon it's good you come when you did."

"No. No." With a shake of her head, Lorena hurried down the hall.

At a look from their father, the girls stayed behind. They huddled together on a sagging couch. Whispering behind their hands, they glanced furtively at Demetri from time to time.

They were all lovely, Demetri thought. The oldest was no more than sixteen or seventeen, the youngest perhaps eleven or twelve. "Halliday, what ails your wife?"

"I'm not sure. One minute she's burning up, the next she's got the chills. I know she needs a doctor, but..." He made a vague gesture with his hand.

Demetri grunted his understanding. Halliday lacked the necessary funds to pay for a physician.

Lorena was crying when she returned to the parlor. Once again, the girls gathered around her, tears sparkling in their eyes as they consoled each other.

"Halliday, would you mind if I looked in on your wife?"

"Are you a doctor?"

"No, but I have some experience with sickness and death."

Halliday considered a moment, then shrugged. "I reckon it'll be all right."

With a nod, Demetri walked down the narrow hallway. He found Lorena's mother lying in bed under a pile of patched blankets, her face deathly pale, her breathing shallow and uneven, her eyes closed. Rolling back his sleeve, he bit into his wrist, then gently pried the woman's mouth open and let his blood drip onto her tongue. She swallowed convulsively. He didn't know what ailed her, only knew that his blood had the power to strengthen those who were ill. Sometimes it healed them completely. After a minute or so, he lifted his arm.

When he turned away from the bed, he saw Lorena standing in the doorway.

"What have you done?" she whispered. "Did you...you didn't...?"

"No. I merely gave her some of my blood. She should be better by tomorrow."

"I don't understand."

143

"One thing I have learned during my long existence is that my blood can heal a variety of ills. Hopefully, it will be effective in treating whatever ails your mother."

"That's … remarkable."

"Indeed. It grows late. We should go home."

"I don't want to leave her."

"There's nothing you can do tonight. And I need to talk to you."

Thinking that sounded ominous, Lorena hugged her father and her sisters, promising to return the next day.

At home, Lorena paced the parlor floor while Demetri headed to the barn to unhitch the mare and looked after the horses. What did he want to talk about? He had been quiet on the way home. Had she said or done something to offend him?

She hardly flinched at all when he materialized in the back parlor.

He gestured at the sofa and she quickly sat down, her hands folded in her lap.

"How old are your sisters?"

"Emma is seventeen now. Alice is almost sixteen. Clara is thirteen, and Anna is eleven. Why?"

"With your father's approval, I intend to ask Sir Everleigh to give Emma and Alice positions in his household."

"But … that would be wonderful! Do you really think he will?"

"I am sure of it."

Jumping to her feet, she threw her arms around him. "How can I ever thank you?"

"Just keep looking at me like that." When she would have moved away, he slid his arm around her waist. "I own a small house on the other side of town. It has been vacant for some time. I want to move your parents and your younger sisters into it. I will, of course, pay your father to look after the place."

Lorena stared at him, tears of gratitude shining in her eyes. "You are the kindest man I've ever known. But...I don't have any way to repay your generosity."

"Your affection is all I ask for." His gaze slid to her lips. "One of your sweet kisses would be payment enough."

Going up on her tiptoes, she cupped his cheeks in her palms and pressed her lips to his. As always, heat suffused her as he kissed her back.

"One more thing," he said when he lifted his head. "I want you to go into town tomorrow and buy your family some new clothes and whatever else you think they need. Just charge it to me."

"Why are you doing this?" she asked, astonished by his benevolence.

"Because they are important to you. And because you are important to me." *And because I love you more than my life.*

Weeping tears of happiness, she rested her cheek against his chest. He was the kindest man she had ever known. And she was sorely afraid that she was falling a little more in love with him every day, not just because of his generosity, but because of the man he was.

"Lorena?"

"Yes."

"Are you happy here? With me?"

She looked up at him. "Yes, very. Why?"

His gaze probed hers. "Do you think you could ever love me?"

"I...I think maybe I already do."

"You think?"

"I've never been in love before. How am I to know?"

He smiled and her heart skipped a beat. Was that love, she wondered, the warmth that spread through her when he looked at her like that? Or the fact that he was ever in her thoughts, and that she missed him dreadfully when they were apart? She enjoyed his company and wanted nothing more than to please him, to make him happy. To see him smile. Was that love, she wondered again? Or just gratitude because he had been so good to her?

He pulled her closer and claimed her lips with his in a long, slow kiss that left her breathless.

"What are you feeling right now?" he asked.

"Hot and shivery all over," she replied, then clapped her hand to her mouth.

"You want me," he said. "Admit it."

Cheeks flaming, she nodded.

"You know I want you?"

She nodded again, embarrassed to be discussing anything so intimate with a man.

"I asked you not long ago to marry me, but you've never given me an answer." He held up his hand when she started to speak. "There is one thing you need to know before you decide. I should have mentioned it before now."

"What is it?" He looked so serious, she quickly imagined the worst.

"I cannot father a child." His wife had been pregnant when he'd been turned. It had been his first and last chance at fatherhood.

She stared at him. Such a thing had never occurred to her.

"Vampires cannot reproduce."

Stunned, she dropped down on the sofa. She had never thought about children. In servitude to Lord Fairfield, she'd had no hope of marriage or family. But now...Would she rather have Demetri, or a child fathered by another man?

"Lorena?" His hands clenched at his sides as he waited for her answer. He wished suddenly that he could call back the words, but how could he keep such a thing from her?

"If I say no?"

A muscle twitched in his jaw. "Nothing will change. I will still love you. I will still provide for you and your family as long as all of you live."

"I do love you, Demetri." A sense of peace, of destiny, washed through her as she spoke the words. "I should be honored to be your wife."

"Lorena!" He swept her into his arms and held her tight, so tight she thought she might break.

Excitement bubbled up inside her. She was going to be his wife, the best wife a man could ask for. She would love him and comfort him and do her best to make him as happy as he made her. She had never been intimate with a man, knew little of the act between a man and a woman save for Lord Fairfield's bumbling attempts at seduction. Would it be different with a vampire? How was she to know?

She reared back when Demetri burst out laughing. "What do you find so amusing about my accepting your proposal?"

He shook his head, sorely tempted to confess that he had read her thoughts.

"Tell me," she insisted.

He blew out a breath. "I suppose I should tell you before we wed."

"Tell me what?" Oh, Lord, she thought, had he been keeping some dreadful secret from her all this time? Did he have a wife somewhere?

"I have the power to read your mind whenever I wish."

She stared at him, wide-eyed, then pushed him away and turned her back toward him.

"Lorena, my love." He slipped his arms around her waist. "I am sorry. I should not have laughed at your naivete," he said, nuzzling the back of her neck. "But rest assured, vampires make love like everyone else." He turned her in his arms and kissed the tip of her nose.

"Have you made love to other women?"

Dammit, he should have seen that coming.

"Demetri?"

"Yes."

She moved out of his embrace and returned to the sofa. He had been a vampire for over three hundred years, she thought as she sank down on the cushion. No doubt he had known a lot of women in that time. How many had he made love to? How many had he loved before her?

"Does this change anything between us?" he asked, his voice quiet.

"No," she said slowly. "But I suddenly realized there are things about you that I don't know."

"Ask whatever you like," he said. "I have nothing to hide."

"How old were you when you became a vampire?"

"Twenty-nine."

"How many women?" She hadn't meant to ask. Now, she wasn't sure she wanted to know.

"I did not keep count."

"Were you in love with all of them?"

"No." He sat in the chair across from the sofa. "I never let myself care deeply for any of them, never met a woman I wanted to spend more than a year or two with. Until I met you. Anything else?"

"No," she said, climbing onto his lap. "I know everything I need to know."

"Now I have a request."

"Yes, my lord?"

"Please don't make me wait too long to make you my bride."

CHAPTER EIGHTEEN

In the morning, Lorena woke with a smile on her face. Demetri loved her and she was going to marry him. All she needed to do was set a date. It was late summer. Perhaps a winter wedding? She laughed softly, thinking she had agreed to marry him and she didn't even know if Demetri was his first name or his last.

Throwing the covers aside, Lorena pulled on her robe and skipped down the stairs into the kitchen. She lingered over breakfast, thinking she had never been happier. She hummed softly while she washed and dried the dishes and put them away.

Back in her room, she combed her hair, pulled on her riding habit, and ran down to the barn to brush and saddle the gray mare.

Lorena arrived in town just as the shops were opening. She spent hours looking at dresses and bonnets for her mother and sisters, pants and shirts for her father, as well as hats for everyone. She grinned, thinking how surprised they would all be when they opened their presents. There had rarely been gifts at their house for birthdays or Christmas, no celebrations other than an occasional cake if they'd had a good year, and those had been few and far between.

She asked the shop clerks to wrap everything and have the packages sent to Demetri's home, then rode down the street to Miss Mavis' Tea Room for brunch. After a leisurely cup of tea and a tart, she bought three dozen assorted tarts and custards to share with her family.

Lorena was halfway to her father's house when she had the oddest feeling that she was being watched. She glanced from side to side and over her shoulder but saw no one. Still, the feeling persisted. Suddenly spooked, she urged the mare into a gallop. When she reached her parents' home, she quickly dismounted and ran inside—only to come to an abrupt halt when she saw her mother in the kitchen.

Grace Halliday smiled at her daughter. "Lorena! Your father told me you were here last night and I didn't believe him." Hurrying forward, she gave her daughter a hug. "I'm so glad to see you!"

Lorena stared at her mother, unable to believe her eyes. Last night, her mother had been pale and only semi-conscious. This afternoon, she looked vibrant and healthy and years younger. Had Demetri's blood done that? "You look wonderful, Mama," she said, holding up the bag of tarts. "Where are the girls? I brought treats."

"They're supposed to be pulling weeds in the garden with your father. What kind of treats?"

Lorena pulled a plate from the cupboard and arranged the tarts.

"Do you know how long it's been since I've had sweets like that?" Grace murmured.

"Well, don't just stand there, have one. Have two. I'll buy you as many as you want."

"Listen to you, talking as if you had money to burn."

"Mama, I have something even better."

❧ ❧ ❧

It was near dark when Lorena bid her family goodbye. She had spent the whole afternoon helping her mother clean the house and do the laundry. She longed to tell her family about Demetri's plans to find employment for Emma and Alice and to move the rest of the family into a new place, but she thought the news should come from him. And she didn't want to get their hopes up in case her father refused or Demetri had changed his mind.

She was halfway home when Demetri suddenly materialized on the road beside her. "Have you been following me?"

He nodded as he vaulted up behind her.

"Were you following me this afternoon, as well?"

"No, why?" he asked sharply.

"I felt like I was being watched the whole time, but I never saw anyone."

"Probably just your imagination," he said reassuringly. Although he didn't believe it for a minute. "For my own peace of mind, I don't want you leaving the house unless I am with you."

"Demetri, you're scaring me."

"I am sorry, my love. It is probably nothing. Just humor me and promise you will do as I ask."

"All right, if it will make you happy."

"You make me happy. How is your mother?"

"Oh, Demetri, she looks wonderful! I've never seen her looking better or so cheerful. She's so full of energy, she was cleaning the house. I wanted to tell her not to bother, but..." She shrugged. "Do you still plan to move them into your other home?"

"We will move them in tomorrow night, if they agree."

"And my sisters? Have you talked to Sir Everleigh?"

"I shall speak to him later this evening."

Lorena leaned back against him, her arm resting on his where it curled around her waist. She was almost sorry when they reached home.

Later, after dinner, they sat on the sofa in front of the fire, wrapped in each other's arms.

She had never felt so content, she thought. Or so loved.

She shivered when he ran his tongue along the side of her neck.

"Lorena, love, let me taste you."

"You promised you wouldn't."

"I said I wouldn't unless you told me I could. So, I'm asking. Just a little taste?"

She worried her lower lip between her teeth. He had bitten her before. She remembered it clearly. There had been no pain, only a sweet rush of sensual pleasure. Would it feel the same the second time? What was she thinking? He wanted to bite her and drink her blood. But, deny it though she might, she wanted to experience it again. "You promise to only take a little?"

"I swear it on my love for you."

"Very well."

She stiffened as he brushed her hair out of the way. What was she doing? No matter how she felt about him, he was still a vampire. She clenched her hands as he rained kisses along the side of her neck. As before, she felt no pain when he bit her, just wave after wave of sensual pleasure that warmed her from head to foot.

She relaxed in his arms, moaned a protest when he lifted his head. How could something that should have been frightening and abhorrent feel so wonderful? She was still puzzling over it when she dozed off.

Demetri stayed where he was, content to listen to the rhythmic beat of her heart, feel the warmth of her body against his. For the first time in centuries, he felt as if he belonged. It was a heady feeling, and he owed it all to the remarkable woman sleeping so trustingly in his arms.

Later, after Lorena had gone to bed, Demetri paid a call on Sir Everleigh.

"What brings you here at this time of the night?" Everleigh asked. "Although, I guess it's not very late for you, is it?"

"With the hours you keep, one would think you were a vampire yourself. I have a favor to ask."

Everleigh gestured for his guest to take a chair by the fire as he poured two fingers of brandy into a snifter and handed it to Demetri. He poured one for himself before carefully easing down into the chair across from Demetri's. "Anything you want, you know that."

"I should like you to hire two of Lorena's sisters as housemaids."

"Of course. Just send them over." Everleigh sipped his drink. "Anything else?"

"Have you heard any rumors about Ainsley and the hunters?"

Everleigh tapped his fingers on the rim of his glass. "Only whispers that made no sense. I did overhear Stanton and Hamilton say something about the council leaving you alone, at least for now. Something about the devil you know," he said, chuckling. "But something else is going on between Ainsley and Fairfield, although I have no idea what it is." He regarded Demetri through narrowed eyes. "What is it between you and Ainsley?"

"In a word? Lorena."

"Ah. If I'm not being too impertinent, how did Lorena come to be in your household?"

"I take it you know her past," Demetri said dryly. The man knew everything that went on in the town and the city beyond.

"If you mean that her father sold her to Fairfield, then yes, I know. I'm also aware that her family is nearly destitute. I assume that's why you're seeking positions for Lorena's sisters?"

"Yes."

"I've heard her mother is very ill."

"She was," Demetri said with a faint smile.

Everleigh lifted one brow. "And are you responsible for that, as well?"

"Indeed." Demetri had used his powers to save Everleigh's life some years ago. The old man was the only human, apart from the hunters and Lorena, who knew his secret. He had often wondered why the hunters had not betrayed him, though perhaps they feared his retribution should they make it known. And now, if Everleigh was right, they had decided to leave him alone. As for Ainsley and Fairfield, he was sure that whatever conspiracy they were concocting had to do with Lorena in one way or another.

"Is there anything else I can do for you?" Everleigh asked as he refilled their glasses.

"Not at the moment. How is your sister?"

"Beatrice is doing well, thank you. There may be a marriage in her future."

"Indeed?"

"As you know, Sir Lancaster's wife passed away last year. He has been courting Beatrice since shortly after her birthday party."

"A good match," Demetri said. "For both of them." Setting his glass aside, he stood. "Is there anything I can do for you?"

"Not at the moment. Just be careful, my friend," Everleigh warned as Demetri headed for the door. "I fear Ainsley will not rest until one of you is dead."

CHAPTER NINETEEN

Lorena woke to the sound of someone knocking at the front door. Pulling on her robe, she belted it tightly as she hurried down the stairs, smiled when she opened the door and saw a young man standing beside a pile of boxes.

"Delivery for Miss Halliday," he said.

"Oh. Thank you."

He tipped his hat at her, then strolled down the walkway, whistling a cheerful tune.

She had no sooner carried the boxes inside then there was another knock at the door. And another delivery. It was amazing how quickly things got done when Demetri's name was mentioned.

Lorena regarded the boxes, thinking how excited her family would be with their new finery. The only things she hadn't bought were shoes, since she had no idea what sizes to buy.

She hurried upstairs, eager to change her clothes and deliver the presents, then slowed. She had promised Demetri she wouldn't leave the house unless he was with her.

Disappointed, she bit down on her lower lip. For a moment, she thought of disregarding her promise but then, perhaps Demetri *should* go with her. After all, he had paid for everything. Then, too, she hadn't forgotten that disquieting sense of being followed the day before. She could have imagined it, she thought. But what if she hadn't? Did she dare take the risk? Did she dare break her promise to Demetri?

Best to wait, she decided as she made her way down the stairs to the back parlor. Picking up her needlepoint, she settled on the sofa, her thoughts straying to her promise to marry Demetri. What would her parents say? Distracted by thoughts of the future, she let out a soft cry of dismay when she accidentally pierced her finger with the needle.

She stared at the bright red drop before licking it away, and then shuddered. Blood. Drinking it was how Demetri survived. She had a sudden image of her future husband bending over the necks of his helpless victims, biting them, drinking from them.

As he had bitten her last night.

She lifted a hand to her neck, remembering how pleasurable it had been. Did it feel the same for those unsuspecting people he … he preyed on, too? Did they experience that same warm and oddly sensual pleasure? Did it give him the same kind of pleasure when he drank from them? From her? What if he accidentally took too much? Was her life in danger?

She pushed the thought away, dropped her needlework on the table, grabbed an apron to protect her skirts, and hurried outside, where she set to work weeding the garden with a vengeance, anything to take her mind off questions she didn't want to ask.

She had managed to calm herself by the time Demetri appeared that evening. She told herself she was just over-reacting, that he had been a vampire long enough to know when to stop...feeding. He didn't kill his...prey. Would she ever get used to terms like *hunting* and *prey* and *feeding*? He loved her, of that she had no doubt. And she loved him. Wasn't that enough?

"How was your day?" he asked as he took her in his arms.

"Fine. I worked in the garden. I was thinking of buying some new rose bushes, if it's all right with you."

"It is *your* house, my love, remember?"

"I know, but, well, it's your money."

"Our money," he said, kissing the tip of her nose. "Or it will be when we wed. Have you set a date?"

"Not yet. I thought I'd discuss it with my mother, if you don't mind."

"As you should. Are you ready to go talk to them about the move?"

"Yes, just let me get my cloak."

He glanced at the two dozen boxes piled near the door.

"For my family," she called over her shoulder.

Demetri shook his head as he watched her run up the stairs. She delighted him at every turn. How had he ever survived this long without her?

Demetri had rented a horse and carriage but not a driver. Lorena smiled as he climbed up on the seat beside her. She had never ridden up front before and it was rather exciting, plus it gave her a broad view of the countryside. They passed a small flock of sheep in a pasture guarded by a large dog, which barked ferociously as they passed by. A short while later, she saw an owl swoop down and then lift off with a small animal clutched in its talons. Hunter and hunted, she thought, with a shudder. Life and death.

They pulled up in front of her parents' home an hour later. When Lorena started to pull some of the boxes from the carriage, Demetri laid his hand on her arm. "Let's talk to them first. If they agree to the move, we'll unload them at the new house."

"Good idea."

Lorena's sisters clustered around her, all talking at once, the main topic of conversation being Demetri. Where did she meet him? How long had she known him? Was he as forbidding as he looked? Was he kind to her?

He grinned, amused by their girlish questions, as he took her parents aside and explained his proposition.

"How can we ever thank you for your help and generosity?" Grace Halliday asked, blinking back her tears.

"No need. I am happy to do it."

Morton Halliday regarded Demetri through narrowed eyes. "As Grace said, you're too kind. But I can't help wondering why."

"I intend to marry your daughter," Demetri said. "That makes you family. Is that not reason enough?"

Morton and his wife exchanged uneasy glances.

"You object to the match?" Demetri asked.

"How long have you known Lorena?" her mother asked.

"Long enough to know that I love her."

"She has no money of her own," Morton Halliday said, his voice cool. "Are you keeping her?"

"She is my housekeeper. As such, I pay her wages."

Her parents exchanged glances again.

"Does she go to her own place at night?" Halliday asked.

"No."

"Are there others in your employ?" This from her mother.

"No, but she has her own room, quite separate from mine, with a good, sturdy lock on the door." Demetri's gaze met Halliday's. "You may rest assured that I want only the best for your daughter. I know one thing. Lorena is much safer in my house than she ever was in Fairfield's."

Halliday flinched as though Demetri had struck him.

"I love her," Demetri said again. "And I intend to spend the rest of my life caring for her. She will want for nothing so long as she lives. Nor will any of you. Naturally, I would like your blessing."

"And if I refuse to give it?" Halliday asked.

"I intend to marry Lorena, with or without your permission."

"You seem very determined," Halliday remarked.

"You have no idea," Demetri said with a wolfish grin.

With everyone helping, it didn't take long to pack the Hallidays' clothing and few personal belongings. They loaded the suitcases on top of the carriage. The furniture would be left behind as the new place was already furnished.

Grace Halliday and her daughters crowded into the carriage, the two younger girls sitting on the floor. Morton Halliday sat on the box with Demetri.

"What's bothering you?" Demetri asked as he turned the horses around.

"I know nothing about you," Halliday said. "Yet you come into my home and inform me that you're marrying my daughter whether or not I give you my blessing. You offer me a job as caretaker of a house you own and positions for Emma and Alice. I can't help wondering if your generosity is an attempt to win my approval."

"It is not. I am doing it because I love Lorena. And she loves you, though heaven knows why."

Halliday nodded and fell silent.

Lorena followed her mother from room to room, pleased beyond words by what she saw. Demetri's second home was not lavish but it was much larger than her childhood home and in far better condition. The furnishings were simple but adequate, with a large parlor and kitchen, and enough bedrooms that Clara and Anna could each have a room of their own, something none of the girls had ever had before.

Lorena, her mother and the girls spent the next two hours unpacking, and when that was done, Lorena handed out her gifts, smiling with delight as her parents and sisters opened their presents.

Demetri stood to one side, apart from the family. He had eyes only for Lorena, who fairly glowed with happiness as she watched her sisters ohh and ahh over the bounty spread before them.

Finally, it was time for Lorena and Demetri to take their leave. She hugged her parents and her sisters and promised to visit as often as she could.

Demetri informed Mr. Halliday that he would arrange transportation to Sir Everleigh's estate for Emma and Alice.

"You've been most kind," Grace Halliday said. "I don't know how we shall ever repay you."

"No need," Demetri replied, taking Lorena by the hand. "Good evening to you both."

Lorena chatted happily on the drive home. Demetri nodded from time to time, but his attention was on the road behind them.

Thanks to his preternatural senses, he knew they were being followed.

And not by any of the local hunters.

At home, he didn't drop Lorena off at the front door, as he usually did. Instead, he drove the carriage around to the back. He jumped lightly to the ground, then helped her down. She stood watching as he unhitched the horses and led them into the barn, where he forked them some hay. Someone from the town would come for the carriage on the morrow.

"Tonight went well, don't you think?" Lorena asked as they strolled up the path to the back door.

"Indeed. Did you have a chance to discuss a wedding date with your mother?"

"Only briefly. We set a month—December—but not the day."

He frowned inwardly, wondering why she wanted to wait so long. But then, they had only known each other a short time. He supposed he couldn't blame her for not rushing into it, but, damn, it was only August. Good thing he was a patient man. "What kind of wedding would you like?"

"What kind?" Lorena frowned. "Just something small, for our family." She looked up at him as they neared the back door. "Do you have any family? You've never mention any."

"No." For a brief moment, he let himself remember his wife, his mother and father, gone these past three hundred and fifty years. So long, he could scarcely remember their faces.

The faint scuff of a boot heel caught his attention. Reaching around Lorena, he opened the kitchen door and nudged her inside. "Lock up the house and stay inside."

Before she could protest or ask why, he closed the door behind her.

Alarmed, Lorena dashed to the side window and pulled back the curtains. Heart pounding with anxiety, she stared into the yard, but it was too dark to see anything.

Demetri pivoted on his heel as two figures materialized out of the shadows. He recognized their scent as the men who had followed them home.

For a tense moment, the three of them stared at each other. "Did Ainsley send you?" Demetri asked. "Or Fairfield?"

"What's it to you?" the taller of the two asked.

Demetri shrugged. "Just curious."

The second hunter shifted nervously from one foot to the other, then leaned toward his companion. "He's a master vampire," he whispered. "They didn't tell us that."

"Whatever they are paying you," Demetri said, his voice low and ominous, "unless you leave now, you will not live long enough to collect it."

The two hunters exchanged anxious glances.

"I think he's right," the tall man said after a tense moment. "Let's get the hell out of here."

Demetri grinned as he watched the pair turn and walk away. He had to give them credit, he thought. They didn't run.

❧ ❧ ❧

Lorena was waiting for him by the back door when he stepped inside. "What happened?" she asked anxiously.

"Nothing."

"Nothing? I heard voices."

"Two men came to see me."

"Friends of yours?"

"Not exactly. But until I find out what is going on, I don't want you leaving the house alone."

"Demetri! What happened out there?"

Taking her by the hand, he led her into the back parlor and drew her down on the sofa beside him. "Two hunters followed us home."

"Hunters!" Her worried gaze ran over him from head to foot. "Are you all right?"

"Yes. All we did was talk."

She lifted one brow.

"Someone paid them to come after me. Sadly for whoever sent them, they lacked the courage to do the job."

"Are you telling me they left, just like that?"

He nodded.

"So they were afraid of you?"

"Do you find that so hard to believe?"

"Not at all, my lord. After all, I was afraid of you, too, not so very long ago."

His knuckles caressed her cheek. "And now?"

Cupping his face in her palms, she murmured, "Now, I'm only afraid of losing you."

❦   ❦   ❦

Oliver Ainsley met Lord Fairfield in their favorite pub late that night. "Have you heard anything from Beatty and Landon?"

"Not a word," Lord Fairfield replied irritably. "You?"

"No. Maybe they're still waiting for a more opportune time."

Fairfield snorted. "We would have heard from them one way or the other."

"So, they ran," Oliver said, his voice laced with contempt.

"Either that," Fairfield agreed, his voice flat. "Or they're dead."

CHAPTER TWENTY

Yawning, Lorena scuffed into the kitchen. She seemed to be sleeping later and later every day, she thought as she boiled a couple of eggs. She supposed it was to be expected. She wanted to spend as much time with Demetri as she could, and that meant staying up long past the time most people had retired for the night. Doubtless that would be the routine of her life once they were married, she thought, as she spread jam on a slice of bread and poured a cup of tea.

Sitting at the kitchen table, she gazed out the window, thinking about last night. What if the hunters hadn't run away? Demetri could have been badly hurt again, perhaps killed. Would that also be the routine of their lives? Men hunting him? When he went out at night, would she spend every hour he was away wondering if he had been hurt, or worse? He was a powerful being, but even Demetri wasn't indestructible.

It was a sobering thought.

Pushing her morbid worries aside, she wondered how Emma and Alice would like being in Lord Everleigh's employ. He seemed to be a kind man. Surely they wouldn't be subject to the same shameful treatment she had received at Lord Fairfield's hands. Surely Demetri wouldn't have suggested they go there if they would be in any danger.

Assuring herself that her sisters would be well, she turned her thoughts to her upcoming marriage. Did she want to wait until December? True, she hadn't known Demetri very long, so it was probably prudent to spend more time with him before they wed. She would have to ask him to take her into the city so she could talk to a dressmaker about her wedding gown. Her mother and sisters would need new dresses, as well, and her father would need a new suit of clothes.

She giggled with excitement at the thought of being Demetri's wife, only to sober moments later at the prospect of sharing his bed. She loved being in his embrace, trembled at his caresses. But he always stopped before things went too far. What would it be like to feel his body sheathed in hers? While at Lord Fairfield's, she had occasionally overheard new brides whispering together about the wedding night. Some claimed the mating act was painful. Others simply blushed and smiled. But there was no real need to worry. Demetri had promised they could be wed in name only. But when she thought how wonderful it was to be in his arms, how she melted at his kisses, she was no longer certain that was what she wanted.

Rising, she heated a large pot of water and carried it upstairs to her room, where she stripped off her nightgown. She washed her hands and face, blushed as she ran the cloth over her breasts and belly, all the while imagining Demetri's hands caressing her.

After drying off, she padded to the wardrobe to select her dress for the day. It still amazed her that she had so many choices. She finally picked the mauve, wishing again she had a larger mirror so she could see how she looked. The small one she had didn't allow her to see herself from head to toe. She contemplated her hair, wishing she knew

how to arrange it in some of the fancy ways that were popular, or that she had a lady's maid to help her.

With a sigh, she brushed her hair out, then pinned the
sides back with a pair of tortoise-shell combs. Sitting on the
edge of the bed, she laced up her shoes.

Returning downstairs, she searched the library book
shelves for something to read until Demetri arrived. To her
surprise, she found him sitting behind the desk, a large
account book open in front of him.

He looked up when she entered the room. "Good evening, my love."

"You're up early, my lord. The sun has not yet set."

"I have decided to rise earlier," he said, closing the
book, "so you need not spend so much time alone. And
so that I may accompany you when you wish to go to town
or visit your family." And being seen during the day would
help dispel Ainsley's rumors. It had never mattered to him
what people thought, but that was before Lorena entered
his life.

"Demetri, you are too good to me."

"Nothing is too good for you, my love." Pushing away
from the desk, he stood and took her in his arms. "What
would you like to do today?"

"I should like to go shopping." She paused, wondering
what his reaction would be when she said, "For a looking
glass."

He grunted softly.

"Is it true that you cast no reflection?"

"Yes."

"How can that be?"

"I do not know. Some say it is because vampires are no
longer mortal. Some believe it is because we have no soul."
He shrugged. "Take your pick."

Lorena frowned at him. "Does no one notice such a thing?" Yet even as she asked the question, she realized she never had.

"People generally see what they expect to see. A bit of vampire glamour makes sure they do."

"Would it distress you to have a mirror in the house?"

"No, my love, as long as you keep it in your room."

"Does it bother you, not having a reflection?"

"Not anymore." In the beginning, it had bothered him a great deal, made him feel as if he no longer existed.

"Is there a cure for what you are?"

"There are rumors of such a thing."

"Would you take it?"

"Perhaps when I was first turned. But not now. I have been a vampire far longer than I was a mortal man. I am content with my life, now that you are in it." He regarded her a moment, his eyes narrowing. "Would you have me take it, if such a cure existed?"

Lorena started to say yes, of course, and then she paused. She loved him as he was. Would he be the same man if he was mortal again? Would it be fair of her to demand it? As a vampire, he might live another three centuries or more. He had been turned at nine-and-twenty. Most mortals lived to be sixty, a rare few, like Sir Everleigh, lived to be seventy. Would Demetri give up centuries for a few decades? Would she?

"Lorena?"

"I don't know. How could I make a decision like that for someone else?"

"There is no proof that such a cure exists, but if one did, I would take it if you asked me to." He kissed her lightly on the tip of her nose. "This is too sober a conversation for such a lovely day. Come along, let us go and find you a looking glass."

Lorena thought about what Demetri had said on the way to town. Surely no man had ever offered to give up centuries of life to please a woman. And she would never ask it of him. And yet…what would happen when she grew old and he did not? Wouldn't it be better to spend the rest of her life with a man who grew old beside her?

Perhaps. Or you could join me and we could have centuries together. Demetri's voice, whispering in her mind. Centuries, she thought. What would it be like?

When they reached the glazier's establishment, Demetri handed her down from the hackney. A boy from the livery had come by the house early that morning to fetch the horse and carriage Demetri had rented the night before.

"I shall wait for you here," he said. "Order whatever size you wish. More than one, if need be. Spend however much you like." He smiled at her. "Consider it an engagement present."

As usual, when they were in town, they stopped at Miss Mavis' Tea Room for tea and a custard tart before heading home.

"So, what kind of mirror did you buy?" Demetri asked after they were seated.

"I saw the loveliest oval cheval mirror and I simply couldn't resist it. It will fit perfectly in the corner of my room. The man promised it will be ready next week. I fear

I spent far too much," Lorena said, handing him a receipt. "Do you mind the cost?"

He glanced at the price briefly, then tucked the bill into his coat pocket. "Of course not. You should always be able to see how beautiful you are."

His words warmed her heart and brought a blush to her cheeks.

As they were leaving the tea room, they passed the large mirror on the wall. Lorena glanced at her image and for the first time, she noticed that Demetri cast no reflection. She saw herself and the room behind them clearly, but it was as if Demetri wasn't there. It sent a cold chill down her spine and she quickened her pace, eager to get outside.

"It upset you, did it not?" he asked when they were on their way home.

She didn't ask what he meant. "I never noticed before. Did you mean for me to see it for myself today?"

He nodded. "You need to know everything before we wed."

"Is there anything else I don't know?"

"Nothing that I can think of," he said and then frowned. "Perhaps I should shape-shift for you when we get home."

Lorena wasn't sure she was up to watching Demetri change into something else. She was still getting over the shock of realizing that he truly had no reflection. How that was possible when she could see him, hear him, touch him, she had no idea. Did he truly have no soul? The very thought was terrifying. She much preferred to believe it was because he was no longer mortal.

She was trembling as she followed him into the front parlor.

He noticed, of course. "Perhaps we should do this some other time."

"N…no." She perched on the edge of the sofa. "Let's get it over with now."

Moving to the small table that held several bottles of wine, he poured her a glass. "Drink this first."

She cupped the snifter in both hands and downed it quickly, sighed as the port's warmth spread through her.

"Ready?" he asked.

She nodded uncertainly.

"Just remember the wolf is me and I will not hurt you."

She nodded again, blinked in astonishment as a sort of mist appeared around Demetri and when it cleared, a large, black wolf with dark blue eyes stood in his place. Taking one slow step at a time, the wolf moved toward her. Sitting at her feet, it laid its head in her lap. She stared at it a moment, then, whispering, "This is Demetri," she cautiously stroked the wolf's head. Its coat was silky-soft.

The wolf whined softly. A few moments later, it stood and shook itself. And a moment after that, Demetri again stood before her.

"That was…I don't know. Incredible. Amazing. Does it hurt?"

"No," he said. "Not at all."

"Where do your clothes go?"

"I have no idea. There is one more thing," he said, and dissolved into a pale gray mist.

Lorena gasped, one hand pressed to her throat as he seemed to disappear. It took her a moment to realize the cloud-like thing hovering overhead was Demetri. How on earth did he do that? Changing physical shape was one thing! But this...

Noting her distress, Demetri immediately resumed his own shape.

"Please don't ever do that again," she murmured.

"Here, now." Dropping down beside her, he took her in his arms. "You are not going to faint on me, are you?"

"I don't know." Lowering her head, she closed her eyes and took several deep breaths. "Is that everything?"

"Yes, my love."

"Thank goodness," she murmured, as he brushed a kiss across her lips. "I don't think I could take any more surprises."

⚜ ⚜ ⚜

That night, Demetri drove them to her parents' house so Lorena and her mother could plan for their wedding.

Demetri and Halliday sat outside, leaving the women to set the date and take care of the details.

Lorena, her mother, Clara and Anna gathered in the parlor. "It's not going to be very fancy," Lorena said. "Demetri doesn't have any family and on our side, there's just us, so..." She shrugged. "We'll just keep it simple. I was thinking of December first."

Grace Halliday nodded slowly.

"Of course, Demetri and I will pay for everything. It will be an evening wedding, something small and simple." Lorena frowned at her mother's silence. "Mama?"

"Girls, why don't you go in the kitchen and prepare some tea?"

Clara winked at Anna. "I think they're trying to get rid of us."

"I know," Anna said. "But Lorena brought tarts!"

"What is it?" Lorena asked when her sisters left the parlor.

"Are you sure about this, daughter? He's been kind to you, I know. And to all of us, as well. But, Lorena," she whispered. "There are rumors about him. You must have heard them."

Lorena's heart sank. Surely the people in town didn't know the truth. "What kind of rumors?"

"That women have disappeared from his household. That he isn't like other men. That he's never seen during the day—"

"That's not true," Lorena said. "We went into town this afternoon."

"Be that as it may, daughter. You've known him for such a short time. Wouldn't it be wiser to wait a year or so?"

"Mama, I know all I need to know." Lorena squeezed her mother's hand. "In a week or two, we'll go into town so you and the girls can order new dresses."

⚜ ⚜ ⚜

A muscle twitched in Demetri's jaw as he listened to the conversation inside the house. He wondered exactly what Grace Halliday had heard and how far she was prepared to go to keep him from marrying her daughter.

He glanced at Halliday. The man had said little, merely sat on the porch step and smoked his pipe.

"I have the feeling your good wife is opposed to this marriage," Demetri said. "Do you still share her feelings?"

"Aye, that I do. We know nothing about you or your family. How you earn your living. I can't help wonderin' if you're hiding something and that's why you're in such a hurry to wed my girl."

"The same girl you sold into household drudgery," Demetri reminded him. "Perhaps you would feel differently about it if I offered to buy her from you."

"You know nothing about it!" Halliday snapped. "I was desperate, with nowhere to turn. Don't you think I've regretted that decision every day of my life since?"

"I don't know," Demetri said flatly. "And I don't care." He looked up when Lorena stepped out onto the porch. "Ready so soon?"

"Yes."

He frowned when he heard the distress in her voice.

"Demetri, please take me home."

"As you wish, my love."

She gave her father a brief hug, then hurried down the steps and climbed onto the seat of the hackney.

Demetri gave Halliday a curt nod before following Lorena down the steps. Swinging effortlessly onto the seat, he took up the reins and clucked to the gray. When they were out of sight of the house, he pulled to the side of the road. "What is it, love? What happened back there?"

"My mother tried to talk me out of marrying you. She says I'm rushing into this and that I should wait." She sniffed back her tears. "I'll wager my father said the same thing."

"That is a bet you would win." His gaze searched hers. "Would you like to postpone the wedding for a while?"

"I don't know. Mama said she's heard rumors about you. You don't think she knows, do you?"

"She may suspect, but I doubt she knows anything for certain. Few people in town know or suspect what I am."

"There are more besides Oliver?"

"There are hunters who live among us. Apparently they have decided not to pursue me, since I do not hunt here in the town. Sir Everleigh also knows."

"Sir Everleigh!"

"I saved his life once."

"You never told me that."

"It was a long time ago, when he was a young man."

Wiping her eyes, she said, "Tell me."

Picking up the reins, Demetri pulled away from the side of the road. "It happened shortly after I moved here. I found him late one night, lying near death along the side of the road. He had been attacked by highwaymen and left for dead." He saw no need to tell her his first inclination had been to drain Everleigh dry. "He regained consciousness when I knelt beside him. There was something in his eye, some last glint of rage and defiance, a refusal to succumb to the inevitable, that I found admirable. I bit him lightly, only to draw back when he murmured, 'Vampire. Are you going to kill me?'

"I told him that had been my intention, but if he would swear on his honor as a gentleman to keep my secret, I would let him live.

"He vowed that he would never tell a soul, so instead of taking his blood, I gave him some of mine. Imagine our surprise when we met at a cotillion given by a mutual acquaintance two weeks later. We have been friends ever since."

"And he's never betrayed you?"

"Not to my knowledge. But he might regret it were he to do so."

Lorena stared at him, aghast. "But he's your friend. Surely you wouldn't hurt him now?"

"No, love," he assured her. "I would not hurt him." But he would not hesitate to wipe the truth of what he was from Everleigh's mind, and from the minds of those he'd told.

They reached home as his story ended. Demetri let her off in front of the house, then continued on down the path that led to the barn to care for the horse.

Lost in thought, Lorena ran up the steps and unlocked the front door. Inside, she lit a lamp, then moved to the window to stare out into the darkness, wondering what to do about the wedding. Should she wait a few months longer and hope Demetri would win her parents' trust? Would Demetri object?

She turned around when he entered the room.

One look at her face and Demetri knew what was troubling her. "We can postpone the wedding if you are having second thoughts," he said. "Or if you think doing so will appease your parents. I do not wish to be the cause of trouble between you and your family."

"Reading my mind again?" she asked, looking up at him.

"No need. Your face is like an open book. It reveals everything."

"Demetri, you know I love you."

"Yes. Just as I know that, deep down, you have doubts about being my wife."

She didn't deny it. How could she, when he could read her mind? "Perhaps we should wait. Maybe instead of a winter wedding, we could marry in the spring."

"As you wish."

"You're angry."

"No, love. I cannot fault you for having doubts, nor can I blame your parents for being opposed to our wedding. A few extra months might make a difference. To all of you." He kissed her lightly on the cheek. "I need to go out," he said, somewhat brusquely. "Do not wait up."

She stared after him as he walked away from her. In spite of his words to the contrary, his steps were quick and angry as he flung open the door and disappeared into the night.

CHAPTER TWENTY-ONE

Lorena paced the parlor floor. She had never seen Demetri so angry or heard his voice so cool. Where had he gone? Was he coming back? Why did she still have doubts? She loved him with her whole heart and yet, down deep inside, she couldn't help wondering if love was enough when two people were so different. She was day and he was night. The sun and the moon complimented each other but no matter how they might wish it, they could never be together.

Her tears came then, a slow, steady stream that seemed to have no end. Sinking down on the floor, she cradled her head in her hands and wept for what she might have lost.

Demetri cursed long and loud as he headed for the city. He had been a fool to believe Lorena could love him unconditionally, and a bigger fool to think her parents would ever accept him. He knew what stories Grace Halliday had heard. Likely her husband had heard them, as well—how he was some sort of Bluebeard, luring innocent young women into his household, debauching them, murdering them, and hiding the bodies in his cellar. He had little doubt in his mind that Ainsley and his ilk had started the salacious rumors. The hunters had been a thorn in his side ever since he moved to Woodridge. He should have disposed of them all years ago. They were hunters. He was a vampire. He must be getting soft, to allow his enemies to live.

He stalked the crowded city streets, his thoughts turned inward. *Vampire.* He had long-ago made peace with what he was, but tonight he hated the very word and everything it stood for.

Men and women who crossed his path gave him a wide berth. No doubt tonight even the most dull-witted among them recognized the evil that walked among them.

His anger fueled his hunger. He took the first lone woman he met, pulled her into an alley that reeked of garbage, and buried his fangs none-too-gently into her neck. Her blood was warm and filling but he found no pleasure in it. He might have drained her dry if a drunk hadn't stumbled upon them.

Muttering epithets under his breath, Demetri released the woman from his thrall and transported himself to the nearest pub. He stared into the dark, red contents of his drink, wishing that a few glasses of wine would make him as drunk as the two tradesmen sitting at a nearby table. Sadly, the port had no such effect.

He sat there, hunched over and lost in a dreary world all his own until the sound of Lorena's weeping penetrated his thoughts. She was sobbing as if her heart would break, and it was all his fault.

A thought took him swiftly home. "Lorena!" Dropping to his knees, he drew her into his arms. "Hush, love," he crooned. "There is no need for tears. Only tell me what you want and it is yours."

"I thought…you…you were angry with…me…and that I'd never see you again."

"No, love, I was only angry with myself."

"What do you mean?"

"It is of no importance." He trailed his knuckles down her cheek, then kissed her lightly. "Next time we visit your parents, you can tell them the wedding has been postponed until a later date. And now I think you should get some rest."

"But..."

He pressed his fingers to her lips, silencing her. "Go to bed, Lorena." Rising, he took her hands in his and pulled her to her feet. "Things will look better in the morning."

"Won't you kiss me goodnight?"

Cupping her face in his palms, he kissed her, a long slow kiss that held all the love in his heart. "Goodnight, my sweet girl."

Upset by something in his tone, she gazed up at him, but she couldn't decipher his expression.

Demetri stood with his hands clenched at his sides as he watched her slowly climb the stairs, whispered, "Good bye, my love," as she reached the landing.

"Demetri?" Lorena whirled around, certain he was behind her, but when she looked back, there was no one there.

He wandered through the night like a lost soul. Her scent clung to his clothing, teased his nostrils with every breath. For the first time in centuries, he had been happy, content. Foolishly, he had let himself believe it would last. He believed that Lorena loved him as much as she was able. But, deep down, she still had reservations about spending her life with him. And though she tried valiantly to hide it, a small part of her remained afraid of him, afraid of what he was. And he couldn't blame her. He had spent hundreds of years learning to control his hunger and yet he harbored the very real fear that one day he would taste her life's blood, lose his hard-won control, and take it all. If and when that happened, it would be his undoing.

He had made sure she would be well-provided for should anything happen to him. The house, its furnishings, and the property were in her name. She was the beneficiary of his bank accounts. She would never want for anything as long as she lived.

"Lorena." He whispered her name to the wind and it seemed to echo back to him.

Lorena. Lorena. Lorena.

How could he survive without her?

When Lorena woke in the morning, she told herself everything was all right. Demetri hadn't been angry about postponing the wedding. But when he didn't come home that night, or the next, she feared he was gone for good. At first, she refused to believe it. He loved her. She was sure of it.

But a week passed by and then another. The days passed with agonizing slowness. She woke each morning hoping that today would be the day when Demetri returned. And night after night she cried herself to sleep, afraid he had gone for good. Afraid something terrible had happened to him

At the end of three weeks, Lorena gave up all hope that he was coming back. The knowledge sat like a hard, painful lump deep within her.

It was time to face reality. She was on her own now. She was also almost out of provisions.

Vowing that she had shed her last tear, Lorena strode purposefully down to the barn where she spent the next forty minutes trying to figure out how to hitch Lady Gray to the hackney.

She had uttered several of the curse words she had overheard at Lord Fairfield's and broken a fingernail by the time she finished.

Climbing onto the padded seat, she picked up the reins and clucked to the mare.

By the time Lorena had finished her shopping and stowed the bags and boxes under the seat of the hackney, she was ready for a cup of tea before heading home. Although it didn't seem like home without Demetri. She blinked back the threat of tears. She would not cry for that man again, she vowed, even as the first tear dripped down her cheek. Why had he left her just when everything seemed wonderful?

When she reached the tea room, she tethered the mare to the post, then stood there, gathering her courage before she opened the door and stepped inside. She felt decidedly uncomfortable, sitting at a table by herself. Remembering the many times she had come here with Demetri didn't help.

She had just ordered when a male voice said, "This is a nice surprise."

Lorena looked up, a gasp of surprise rising in her throat when she saw Oliver Ainsley standing beside her.

He gestured at the empty chair across from her. "May I?"

She wanted to say no. Instead, she inclined her head.

"How have you been, Lorena?" he asked as he took his seat.

"Very well, thank you."

"I trust Demetri is not…mistreating you."

"Of course not!"

His gaze moved over her, lingering on her neck. "I find it hard to believe that he has restrained himself this long."

"I'm sure I don't know what you mean," she said, her voice icy.

"I'm sure you do. I don't want to quarrel with you, Lorena," he said quietly. "I've been worried about you."

"As you can see, I'm fine."

He grunted softly, then sat back as the waitress approached the table with Lorena's order.

Grateful for an excuse to look away, she busied herself with adding milk and sugar to her tea.

"Forgive my impertinence," Oliver said, "but did you and Demetri ever marry?"

Pain lanced her heart. "Not yet. We decided to postpone the wedding until spring."

"I see."

Still avoiding his gaze, Lorena nibbled on her tart. It tasted like ashes in her mouth.

Oliver pushed away from the table. "I have an appointment in half an hour," he remarked. "But I would love to see you again. Perhaps we could meet here tomorrow afternoon?"

"I don't think so. Demetri wouldn't like it."

A faint smile played over Oliver's face. "We don't have to tell him. I shall be here tomorrow at four if you change your mind."

Lorena stared after him. She had the strangest feeling that Oliver knew that Demetri had left her. And an even stranger suspicion that he knew of Demetri's whereabouts.

Oliver whistled softly as he left the tea shop. Lorena was lovely but she was a poor liar, he thought as he mounted his horse. He wondered how long she would wait for the vampire to return. Not that he cared. He was a patient man. If he played his cards right, sooner or later she would turn to him for comfort. And when she did, he would take great pleasure in detailing his victory in glowing terms to Demetri before he took the master vampire's head and burned the body.

Demetri looked up as Oliver Ainsley strolled into the dungeon located in the bowels of Lord Fairfield's house. The cage that held him smelled of old blood, fear, and death. Many men had died in this foul place, not all of them vampires. He wondered if he would be next as Ainsley strutted toward him like the cock of the walk. He growled low in his throat when he caught Lorena's scent on the other man.

"Comfortable, my lord?" Ainsley asked with a sneer.

Demetri glared at him.

"I had tea with the lovely Miss Lorena Halliday this afternoon," Oliver said, strutting back and forth in front of the cage. "She is a rare gem, that one. I shall see her again on the morrow. Anything you would like me to tell her?"

Demetri clenched his jaw until it ached, but remained mute.

With a triumphant grin, Oliver swaggered out of the dungeon.

Demetri stared after him, silently cursing the man even as he castigated himself for letting his guard down. He tugged against the thick, silver cuffs that chained him to the wall. The heavy silver band around his neck scorched his flesh and drained his strength, but not as much as the blood Oliver and Fairfield had siphoned from him. He wondered briefly if Oliver knew about the healing properties of vampire blood. You could buy it from unscrupulous men in dark alleys if you knew where to look.

But none of that mattered as much as the thought of Ainsley spending time with Lorena, working his way into her affections. Or worse, Lord Fairfield dragging her back to his estate and violating her.

Knowing it was useless, he tugged against his bonds, but it only served to lacerate the skin on his wrists. The silver against his flesh was a constant torment. And he had only himself to blame. He had been so lost in self-pity after he left Lorena that he had wandered aimlessly through the dark, deserted streets, not caring if he lived or died. And his carelessness had cost him his freedom, and would likely cost his life, as well.

Closing his eyes, he summoned Lorena's image. If he concentrated hard enough, he could almost hear her laughter, see her smile, smell her warm, womanly scent. Lorena. His heart cried out for her, echoing in the darkness like the wail of a lost soul.

Lorena looked up from the book she'd been reading as Demetri's voice whispered through her mind. She glanced around the parlor fully expecting to find him there. "Demetri? Demetri, are you here?"

Shoulders sagging with disappointment, she bowed her head and let the tears fall.

In the morning, Lorena's first thought was for Demetri. She had heard his voice in her mind last night. It hadn't been her imagination, she was sure of it. He had been in pain and he had called for her.

But how was she to find him?

Yesterday, she had been certain Oliver knew Demetri's whereabouts. This morning, she was even more sure of it, though she couldn't say why.

She glanced at the clock. Oliver had said he would be at Miss Mavis' Tea Room at four o'clock this afternoon.

Perhaps she should meet him there.

Oliver was waiting for her when she arrived, fashionably late so as not to appear anxious.

He rose, smiling smugly as she wended her way toward his table. "Miss Halliday, how good of you to come." He held her chair for her before resuming his own.

"I'm sorry I'm late," she lied. "I had some errands to run."

He pressed a hand to his heart. "Alas, and here I had hoped you were as eager to see me again as I am to see you."

She shrugged her indifference.

"Sir Everleigh is hosting a party tonight. I was hoping you would accompany me."

"I'm afraid I must decline," she said. "I've promised my family I would visit them."

"Can you not make it some other evening?"

"No. You see, it's my sister, Anna's, birthday and she's expecting me. I see her so seldom, I can't disappoint her."

"Very well. Another night, then?"

She smiled but didn't answer.

"I heard that Lord Demetri has left town," Oliver remarked.

"Did you?"

"It's true, is it not?"

"I'm afraid so."

"I'm sorry, Lorena. But it's for the best. The man is a monster."

"So you've said." She took a deep breath. "Do you know where he's gone?"

"As a matter of fact, I do."

CHAPTER TWENTY-TWO

Lorena stared at Oliver. "Where is he? What have you done with him?"

"Me?" He lifted one shoulder in an elaborate shrug. "I've done nothing."

"I don't believe you."

"No?"

"I know what you are. Demetri told me."

"Ah, so you do know the truth."

"Where is he?" She reached across the table and grabbed his hand. "Tell me, Oliver!" Her gaze searched his. "Is he still alive?"

"You really believe you're in love with him, don't you?"

"I am in love with him. And he loves me."

Oliver snorted. "His kind are not capable of love." Leaning toward her, he whispered, "Lorena, he is not even a man, nor is he alive. He is undead, a living corpse."

"And you're a hunter," she hissed. "A murderer!" She sniffed back her tears. "You've killed him, haven't you?"

"Not yet."

Relief washed through her, so intense it was almost painful. "Where is he? Please, Oliver, tell me where he is."

"I can do better than that. I can take you there, if you like."

"Oh, yes! Please!"

❧ ❧ ❧

Filled with equal measures of hope and distrust, Lorena sat beside Oliver as he drove out of town. She didn't know where she had expected to find Demetri, but it certainly wasn't at Fairfield Green, the country home of Lord Fairfield. She shuddered as Oliver pulled up in front of the manor. "What are we doing here?"

"You wanted to see the vampire. This is where he is."

"But... how? Why would he be here?"

"Fairfield is also a hunter."

Lorena stared at him in disbelief. That fat old lecher, a vampire hunter?

Leaping lightly to the ground, Oliver reached for her.

Lorena recoiled from his touch. "I can't go in there."

"You've nothing to fear," Oliver assured her with a sly grin. "I bought you from Fairfield two weeks ago."

"You. Bought. Me?"

"Did you think I didn't know you belonged to him?"

Lorena bit down on her lower lip. He had known of her humiliation from the beginning. Embarrassment warmed her cheeks. All this time he had known she was nothing but a servant, bought and paid for. And now he owned her.

She was too shocked to resist when he lifted her from the cabriolet. "Come along, Lorena."

At Oliver's knock, Hamish, the butler, opened the door. If he was surprised to see her, it didn't show on his face.

"Lord Fairfield is not in residence," Hamish said. "He has gone to spend a few days in his other residence."

"We're not here to see him," Oliver said. Taking a firm hold on Lorena's hand, he took a step forward.

With a faint shrug, the butler stepped back to allow them entrance.

Lorena felt numb as they crossed the entryway. Memories crashed down on her. All the nights she had fought off Fairfield's unwanted advances, the revolting smell of his breath, his vile touch, his tongue plundering her mouth.

Oliver dragged her down the corridor that led to Lord Fairfield's den.

Still clutching her hand, Oliver pulled back a black velvet drape, exposing a narrow door she had never known was there. He took a key from a hidden compartment in the top desk drawer and inserted it into the lock. "Almost there," he said cheerfully as he lit a candle. "Watch your step."

The taper's wavering light revealed a narrow set of wooden stairs. Lorena shivered as she preceded Oliver. When they reached the bottom, he lit several candles. She didn't know what she had expected to find—a wine cellar, perhaps, but there was nothing in the low-ceilinged room save for a square table that held a variety of knives and other deadly-looking instruments.

And a metal cage barely large enough to hold its occupant.

She let out a gasp when she realized it was Demetri inside. Crying his name, she ran toward him, bit back a scream at what she saw. He sat slumped against the wall, his hands bound behind his back, a thick silver collar around his neck, so tight she wondered that he could breathe. His skin was deathly pale, his cheeks sunken.

Alarmed, she glanced over her shoulder at Oliver. "Is he dead?"

"No. Just at rest."

Of course, she thought. The sun was high in the sky. "What have you done to him?"

"Deprived him of the blood that keeps him alive."

"But... he'll die."

"It won't kill him. It merely drains his strength, as does the silver that binds him. Even master vampires have a weakness."

Tears welled in her eyes and dripped, unheeded, down her cheeks. He looked subdued. Yet, even now, when he seemed to be helpless, a latent sense of power clung to him. Did Oliver feel it, too? Or was he too busy gloating? "How long do you intend to keep him here, like this?"

Oliver shrugged. "A year. A day. Forever." He shrugged again. "It's up to you."

"Me?"

"I own you now. You can be my servant, or you can be my wife and bear my children."

She shook her head. "Surely your family will never allow it. I'm a commoner…"

He held up a hand to stay her words. "If you refuse to marry me, he dies tomorrow. If you agree to be my bride, I will let him live as long as you do."

She stared at him in disbelief.

"Lorena."

She turned at the sound of Demetri's voice.

"Do not believe him. I know his thoughts. He will not keep any promise he makes you."

Wrapping her hands around the bars, she leaned forward as far as she could, tears again stinging her eyes. "I can't let him kill you."

"I would prefer it to this. Please, my love, do not agree to his terms. I would rather be dead than think of you in his arms."

Lorena glanced over her shoulder to glare at Oliver. "I'll agree to marry you if you let him go."

"I'm afraid that's quite impossible, my dear," Oliver said with feigned sorrow. "He would surely kill me the instant he was free."

"If you will swear to me on your honor as a gentleman that you will not harm him, I will agree to your terms. But only if you let me come here each night to make sure you are keeping your word, as I will keep mine."

Demetri tugged against his bonds. "Lorena, no!"

Ainsley smiled triumphantly. "You drive a hard bargain, my dear."

"And you must give him what he needs."

Oliver grimaced. "Very well."

"Swear it!"

"I swear."

"I want to be alone with him."

A muscle throbbed in Oliver's jaw before he said, grudgingly, "Only for a few minutes."

She waited until Oliver left the room before going around to the side of cage where she dropped to her knees. "Demetri, what can I do?"

"You cannot marry him. Promise me, love."

"I can't let him destroy you." Tears stung her eyes. "I can't. I implore you, please don't ask it of me."

"Would you rather have me spend decades in this hell?"

"Of course not, but…"

He closed his eyes as the scent of her blood aroused his hunger. He craved it as he had never craved anything before. Needed it to ease the agony that throbbed relentlessly through the length and breadth of his being. Days without feeding had left him with a hunger like no other.

"There must be something I can do," she murmured.

"There is." His gaze settled on the pulse throbbing slow and steady in the hollow of her throat. "Let me drink from you."

Of course. He needed blood. She quickly rolled up her sleeve and thrust her arm through the bars. Chains rattling, he moved as close to her as he could.

"Don't let me take too much," he warned, and sank his fangs into her wrist.

There was no pleasure in his bite, as there had been before. Only a desperate need.

She let him drink until she began to feel light-headed. Suddenly frightened, she jerked her arm away, recoiled when he growled a protest low in his throat.

He took a deep breath, and when he met her gaze, his dark eyes were filled with gratitude. "Bless you, my love."

"Demetri, why did you leave me without a word?"

"It doesn't matter now. I was a fool to do so."

"You did it because you thought it was best for me, didn't you?"

He nodded.

"Have you been here all this time?"

"No, my love. Only a few days." Days that seemed like centuries.

"I'll get you out of here somehow." She scrambled to her feet and backed away from the cage when she heard the cellar door open. "I love you," she whispered as she quickly pulled her sleeve down to cover the tiny bites in her wrist.

Oliver's footsteps echoed off the cold, stone walls as he strode toward her. "It's time to go."

She didn't argue, nor did she pull away when he reached for her hand.

Demetri watched her ascend the stairs, then closed his eyes. The taste of her life's blood lingered on his tongue, warm and sweet. Already, he could feel it warming him. Strengthening him. Solidifying the link that bound her to him. And him to her.

Closing his eyes, he listened to the sound of her footsteps leaving the manor, the muted laughter of two of the house-maids, the tread of another servant moving about in Fairfield's den, which was directly above the dungeon. Summoning what little power he had left, he called the maid to him, praying that Oliver had neglected to lock the cellar door.

He breathed a sigh of relief as he heard the girl's foot-steps on the stairs. She was young, as were all of Fairfield's female servants. She walked stiffly toward him, her expres-sion blank.

"Give me your arm."

Kneeling beside the cage, she obediently thrust her arm between the bars.

Her blood was not as sweet or satisfying as Lorena's, but he was too desperate to care. He yearned to drink her dry. Only the thought that she would be missed, her body found outside the cage, kept him from doing so. He couldn't take a chance on alerting Fairfield or Oliver that their prisoner had regained some of his strength.

When he had taken all that he dared, he sent the maid back upstairs. As soon as heard her footsteps overhead, he wiped the memory of what had happened from her mind. Later, after everyone had retired for the night, he would summon one of the other servants. If only he could mesmer-ize Fairfield as easily. But the hunters were not as suscep-tible to mind control as most mortals. They were aware of his power and rarely let their guard down. Years of practice had taught the more seasoned among them how to shield their minds and block his influence.

Leaning back against the wall, he closed his eyes and surrendered to the darkness.

CHAPTER TWENTY-THREE

At home, Oliver walked Lorena to the door. "As much as I would like to come in, I fear I have urgent business to attend to," he said. "However, now that we are betrothed, I believe a kiss is in order. Do you not agree?"

She tried not to cringe as he took her in his arms and slanted his mouth over hers.

"I shall call on you tonight."

"Have you forgotten? I'm going to my sister's birthday party this evening. I may stay until the morning."

He stared at her, his gaze intense. "Tomorrow night, then. At eight."

"Yes," she said, forcing a smile. "Tomorrow."

With a curt nod, he descended the stairs.

Shoulders sagging, Lorena closed and locked the door. She had to get Demetri out of that dreadful place, but how?

She paced the parlor floor. Even if she had a plan, she couldn't carry it out alone, but she had no one to turn to. No one who would help her. No one she could trust to keep his secret. No one … she paused. What of Sir Everleigh? He was Demetri's best friend. And he already knew Demetri's secret. If only she had agreed to go to Sir Everleigh's party tonight, she might have had a chance to see him alone.

She found a sheet of paper, intending to send Oliver a note, then put the pen aside. She had told him she was going to her sister's party. What plausible excuse could she make for changing her mind now? She was afraid he already suspected she had lied about it. If she now changed her mind, it might only fuel his suspicions.

It might be wise to actually go and visit her family, just in case Oliver decided to check up on her. Besides, she hadn't seen her family in weeks.

And tomorrow afternoon, she would go visit Sir Everleigh. She would tell him she missed Emma and Alice and hoped to visit with them for a short while.

Sinking down on the sofa in the back parlor, she closed her eyes. Demetri's image immediately came to mind. How did he endure being caged like that? Deprived of nourishment, at the mercy of hunters. Vampire hunters. How many were there? And who would have thought that Lord Fairfield would be one of them?

"Demetri." She whispered his name, her heart aching for his suffering, his loneliness.

Lorena, my love.

"Demetri?" She opened her eyes, her gaze darting around the room.

I'm here.

"But, how is that possible?"

I can hear your thoughts.

"Even though we're miles apart?"

Yes.

"Can you read everyone's mind?"

If I wish.

"That's...amazing. Is there anything I can do for you?"

Change your mind. Refuse to marry Ainsley.

"I can't do that. I can't let you die if I can save you."

Stubborn woman, he muttered.

"Demetri, I..."

Fairfield is here.

She started to reply and then stopped. Even though she hadn't been aware of it when his mind joined hers, she knew the moment the connection between them was gone.

Fairfield strolled across the floor, a satisfied smirk on his face. "How the mighty have fallen."

Demetri glared at him, but said nothing.

Like a farmer examining a bull he intended to buy, Fairfield walked back and forth in front of the cage, eyes narrowed in contemplation. "I hear Ainsley brought Lorena to visit you. She's a lovely bit of skirt, that one. Did you know he bought her from me?"

Demetri bolted upright, eyes blazing with anger. "Damn you to hell! She isn't some piece of meat, to be bought and sold by the likes of you."

"Fetched me a fair price, she did. Four times what I paid for her."

Demetri tugged against the chains that bound him, wanting nothing more than to get his hands around the man's neck.

Fairfield laughed. "You'll never break those chains, my lord," he said with a sneer. "Too bad you'll miss Ainsley's wedding. It will likely be the social event of the year."

Demetri tensed as Fairfield picked up a wicked looking knife from the table.

Fairfield held it up, turning it this way and that as he walked closer to the cage. The silver blade glinted in the candlelight. "Time to bleed you, my lord." He drove the blade deep into Demetri's left thigh and dragged it through meat and muscle to his ankle. Dark-red blood welled in the long, narrow gash.

"Until tomorrow," Fairfield said. Whistling softly, he swaggered up the stairs.

Demetri released the breath he'd been holding, grateful that Fairfield hadn't lingered. Thanks to the blood he had taken from Lorena and the maid, the wound in his leg healed quickly. Without it, he would have bled for several minutes.

He grinned into the darkness. Perhaps there was hope, after all.

Her family was surprised to see her when Lorena arrived at the house, since she had not visited them since Demetri left her.

"Where's the future bridegroom?" her father asked.

"He couldn't make it this evening," Lorena said. "Stop looking so glum, papa. You'll be happy to know we've postposed the wedding."

"Indeed?"

"What happened?" her mother asked.

"We didn't want to upset you. I have a favor to ask," she said, glancing at each member of her family in turn. "In order to avoid a gathering I didn't wish to attend, I told a lie. I said I couldn't go because it was Anna's birthday. So, please, back me up if anyone should inquire about my whereabouts on the night in question."

"Who were you trying to avoid?" Grace asked.

"Oliver Ainsley."

Her father's brows shot up. "You could do worse than associate with him. The man not only comes from an old and respected family, he is well-liked by one and all."

"Not by me." No doubt her parents would be delighted when they learned she had agreed to marry the despicable man, but she didn't feel like talking about it tonight, not when she hoped it would never happen.

Later that night, as she waited for sleep to claim her, she clung to the hope that Sir Everleigh could help her rescue Demetri before it was too late. Because, like Demetri, she didn't believe Oliver would keep his word.

It was late afternoon when Lorena bid her family goodbye. Anna hugged her fiercely and begged her to visit more often and Lorena promised she would try. But it was Clara who touched her heart when she whispered, "I hope you bring Demetri with you the next time you come calling."

Blinking back her tears, Lorena nodded.

At home, Lorena tethered the mare to the hitching post before hurrying into the house. In her room, she quickly changed into her favorite dress, then combed and brushed her hair. Certain she looked her best, she ran outside, climbed into the saddle and headed for Sir Everleigh's estate, praying that he was home and that he would receive her.

The butler answered the door. "May I help you, miss?"

"I should like to see Sir Everleigh, please."

"Is he expecting you?"

"No, but..."

"I'm sorry, the master doesn't entertain unchaperoned ladies."

"Please, wait!" she cried as he stepped back to close the door. "Tell him I'm a friend of Lord Demetri and I must see him. It's urgent."

The butler regarded her through narrowed eyes. "Very well. Wait here," he said, and shut the door in her face.

Lorena tapped her foot impatiently. What if Sir Everleigh refused to see her? He was her only hope.

After what seemed like an hour, the butler returned. "Sir Everleigh will see you in the library, Miss. If you will please follow me."

Lord Fairfield's house was lovely, but Sir Everleigh's home was magnificent. She hadn't seem much of the house either time she had been here, hadn't paid much attention to the many paintings, the expensive carpets, or the lavish décor. Gilt-edged mirrors reflected the light. A glass-fronted cherrywood cabinet held dozens of delicate China plates and figurines.

The butler paused before a closed door. He knocked once before opening it. "Miss Halliday to see you, Sir," he announced.

"Come in, come in," Sir Everleigh said as he rose from his chair to greet her. "This is a pleasant surprise. But where is Demetri?"

"That's what I've come to talk to you about."

Sir Everleigh's brows rushed together. "You look troubled, my dear. Please, sit down. Is something amiss?"

Lorena perched on the edge of the chair he indicated. "Demetri told me of your friendship, of how you met."

"Did he now? I find that... unusual. To my knowledge, there are few who know the truth."

"He's in terrible trouble. I have no one else to turn to, my lord. I was hoping you could help me."

"Trouble?" Everleigh muttered something unintelligible. "No doubt Ainsley is behind it."

Lorena stared at him. "You know about him?"

"Yes, I'm afraid I do. A vile man, to be sure, one known to indulge in, shall we say, questionable practices not spoken of in polite society. I warned Demetri to be wary of him." Sir Everleigh's gaze searched hers. "Knowing Demetri, it's hard to believe he's gotten himself tangled up in something he cannot handle. So, tell me, what is going on?

"Oliver and Lord Fairfield have him locked in a cage. They are slowly starving him."

Sir Everleigh swore a vile oath, then quickly apologized. "Where are they keeping him?"

"In a dungeon. In Lord Fairfield's country home."

Everleigh swore again. "I've heard rumors of such a place, but of course, I could not believe them to be true. Do they plan to destroy him?"

"Only if I refuse to wed Oliver."

Everleigh leaned back in his chair and folded his arms across his chest. "I see."

"Can you help me?"

"I shall do my best. You look a bit pale, my dear. Can I offer you some refreshment?"

"Yes, thank you."

Rising, he poured a finger of brandy for her, two fingers for himself. Sipping his own, he paced the floor for several minutes before resuming his seat. "This will take some thought and some planning. There are other hunters in town besides Fairfield and Ainsley. We must move carefully. If threatened, they may destroy Demetri and dispose of the remains rather than let what they're doing be known."

"Perhaps that's the answer!" Lorena exclaimed. "I can threaten to tell everyone what they're doing if they don't release him!"

"Here, now, let us not be hasty. Such a threat might well put your own life in danger."

"I don't care!" she exclaimed, blinking back her tears. "You haven't seen him."

"But Demetri would care. Perhaps he would blame me. I should not like to be on the receiving end of his anger."

She smiled faintly. "Nor would I."

"My advice is that you delay the wedding as long as you can. Demetri may be in chains, but he is not yet defeated. He is a powerful being. I should not be surprised if he finds a way to free himself. In the meantime, I will ask around and see if I can learn anything." Reaching forward, he patted her hand. "Do not lose hope, my dear. We will see the better side of this yet."

Lorena felt somewhat better when she left Sir Everleigh's home. Just sharing her worries had helped relieve some of her anxiety. Sir Everleigh was the wealthiest and most influential man in the town. If he couldn't help her, no one could.

As she rode home, she hoped Sir Everleigh was right, and that Demetri might be able to free himself.

Demetri roused with the setting of the sun. His arms ached from being chained behind his back for so long, but it was only a minor irritation. Opening his vampire senses, he searched for Lorena, breathed a sigh of relief when he realized she was safe at home.

He cursed softly when he heard footsteps on the stairs. Fairfield, come to bleed him again. He clenched his hands as he imagined them around the man's throat, slowly squeezing the life out of him.

Fairfield smiled as he picked up his favorite knife and approached the cell. He frowned as he drew closer. "If I didn't know better, I'd think you had found sustenance somewhere."

"Any blood would be welcome, even yours." Demetri flashed his fangs, grinned when Fairfield took a hasty step back.

Eyes narrowed with anger, Fairfield strode up to the cage and jammed the blade into Demetri's thigh. Demetri sucked in a breath as the blade went all the way through to the floor.

Fairfield sneered at him. "Who's laughing now?" he gloated as he jerked the blade free, then dragged it down the length of Demetri's leg. "See you tomorrow," he said, as he turned to leave. "My lord."

"When I get out of here, I will rip out your heart," Demetri hissed as the man turned away. "And shove it down your throat."

Fairfield paused a moment, then stiffened his shoulders before heading up the stairs.

Chapter Twenty-Four

L orena worried and fumed the rest of the day. She came up with a dozen ways to free Demetri, but none of them had the least chance of success. Her only hope remained with Sir Everleigh.

At seven, she hurried upstairs to get dressed.

Oliver arrived promptly at eight. He looked quite dashing in a blue velvet jacket and black breeches. Once, she might have been quite taken with him. Now, all she saw was a monster far more cruel than the man she loved had ever been. For she did love Demetri, nothing wavering.

"You look quite lovely, my dear," Oliver said as he bowed over her hand. "I trust you had a good time at your sister's birthday party."

"Yes, I did. Thank you."

"I have tickets for the opera, or we could just go for a drive through the park."

"The opera sounds wonderful," she said, forcing a note of enthusiasm into her tone. The last thing she wanted was to be alone with Oliver in a carriage or anywhere else.

Oliver had bought the best seats in the house, though for what little attention she paid to what was happening on the stage, they might as well have been sitting in the last row. She could think of nothing but Demetri.

My love?

Demetri! Are you all right?

As well as can be expected. Are you home?

No. I'm at the opera with Oliver. She felt Demetri's jealousy as if he were there beside her. *I wish we could be together. I miss you.*

Tell Ainsley you want to see me again, to make sure I am still alive.

I will.

Whatever happens, remember that I love you to my dying breath.

Don't talk about dying. I love you!

Lorena!

How will I bear it if they kill you?

They will not.

I pray you are right.

"Lorena?"

She blinked, surprised that the opera was over.

"My dear?" Oliver asked. "Are you well?"

"Yes, of course. Why do you ask?"

"You look troubled."

"I am," she replied curtly. "You've imprisoned the man I was going to marry."

"I do not wish to speak of him."

"But I do. I want to see him tonight before I go home, to make sure he is still alive."

"How many times must I tell you he is not alive? He is the walking dead. An abomination!"

"Whatever he is, I wish to see him."

"Very well," Oliver said, his voice tight with anger. "But this is the last time until we are wed."

❧   ❧   ❧

Lorena's heart was pounding as they reached Lord Fairfield's country estate. Oliver guided her through the house and into the den with the hidden door that led to the dungeon. She waited impatiently as he unlocked it, then lit a candle.

When he started to follow her down the stairs, she stopped. "I wish to be alone with him," she said.

"But..."

"Alone!"

Face purple with rage, he handed her the candle.

Lorena waited until he closed the door before carefully making her way down the narrow flight of stairs. She lifted the candle high as she approached the cage. He sat on the floor, back to the wall, his eyes closed. "Demetri?"

He looked up at her, a faint smile playing over his lips when he saw her.

"Are you all right?" she asked anxiously.

"I am now."

"You always know just what to say. How are you, really?"

"Unbeknownst to Fairfield, I have been feeding on his servants after the household has gone to bed."

Lorena stared at him. "How have you managed that?"

"Your blood has strengthened me. I merely call them to me as with any other ... prey, and then wipe the memory from their minds." He smiled inwardly. Last night, he had taken his fill, albeit from several maids and the butler. Had any of them known how to find the key to his cell and the shackles that bound him, he would have been free long ago.

She smiled. "Very clever, my lord. I guess you do not need my blood then."

"No," he said, his gaze caressing her. "But I would not refuse a drink."

Sitting as close to the bars of the cage as she could, she rolled up her sleeve and offered him her arm. She closed her eyes as he bit her gently. Unlike the last time, pleasure spread to every nerve and fiber of her being. She sighed with regret when he lifted his head.

"Bless you, my love."

"Oliver said this is the last time he will let me see you until we are wed."

"We will see each other before that happens, my love. Do not doubt it."

"I went to see Sir Everleigh."

"Indeed?"

"He said he would try to help, although I don't know what he can do."

"He is a good friend, but I should not like him to be involved. In any case, there is nothing he can do except put his own life in danger."

"I could go to the police."

"No. I doubt they would believe you. You have no proof other than your word. And I would be no safer in their hands, believe me."

"There must be something!"

"Leave it to me, love."

Needing to touch him, Lorena reached through the bars and stroked his cheek, only to jerk it back when she heard the door open. Springing to her feet, she pulled her sleeve down and backed away from the cage.

"Lorena, it's time to go," Oliver said brusquely.

"Goodbye, Demetri," she murmured.

"Goodbye, my love." He fought a wave of jealousy as Ainsley grabbed her arm and practically dragged her up the stairs. "You will live to regret this, Ainsley," he murmured, his gaze boring into the man's back. "But not for long."

❧   ❧   ❧

When they reached her house, Oliver walked her to the door and followed her, uninvited, inside.

"Really, my lord, what will people say?" she asked as she pulled the pins from her hat and set it on the table beside the sofa.

"Who's to know?"

"I have my reputation to think of, sir."

He snorted. "I fear you lost that when your father sold you to Fairfield."

She glared at him, too angry to speak.

"Whatever happens in the future, never forget that you are mine. Married or not, my dear, you belong to me now."

"I will *never* belong to you!"

"Once we are wed, you will be even more in my control," he said, each word cutting like a knife. "I have made arrangements for us to marry a week from today. Go find yourself a dress."

"So soon?"

His gaze burned into hers. "Did you share Demetri's bed?"

"Of course not!"

"I hope you're telling me the truth," he said, as he dragged her into his arms. "I would not like to discover that my wife is another man's leavings."

She stared at him, horrified by his crude words. To think she had once thought him a gentleman.

He grasped a handful of her hair, then covered her mouth with his.

Lorena gagged as his tongue plundered her mouth. When his hand closed over her breast, she raked her nails down his cheek, let out a hoarse cry of pain when he slapped her, once, twice.

"You will never raise your hand to me again," he warned. Pulling a handkerchief from his pocket, he wiped the blood from his face. "You will not like the consequences if you do."

Eyes glittering with outrage, he stalked out of the house.

Lorena collapsed on the floor, her head bowed as she wept bitterly. How could she marry such a man? How could she not, when Demetri's life hung in the balance?

CHAPTER TWENTY-FIVE

Sir Everleigh paid a visit to his club the night after Lorena's visit. It was the best place to hear the latest gossip.

Taking a seat at one of the card tables, he listened to the conversations around him. There was the usual bragging of the young men boasting of their recent conquests, whispers about one lord who was cuckolding another.

Several of the vampire hunters—Minton, Whitfield and Dutton—were gathered at a table in the corner with their heads together. But he heard no mention of Demetri, no hint of anything amiss at Fairfield's country estate, no rumors that Ainsley had been up to anything suspicious.

Other than confronting Ainsley outright, he could think of no subtle way to bring up the subject of Demetri, or of Lorena's knowledge of a dungeon in Fairfield's cellar. He considered contacting the police, but could think of nothing that would get Demetri killed faster. Fairfield had several constables on his payroll. They would warn him of any warrants issued to search his premises. Fairfield would immediately destroy Demetri and burn his remains.

Everleigh lingered until the club closed, none the wiser, but his purse ten pounds lighter.

CHAPTER TWENTY-SIX

Demetri listened to the sounds of Fairfield's household as they prepared to retire for the night. Always the same. The kitchen maids preparing for the morning, the house-maids going from room to room to make sure the lamps had been extinguished, the muted sounds coming from Fairfield's bedchamber as he ravaged one of the maids.

He waited in anticipation for the man to finish, forced himself to relax as the cellar door opened and he heard Fairfield's heavy foot falls on the stairs.

"Have you heard the news?" Fairfield asked jovially. "Oliver is wedding your woman next week. No doubt you won't survive long after the ceremony."

Demetri choked back the words, *You won't live that long,* as Fairfield picked up his favorite silver-bladed knife and jabbed it into Demetri's leg.

Exerting all the power at his command, Demetri ripped the chains out of the wall, reached through the bars and wrapped one hand around Fairfield's lily-white throat. "Have you forgotten what I told you?" he growled as he jerked Fairfield up against the cage, smashing the side of the man's face against the bars.

Fairfield struggled to free himself, his hands clawing at Demetri's. "Let me go," he begged. "I'll give you anything you want, I swear."

"I promised to tear out your heart and shove it down your throat. Remember?"

Fairfield kicked and scratched like a man gone berserk but he was held fast in the vampire's grip. His face went pale, his eyes bulging with terror as Demetri's eyes went red.

Fairfield managed one last desperate plea for help but to no avail.

Eyes blazing, Demetri plunged his hand into Fairfield's chest, ripped out the man's heart and tossed it aside. Shoving it down the hunter's throat had been an empty threat, he mused as he released his hold on Fairfield. There was a muted thump as the body hit the floor.

Rising, Demetri summoned his remaining power, wrapped his hands around two of the steel bars and pulled them apart, then stepped sideways through the narrow opening. Seething with rage, he searched the table for the keys to the manacles on his wrists and the thick silver collar around his neck.

Finally free of his bonds, he took several deep breaths, then made his way up the stairs into the den. He closed the cellar door behind him and pulled the drape across it before ghosting up the stairs to the servants' quarters, where he quickly satisfied his thirst before leaving the estate.

He considered going after Oliver, but his need to see Lorena was stronger than his desire for vengeance.

A thought took him to the front parlor. He cursed long and loud when he caught Ainsley's scent. The man had been in the house only hours ago.

Striding into the kitchen, he removed his boots, then peeled off his blood-stained shirt, vest, trousers, and underwear, and tossed them in the trash bin. After filling a large pail with water, he washed from head to foot.

In spite of his longing to see Lorena, he told himself to stay away from her even as he swiftly climbed the stairs. He made a detour to his room where he donned a pair of trousers. Barefooted, he padded down the hall to her bed chamber. He paused outside her door, once again telling himself to wait until the morrow when his lust for blood and vengeance had cooled.

But it was no use. He had to see her with his own eyes, know that she was well, that she was still his.

He eased the door open and stepped into the room. She lay on her side, the wealth of her hair spread across the pillow like skeins of scarlet silk, her cheeks tracked with tears. Her scent called to him and he was helpless to resist.

He moved silently toward the bed. Reached out to caress her cheek.

In her sleep, she murmured his name. It was his undoing. Drawing back the covers, he slipped into bed beside her and drew her into his arms. Her hair smelled of lilacs. But it was the scent of her blood that surrounded him.

She stirred in his embrace and woke with a start.

"Hush," he murmured. "'Tis only me."

"Demetri?" She ran her hands over his face, his hair. "Oh, Demetri!" she exclaimed, and threw her arms around him. "How did you get away?"

"I am a master vampire, my sweet. No mere mortal can hold me."

"I'm holding you," she whispered, a smile in her voice.

"Ah, my love, you are no mere mortal."

"I missed you so much. I was so afraid I would never see you again."

"I will never leave you again, my love, unless you tell me to leave."

"We can be married now," she said. "If you still want me."

"Never doubt it." He cupped her face in his hands and kissed her. He had meant it to be a mere touch of his lips to hers, but that small touch lit a spark that quickly turned to flame. He drew her body tight to his, his hands caressing her, arousing her, until she writhed against him.

He told himself to stop, to wait. She would soon be his bride. But the fire would not be quenched, nor did she resist when he removed her gown and his trousers. Her skin was as smooth as the finest satin, her lips the soft velvet of rose petals.

Lorena made no move to stop him, gave no thought to right or wrong. There was only Demetri, holding her close in the dark when she had thought never to see him again, whispering that he loved her. She ran her hands over his chest, the length of his arms, his hard, flat belly, and marveled that this mysterious, amazing man desired her.

When he rose over her, she lifted her hips to receive him, let out a faint cry as his body melded with hers. Lost in the wonder of it, she closed her eyes, desperate to be closer, to surrender herself to him completely. She cried his name, her nails clawing his back, as sunlight burst deep within her. His own release quickly followed.

A sigh escaped her lips and then, safe in his arms, she fell asleep.

In the morning, Lorena woke feeling blissfully happy and content. Eyes still closed, she thought about the dream she'd had last night. Such a wonderful dream. In it, Demetri had come into her room in the dark of the night and made love to her. She wondered if the real thing would be as unforgettable.

Smiling, she flung her arms out to the side, let out a shriek when her hand struck flesh.

Sitting up, she stared at Demetri, who was bare to the waist and appeared to be naked beneath the sheet.

It hadn't been a dream at all.

Her gaze moved over him. He was beautifully made, his arms muscular, his chest and shoulders broad, his stomach flat and ridged with muscle. The sheet covered the rest of him. It had been pitch black in her room last night. Almost, she was tempted to peek under the covers, but her courage deserted her when she looked at him and saw him watching her, an amused smile on his face.

"I promise to keep my eyes closed if you want to take a look beneath the sheet."

She blushed from head to foot.

He sat up, his knuckles caressing her cheek. "Are you sorry about last night?"

Her gaze slid away from his as she felt her cheeks grow hotter. "No, my lord."

"Lorena, let there be no lies between us."

His voice was so soft, so filled with love, it brought tears to her eyes. "I'm not sorry, Demetri. Truly."

He drew her into his embrace, his hand lightly stroking her hair, her back. "You have given me the most precious gift I have ever received," he said quietly. "I did not mean to steal your virginity."

"You didn't steal it," she said. "It was freely given."

"If you have no objection, we will wed as soon as possible."

"I have no objection, my lord. Would it be terribly shameful if we made love again now, when I can see you?"

His laughter rang off the walls as his arms tightened around her. "I see I have fallen in love with a lusty wench," he teased. "How did I ever get so lucky?"

Oliver Ainsley scowled as someone pounded on his bedroom door. Who the devil dared come calling at this hour of the morning? He hadn't even had his tea yet.

Rising, he threw on his robe and flung the door open. "What is it, Moss?"

"A message for you, sir. From Fairfield Manor."

Brow furrowed, he reached for the envelope. "Thank you, Moss."

"Will there be a reply?"

"Not at the moment." After closing the door, Ainsley slit the envelope and removed a sheet of stationery. The message was brief—*Lord Fairfield is missing.*

Missing? Ainsley's frown deepened. Where would he have gone?

He didn't waste time calling for his valet. He dressed quickly, hurried to the stable and saddled his horse. Something must be wrong. Fairfield would have told him if he planned to leave town.

When he reached Fairfield's country estate, he knocked several times before one of the maids answered the door.

"Mr. Ainsley, Lord Fairfield isn't in residence."

"Did he say where he was going? Back to Fairfield Manor, perhaps?"

"No, sir."

"When did you last see him?"

"He retired to his bed shortly after ten o'clock last night. He had an early meeting this morning. When his valet went to wake him, his bed was empty. No one has seen him since last night. His horse is in the stable. There was no call for his carriage."

Muttering under his breath, Ainsley pushed the maid out of his way and hurried toward Fairfield's den. A quick glance showed nothing amiss. The drape that covered the hidden entrance to the basement was in place, the door obviously closed.

Oliver locked the door to the den and crossed to the desk. His hand trembled as he opened the secret compartment in the desk drawer. And then he frowned. The key was missing. He stood there a moment, trying to put the pieces together—the drape had been in place when he entered, the door to the cellar closed, but the key was missing. Had Fairfield forgot to return it to the desk after checking on the prisoner?

Taking a deep breath, he tried the cellar door. It opened on silent hinges. Ainsley stared into the dark maw beyond, his heart pounding, before slowly moving down the stairs. His footsteps echoed off the silent walls.

Holding the candle high, he stared at the cage, felt the bile rise in his throat when he saw the empty cell, and the body sprawled beside it. A body with a gaping hole in its chest. The missing heart lay on the floor not far away.

Ainsley broke out in a cold sweat as he turned away, his stomach heaving violently.

When he was again under control, he made his way blindly up the stairs, his only thought to get away from the horror he had left behind.

❧ ❧ ❧

Lorena hummed as she skipped into the kitchen, thinking how wonderful it would be to fall asleep in Demetri's arms each night and wake beside him each day. She felt her cheeks grow warm as she wondered if they would make love every morning. She had fallen asleep again after they made love the second time. When she woke, he was still asleep. She had spent several minutes just looking at him. He really was the most handsome man she had ever seen, perfectly formed, strong, filled with a power she would never understand. A power that was fascinating and frightening.

She had just finished breakfast and poured herself a cup of tea when someone knocked at the door.

Fearing it was Oliver, she didn't answer.

But the knocking came again, louder and more insistent this time.

Taking a deep breath, she lifted the latch, her eyes widening when she saw two men in uniform.

"Good morning, miss," one of them said. "I am Constable Parker. Is Lord Demetri at home?"

"Has he done something wrong?"

"Are you his wife?"

"No. I'm his ... his betrothed."

"Is he at home?" the officer asked again, his voice sharp.

"He's ... he's still in bed."

"We need to ask him a few questions. Would you wake him, please?"

"What is this about?"

"Just wake him, please."

"As you wish." Filled with trepidation, she showed them into the front parlor. Hurrying to her room, she quietly closed and locked the door behind her. "Demetri. Demetri, wake up!"

He jackknifed to a sitting position. "Lorena, what is wrong?"

"The constable is here. To see you. He wouldn't tell me why."

"I know why." Damn Ainsley, he must have discovered Fairfield's body and gone straight to the constable's office. "Go and tell them I will see them directly."

"But…"

"Do as I say, love."

Returning to the parlor, Lorena took a seat on the sofa and folded her hands in her lap to still their trembling. "Lord Demetri will be here shortly."

"Thank you, miss."

She saw no reason to invite them to sit, started when Demetri strode into the room.

"Gentlemen," he said, "how may I help you?"

The constable glanced at Lorena. "Perhaps it would be better if the lady left the room."

"I have nothing to hide," Demetri said.

"When was the last time you saw Lord Fairfield?"

"I am afraid I do not recall. We are not friends."

"He was murdered in his home last night. Would you know anything about that?"

"No."

"Where were you last night after ten o'clock?"

"I was here."

"Was anyone else at home at the time?"

"Miss Halliday."

The constable lifted one brow. "She lives here, with you?"

"Yes."

"Does anyone else reside here?"

"No."

The constable glanced at Lorena. "Was Lord Demetri here all night?"

"Yes, of course."

"Is there anything else you wish to know?" Demetri asked.

"Not at this time."

"Then I shall show you to the door."

"Good day to you, sir. Miss."

Demetri showed them out. After locking the door, he stood there, his brow furrowed, wondering exactly what Ainsley had told them.

"Is it true?" Lorena asked.

Demetri turned to find Lorena at his elbow.

Her gaze searched his. "Is it true? Did you kill Lord Fairfield?"

"Yes."

He saw the question in her eyes, knew she wondered if he had drained the man dry. But she didn't ask, and he didn't enlighten her.

"What are we going to do now?"

"Do?" He smiled at her. "You promised we would wed as soon as possible, remember?"

She blinked up at him. "How can you think about marriage at a time like this? What if they can prove you did it? What if they come back and arrest you?"

Taking her by the hand, he led her to the sofa and drew her down beside him. "Do you think they could catch me if I didn't wish to be caught?"

"Fairfield and Oliver did."

"Only because I let my guard down one night. It will never happen again."

"Has it ever happened before?"

"Once, when I was a very young vampire."

"How did it happen?"

"I mistakenly tried to prey upon a female hunter, not knowing who she was, or that she had a partner nearby. They caught me quite by surprise."

"How did you get away?"

"They were also young. And over-confident."

"So you escaped?"

"Yes." He hesitated a moment, debating whether to tell her the rest. But if she was going to spend her life with him, she had a right to know. "I killed the young man when he tried to drive a stake into my heart."

"And the girl?"

"I let her go."

Lorena rested her cheek against his chest. She told herself he was here and he was safe and that nothing else mattered. But he had killed the hunter. And Lord Fairfield. Still, he had killed the hunter in self-defense. And, in a way, Lord Fairfield, too. But how many others had he killed in his long life?

He caressed her cheek. "Has what happened last night changed your feelings for me?"

"No, but..."

"You wish I had not killed Fairfield."

"Yes."

"He deserved what he got," Demetri said flatly. And more, for daring to lay his filthy hands on Lorena, if for no other reason.

"Are you going to...to kill Oliver, too?"

"What do you think?"

"I wish you wouldn't."

"You care for him?"

"No! No, but I care for you, Demetri. I love you and I don't like to think of you killing anyone, even if they deserve it."

Jaw clenched, he stared into the distance. Let Ainsley live? How could he? Fairfield wasn't the only who had taken pleasure in bleeding him until he thought he'd go mad with thirst. True, he had been their prisoner only a few days. True, he was a master vampire, the strongest of his kind. But he was not immune to pain, and they had gloated as they tortured him. The silver against his skin had been a constant agony. But for Lorena giving him her blood, it would have been much worse. Her generosity had strengthened him when he needed it most.

"Please, Demetri?"

"Very well, my love. I will spare his life, but only because you asked it of me."

Later that night, after Lorena had fallen asleep, Demetri left the house. A thought took him to Ainsley's vast estate. Masking his presence, Demetri prowled the outskirts of Ainsley's home. There were armed servants at every door and window, inside and out. Lights burned behind the windows, even though he knew Ainsley had retired for the night. He could hear the man tossing and turning in his bed.

Demetri grinned inwardly. It was obvious that Oliver had seen Fairfield's body, or at least knew the manner of his death and feared he would be next. He had no doubt it had been Oliver who had gone to the constable and suggested that Demetri was the guilty party.

His need to confront the man, to bury his fangs in Ainsley's throat and slowly drain the life out of him was almost overwhelming. Still, he had promised Lorena he would spare Oliver's miserable life. But Ainsley did not know that.

Demetri grinned into the darkness. Ainsley would live in fear for weeks, perhaps for the rest of his life, hiding behind his threshold, afraid to open his door, not daring to venture outside after the sun went down. He would avoid invitations, be afraid to open his door to strangers, never knowing if Demetri had sent someone to drag him out of his house so Demetri could claim his revenge.

Perhaps, as the French were fond of saying, revenge was, indeed, a dish best served cold.

Whistling softly, he returned to his lair.

CHAPTER TWENTY-SEVEN

Lorena woke expecting to find Demetri beside her. It troubled her that he wasn't there. He had shared her bed last night, made slow, sweet love to her. Why did he now stay away? Had she displeased him? Was he angry, or maybe jealous, because she had begged him to spare Oliver's life?

She fretted all that day. Had she truly offended him, or had he simply taken his rest elsewhere? He had told her once that he had a secure location where he passed the daylight hours. She wondered now if it was nearby. Would he tell her where it was after they wed?

Needing to be busy, she dusted and mopped until her back ached and then she walked down to the barn and mucked the stalls, fed and watered the horses, fed the chickens.

Refusing to worry over his whereabouts until she knew there *was* something to worry about, she washed her hands and face, prepared a quick midday meal, then curled up on the sofa with *The Man in the Iron Mask*.

She had just turned the last page when Demetri materialized inside the parlor. Just looking at him took her breath away. Tall, dark, and dangerous, she thought, with a faint smile. Her heart skipped a beat as he closed the distance between them, took her hands in his, and lifted her to her feet and into his arms.

"I miss you every minute we are apart," he murmured, and all her doubts and fears melted away like morning dew.

"I missed you, too," she said, stroking his cheek. "I … this morning … never mind."

His gaze caressed her, an invisible touch that made her toes curl with pleasure. "Tell me."

"I … after the other night, I thought that you … you would rest beside me."

"Ah. And would you like that?"

Her cheeks grew hot as she nodded. "Is it very wicked of me to want you to share my bed?"

"Some would say so."

"Why do you not sleep in the house?"

His hand skimmed up and down her spine, eliciting shivers of delight. "I have never done so, save that one night with you." He kissed the tip of her nose. "But I shall sleep here beside you from now on, if that is your wish."

"I love you, Demetri." Her gaze slid away from his. "I'll understand if you no longer wish to marry me."

He threaded his fingers through her hair. "Why would I not?"

"My mother always said men don't marry spoiled goods."

"Hardly true in this case, since *I* am the one who took advantage of *you*. Only name the day."

"Is the day after tomorrow too soon?"

"That depends."

"On what?"

"On what kind of wedding you desire. It will take time to have a new gown made. To invite your guests."

"Shall we make it next Wednesday night?"

"Any reason for that particular day?"

"Of course," she said with a grin. "Marry on Monday for health, on Tuesday for wealth, on Wednesday for the best day of all. Marry on Thursday for crosses, on Friday for losses. But Saturday is the worst day of all."

"I must say, I've never heard that before," he said with a laugh. "Wednesday it shall be."

"I'm sure you can persuade Madam Tomlinson to make me a gown by then," she said, remembering their first visit to the dressmaker's shop.

Demetri laughed softly. "I am sure I can. We will go in the morning."

She smiled up at him, happier than she had ever been in her life. "Will you go with me to tell my parents tonight?"

"You know they will not approve."

"I know. But my sisters will be delighted. They are quite smitten with you. Anna, especially."

"Indeed?"

"Oh, yes. I know it's unlikely that you and my parents will ever be good friends, but you don't have any objection to having them at the wedding, do you?" "None at all, my love. They are your kin and I shall treat them as such."

' She blew out a sigh. "Let's go now and get it over with."

As Lorena feared, her parents were still opposed to her decision to marry Demetri but when they realized they couldn't dissuade her, they agreed to attend the wedding. Clara and Anna were excited for her. The girls hugged her and then shyly hugged Demetri.

"I would like to buy you and the girls new dresses for the occasion," Lorena told her mother when they were alone in the kitchen.

"With *his* money?" her mother asked.

"Mama, why do you dislike him so?"

"I do not trust the man. There's something about him, something not right."

"Please don't believe the rumors," Lorena begged. "He is a fine man and he treats me like a queen. And I love him more than anything."

Grace Halliday shook her head. "I know you do, daughter. I can see it in your eyes. More's the pity." Sighing, she took Lorena's hands in hers. "We will see you at the wedding. I pray you will not regret this decision."

"If you only knew…" Lorena clamped her lips shut. Eager to change her mother's poor opinion of Demetri, she had almost blurted that, if not for Demetri, Grace would have died weeks ago. But doing so would betray Demetri's secret, and that was something she would never do.

"Knew what?" Grace asked.

"Nothing, Mama. I'll see you at the wedding. Demetri and I are going to stop at Sir Everleigh's on our way home to let Emma and Alice know my good news." Lorena gave her mother a quick hug, then went to find Demetri and let him know she was ready to leave.

Demetri glanced at Lorena as they left her parents' house behind. She sat stiffly beside him, trying not to cry. When they were out of sight of the house, he reined the horse to a halt and wrapped his arm around her. "You knew they would not approve."

"I know."

"But it still hurts."

She nodded as she wiped away a tear. "They owe you so much. How can they be so ungrateful? They would still be living in our old house. Mama would likely be dead now if not for you, and I almost told her so. But I didn't," she added hastily.

"I know, love. Perhaps, in time, they will forgive you."

"It doesn't matter."

"A poor liar," he murmured, as he kissed her lightly. "Do you still wish to stop at Everleigh's?"

"Sir Everleigh!" she exclaimed. "I never told him you were home."

"What are you talking about?"

"You remember I told you I went to see him when you missing? To ask for his help? But I was so excited when you came home, I forgot all about him. He must still believe you to be in danger. Or worse."

Demetri laughed softly. "I imagine he will be surprised to see me still alive and well."

"Demetri! Good lord, man, when I heard no more from Miss Halliday, I thought you dead."

"I'm so sorry for that, my lord," Lorena said. "I was so relieved to see him, I could think of nothing else."

Sir Everleigh threw back his head and laughed. "Ah, to be so young and madly in love again. Will you come in?"

"Only for a moment," Demetri said. "Lorena wishes to see her sisters."

"Of course. Just go on upstairs. Third floor," Everleigh said.

"I won't be long," Lorena promised, and hurried toward the winding staircase.

"We would like to invite you and Beatrice to our wedding," Demetri said.

"A wedding! Congratulations! We'll be there, of course."

"I shall let you know where and when."

"At least my sisters are happy for us," Lorena remarked as they left Sir Everleigh's house a short time later.

"And Sir Everleigh, also," Demetri added as he lifted her onto the seat of the hackney. "But the only happiness I care about is yours," he said as he took up the reins. "And I will devote the rest of my existence making your every wish come true."

Lorena glanced at Demetri as she readied for bed. Despite asking him to spend his nights with her, she was suddenly nervous. It had been one thing to have him in her bed in the throes of passion. That had happened spontaneously, with no thought of right or wrong. But now . . . she licked her lips as she turned her back to him, her fingers trembling as she unfastened the long row of buttons down the front of her dress. Oliver claimed Demetri was undead. But she had seen him at rest and he hadn't looked dead. Just asleep, like anyone else.

She stilled as he came up behind her, his arms sliding around her waist.

"Relax, my love," he murmured. "We are just going to sleep." And then, as his mind brushed hers, he laughed softly. "Vampires are not undead. Our hearts beat. We breathe, though not as frequently as mortals. But if you've changed your mind about my spending the night in your bed, I will understand."

She turned in his arms. Once, she had been upset to know he could read her thoughts. Now, she rather liked the idea. "I haven't changed my mind."

"And if I should reach for you in the night before we are wed, would you refuse me?"

Her cheeks flushed with embarrassment. There seemed little point in denying him after the other night. In her heart, she felt as though they were already man and wife. But they weren't.

"I can wait, my sweet," he murmured as he rained kisses on her cheeks, her brow, the tip of her nose.

With a nod, Lorena rested her cheek on his chest. She should have been relieved, she thought. So why was she disappointed instead?

Lorena woke slowly, all too aware that she wasn't alone in bed. Demetri lay beside her, his breathing slow and regular.

Propped on one elbow, she studied his face, the length of his neck, the breadth of his shoulders, the line of fine black hair that led down to his waist and disappeared beneath the sheet. They had made love, but she had never really seen *all* of him. Unable to resist the temptation, she lifted the sheet and peeked underneath.

"Like what you see?"

She jumped like a scalded cat, her cheeks flaming at the sound of his laughter. When she would have scrambled from the bed, he caught her hand.

"Lorena, look at me."

She shook her head vigorously.

"You have nothing to be embarrassed about, my love," he said, his voice kind. "It is not a sin to be curious." His fingers stroked her arm, her neck, slid up her nape to delve into her hair.

His touch sent a shiver of longing down her spine.

When he tugged her down beside him, she didn't resist but rested her head on his shoulder. "I have so much to learn."

"And I have so much to teach you. But, like I said, I can wait."

She turned onto her side and pressed herself against him. "Don't wait, Demetri," she whispered. "Teach me now."

As promised, Demetri took her to visit Madam Tomlinson's shop, although they didn't leave as early as they had originally planned. The modiste did not look pleased by the thought of sewing a wedding gown on such short notice, but when Demetri offered to pay her double her regular fee, she acquiesced and promised it would be ready the following Wednesday morning.

"Have you any other business to attend to while we are in town?" Demetri asked as they returned to the hackney.

"No. We should go home. I know how the sun bothers you."

He didn't argue. Thankfully, the sky was overcast, with a promise of rain before day's end.

When they reached home, Lorena stood by while he unhitched the mare and led her into the barn. Hand in hand, they walked up the path to the back door and into the kitchen.

Inside, Demetri drew her into his arms. "I must rest a while."

"I'll walk you upstairs."

He winked at her as he took her hand.

"Maybe, after we are wed, I should start keeping the same hours you do," she remarked as they climbed the stairs.

"Maybe I should just rise earlier in the day. You are too rare a flower to live only in the darkness."

"It won't bother you to do so?"

"Not anymore."

She frowned at him. "If you can be awake during the day, why don't you rest at night instead?"

"Darkness is my natural habitat," he explained. "I belong to the night. Young vampires are unable to fully function during the day, but we grow stronger as we age, more able to endure the heat and the light of the sun." His gaze caressed her. "Until you came into my life, I had no reason to rise before sunset."

When they reached the bedroom, he took her in his arms again. Warmth unfurled within her as he cupped her face in his palms and kissed her, long and slow and deep.

"Sweet dreams," she murmured.

"Only if they are of you, my love." He kissed her once more, quickly, then stepped into the bedroom and closed the door.

Humming softly, her head in the clouds, Lorena made her way down the stairs. In a week, she would be his wife. The thought made her insides curl with anticipation. He would be hers and she would be his and nothing in the world would keep them apart.

In the kitchen, she brewed a pot of tea and prepared a midday meal, all the while thinking about their upcoming wedding. It would be small, just the two of them, her family, and Sir Everleigh and his sister. There had been a marriage at Lord Fairfield's house when she had been his servant. It had been held in the back yard of the manor, attended by over a hundred people. It had been the most lavish affair she had ever seen. Tables covered with damask, sagging under the weight of enough food and drink to sustain a small country. There had been music and dancing and laughter. And even fireworks.

Not that she yearned for anything like that. She needed only Demetri. He would love her as long as she lived... *As long as she lived.* She wondered if he would marry again when she was gone. She told herself she hoped so, that she didn't want him to be alone, and knew it was a lie. What kind of person did that make her, to wish him an eternity of loneliness?

She imagined herself growing old, her skin wrinkling, her body aging, her hair turning gray, while he remained forever as he was now, young, handsome, and virile.

It was not a happy thought.

And then another thought occurred to her. What if she became a vampire? Wouldn't that solve everything? She thought about Demetri's life... and grimaced. Did she want to live only at night until she had survived for hundreds of years, drink blood, hide what she was from everyone she knew? And what about vampire hunters? She wasn't strong enough to fight them off, nor did she want to be forced to take a life to defend her own.

But she didn't want to get old, either, nor did she want Demetri to have to look after her if the time came when she couldn't look after herself.

Why did she have to think of this now?

Why hadn't she thought of it before?

Demetri rose three hours before the sun set. He blinked against the light. He had assured Lorena it wouldn't bother him to be awake when the sun was up, and it was mostly true. But he couldn't help wondering how it would affect him over a prolonged period of time. He thrived in the dark. It was an integral part of who and what he was. But for Lorena, he would endure the daylight hours as long as he could.

His head snapped up when he caught snippets of her thoughts. Startled, he opened his senses, a curse whispering past his lips when he realized she was considering becoming a vampire because she didn't want to burden him with caring for her when she grew old and feeble. As if caring for her could ever be a burden.

He dressed quickly, ran a comb through his hair, and willed himself into the kitchen. "What the hell are you thinking?"

Startled by his abrupt appearance, she looked up from the table. "My lord?"

"Do you want to be a vampire?"

"You've been reading my thoughts again."

"Not because I wanted to." He closed the distance between them, his gaze searching hers. "Loving you will never be a burden, Lorena. I will love you forever."

"But I won't live forever. I'll grow old. And ugly."

"You will always be beautiful in my eyes."

"Demetri, when I'm old and infirm, you'll still be as you are now. What if I start to hate you because of it?"

He stared at her, troubled by her words. He could abide anything but her hatred. He lifted her to her feet and into his arms. "You are still very young to be worrying about such things. If you still want to be as I am when you are older, we can discuss it. But for now, you need to enjoy your life. Bask in the sun's light. Enjoy the things you love, the people you care for. If you decide to become a vampire, there is no going back, no changing your mind. Once it is done, it is forever."

His words sobered her. He was right, of course. She had not yet turned twenty.

She had years to make up her mind. Smiling, she threw her arms around his neck and kissed him. "I love you, Demetri," she said, and then she frowned. "Is Demetri your first name, or your last?

"My first. You will be Lady Sadalas of the house of Thrace."

"Are you royalty, then?"

"There are kings and queens somewhere in my line."

"Imagine that," she said with a grin. "From lowly house-maid to Lady Sadalas. Wait until I tell Mama!"

Chapter Twenty-Eight

Oliver glanced at the hunters gathered in his den. "He has to be stopped and soon," he said.

"Damn right!" Lord Hamilton exclaimed. "Something has to be done."

With a shake of his fist, Lord Devereaux said, "I agree."

The others nodded in agreement.

Earlier, they had all attended Fairfield's funeral. The casket had been closed, of course. The few servants who had seen the body had been sworn to secrecy as to the condition of the corpse. The cage had been dismantled and removed from the cellar, the floor scrubbed clean, the table and its implements of torture disposed of.

The story told to the public was that Lord Fairfield had fallen down the stairs and broken his neck. It had taken a considerable amount of money to convince the head constable to perpetuate the lie.

"What do you suggest we do?" Lord Stanton asked as he helped himself to another brandy.

"I, for one, have no desire to end up like Fairfield," Lord Tinley remarked with a shudder.

"Nor I," agreed Lord Whitfield.

"We've hunted vampires before," Oliver said. "What's happened to your courage?"

"What's happened to yours?" Lord Devereaux retorted. "I'm told you haven't left your house since Fairfield's unfortunate demise, and that your servants guard the doors and patrol your estate day and night. Who's the coward now?"

A faint flush heated Oliver's cheeks. "The man threatened me personally. You can hardly fault me for taking precautions after what happened to Fairfield."

"It never would have happened if the two of you had simply left the bloodsucker alone, as we agreed," Lord Hamilton remarked. "Whatever were the two of you thinking, to try and take down a master vampire as powerful as Demetri?"

"It's because of the woman in the vampire's house," Lord Stanton said. "Oliver wants her, but she doesn't want him."

Oliver leaped to his feet. "How dare you!"

"We all know it's true," Lord Devereaux said, refilling his glass. "Not that we blame you. Even though she has no breeding, she's a comely wench."

"That may be true, but no woman is worth dying for," Lord Tinley said, rising. "As long as Demetri isn't bothering the people of the town, or hunting us, I say leave the man alone."

Lord Dutton grunted. "I might be willing to die for the woman I loved, but not for yours, Oliver. I'm sorry."

Ainsley stared after them as, one by one, they filed out of the house. "Some vampire hunters," he muttered. Like it or not, he was on his own. How in Heaven's name was he to prevail with no one to back him up? It had been sheer luck that he and Fairfield had managed to overpower Demetri the last time.

And look how that turned out, whispered a little voice in the back of his mind. Just thinking about what the vampire had done to Fairfield made the bile rise in his throat. No woman was worth that. But how could he live with himself if he didn't avenge Fairfield's death? If he didn't rescue that misguided woman from that soulless creature of darkness?

Cursing softly, Oliver hurled his glass against the wall. Dark red drops of wine splashed across the pale wallpaper, reminding him of the blood that had streaked the floor in Fairfield's cellar.

Chapter Twenty-Nine

Lorena kissed Demetri, then stood in the doorway as he descended the porch stairs. There was no need to ask where he was going. He left the house at the same time every night. He was never gone long, and they never discussed his reason for leaving.

The last few days had flown by, she thought as she closed and locked the door. In the parlor, she settled on the sofa with a book to await his return. Demetri had driven her to town twice to be fitted for her wedding gown. They had chosen a church for the ceremony. And he had insisted on inviting her family to their house for a reception afterward. To that end, she had ordered a cake and champagne, as well as several trays of *hors d'oervres*.

With every passing day, she loved him more. She loved having him in bed beside her. His face was the first thing she saw when she woke, the last thing she saw before she fell asleep in his arms. There were no words to describe what it was like when they made love. Sometimes he was gentle, treating her as if she were made of spun glass that might shatter at his touch. Other times, his kisses bruised her lips, his hands were more demanding though never rough, and he made love to her as if it might be the last time, as if he wanted to burn the memory of their coupling into his mind. And sometimes he stretched out on the bed and let her be in control, touching and tasting and exploring to her heart's content.

Tomorrow night, she would be his wife. Just thinking about it made her heart skip a beat.

Demetri prowled the streets of the city. It was Tuesday night and the pickings were scarce. A haggard trollop. A smelly drunk passed out in an alley. A homeless lad in patched pants who looked like he hadn't had a decent meal in a month.

Demetri called the boy to him and after taking a small drink, he shoved a handful of bank notes into the lad's pocket and sent him on his way.

A thought took him back to town where he stopped in at his favorite tavern. He smiled when he saw Sir Everleigh sitting alone at one of the tables.

"Ah, Demetri," Everleigh exclaimed. "Ready for the big day?"

"More than ready," he said, taking an empty chair.

"I must say, I envy you. She is a delightful young woman. And she loves you dearly."

"As I love her."

"I can see that you do. I often wish I had remarried after Evelyn passed away. A man shouldn't live alone."

"I feel certain you could find a woman who would be more than willing to share your life," Demetri said.

"And my wealth?" Everleigh said with a grin. "I can think of no other reason why a woman would marry an old codger like myself."

"Ever the pessimist. I think…" Demetri paused as the door opened and Oliver Ainsley stepped inside, accompanied by his coterie of hunters. Ainsley was halfway to a table when he spied Demetri. He stopped abruptly. His companions fanned out alongside him. Ainsley turned and headed for a table in the far corner of the tavern.

"Looks like he finally found the nerve to leave his house," Demetri muttered.

"Is what I heard about Fairfield true?" Everleigh asked.

"It depends on what you heard."

"That he met a rather grisly end."

"You could say that," Demetri muttered, his gaze still on Ainsley. "Are you shocked?"

"It depends on the provocation."

"He locked me in a cage in his basement and bled me every night for a week."

"And Ainsley?"

"He was there, too. He kidnapped Lorena and told her I would be killed if she refused to marry him."

"I see. And have you similar plans for Oliver?"

"I did, but Lorena begged me to not to touch him."

"And will you abide by that?"

A muscle twitched in Demetri's jaw. "As long as he leaves me alone."

Brow furrowed thoughtfully, Everleigh considered what Demetri had said for a moment, then remarked, "I would say the punishment, though severe, fits the crime."

"So we are still friends?"

"You saved my life, sir. I will always be in your debt for that. And steadfast in my loyalty and my friendship."

Demetri nodded, his attention still on Ainsley and the hunters, who one after another sent sideways glances in his direction. "Enjoy the rest of your evening, my friend," he said as he stood. "Give my best to Beatrice when next you see her."

"Be careful," Everleigh warned. "It would be a shame if you missed your wedding."

"No fear of that," Demetri assured him, keenly aware of Ainsley's malicious glare as he strode out of the tavern.

"You look a little pale, Ainsley," Lord Dutton remarked with a smirk.

"Shut up."

"I think you're worrying for nothing," Lord Whitfield said. "If he was going to make a move against you, don't you think he would have done so by now?"

"Who the hell knows?" Oliver picked up his brandy snifter and tossed the contents back in a single swallow. "But it doesn't matter. I can't take him alone, and since none of you have the guts to back me up, I've hired someone to take care of him for me."

Lord Hamilton stared at him. "Tell me you didn't."

"Didn't what?" Devereaux glanced from Hamilton to Ainsley and back again. "What's he talking about?"

"I'll tell you," Hamilton said, when Oliver remained mute. "He's sent for Serghei."

Oliver flinched as all eyes settled on him.

"You're not only a coward, but a damn fool," Dutton hissed. "Don't you realize you've put all of our lives in danger now?"

Demetri found Lorena in the back parlor. She looked up, her expression worried, when he entered the room.

"You're late!" she exclaimed, laying her book aside. "Is everything all right?"

"Nothing to fret about," he said. "I stopped at the tavern and had a few words with Sir Everleigh."

Her relief was palpable as he settled on the sofa beside her. "How is he?"

"The same as always. I count myself fortunate to have him as a friend, especially when I have so few."

"He's a true gentleman. I look forward to seeing him tomorrow night."

"Is that all you're looking forward to?" Demetri asked, a teasing glint in his eye.

"What else is there?" She tapped her chin thoughtfully. "Oh! I believe I have an appointment at the church."

"I believe you do."

"I need to pick up my gown tomorrow morning."

"I cannot wait to see you in it. I have no doubt you will be a beautiful bride."

"We need to pick up the refreshments, too."

"Relax, love. We have all day to run your errands."

"I know." She rested her head on his shoulder. "Just think, tomorrow night we'll be man and wife."

He brushed a kiss across the top of her head, thinking that after over three hundred years he had finally found happiness, and it was all wrapped up in the woman beside him.

Demetri stood in front of the fireplace as he listened to Lorena move about upstairs, getting ready for bed. He still couldn't believe his good fortune, couldn't believe that tomorrow she would be legally and lawfully his. He found himself wondering if she'd been serious when she talked about the future, about becoming a vampire. Becoming Nosferatu sometimes changed a person. He had seen gentle souls turn into ravening monsters, seen priests turn into killers. But those cases were rare.

He was about to go up to bed when someone knocked at the door. Demetri frowned as he recognized Everleigh's scent. Something must be wrong, he thought as he opened the door. No one came calling this late for a social call.

"Demetri," Everleigh said, "I have news, although I don't know if it even concerns you."

"Come in. Can I get you a drink?"

"A brandy, please." He followed Demetri into the parlor and eased his bulk down on the sofa.

"What is it?" Demetri asked as he handed Everleigh three fingers of brandy. "You look worried."

"I am, although I'm not sure it's warranted. Do you know anyone who goes by the name of Serghei?"

"I have heard of him. Where did you hear it?"

"I overheard Ainsley say he'd hired him. It upset his cronies. Something made me think it might concern you, so I thought you should know."

Demetri swore a pithy oath.

"Who is he?"

"Serghei is a very old Romanian vampire who was a hunter before he was turned. Now he hunts both hunter and hunted, if the price is right."

"Older than you?"

"By a decade or two, perhaps."

"Good Lord." Looking worried, he sipped his drink, then put it aside.

"Thank you for letting me know."

"I shall pray for your safety," Everleigh said as he hauled himself to his feet. "And for your lovely lady, as well."

"I am not sure any prayers uttered in my behalf would be heard," Demetri said with a wry grin. "But I welcome the thought."

They shook hands at the door.

"Be careful," Sir Everleigh said, his voice tinged with worry.

"Always. I will see you tomorrow night at the church."

"Yes," Everleigh murmured. "The good Lord willing."

Demetri stood on the porch watching Everleigh's carriage until it was out of sight. So, Ainsley had hired a killer. Well, he had no one to blame but himself. He should have ripped out the man's heart long ago. Now, not only was his own life in danger, but Lorena's, as well.

She was sitting up in bed, her hair falling over her shoulders like a waterfall of red silk, when he entered the room. "Who came calling at this hour?"

"Sir Everleigh."

"Is he all right?"

"Yes." He sat on the edge of the mattress and pulled off his boots, then stood and removed his coat, shirt and trousers before climbing into bed beside her.

"What did he want?"

"Nothing that can't wait."

"Demetri, what aren't you telling me?"

"Not now, love. Get some sleep. We have a busy day tomorrow." Cupping the back of her head in his hand, he kissed her, then stretched out on the mattress and closed his eyes.

Lorena stared at him. What wasn't he telling her? As she slid under the covers, she wished she had the ability to read his mind, the way he read hers.

❧ ❧ ❧

A busy day, indeed, Lorena thought in the morning as she dressed to go into town. She took a last glance in the mirror before hurrying downstairs and out the door where Demetri waited with the buggy. He wore gloves, and a long black cloak with the hood up and pulled forward to shield his face from the sun.

Their first stop was Miss Tomlinson's shop. Demetri parked the buggy in the shade as Lorena hopped to the ground and hurried inside.

The modiste had the gown waiting for her. In the dressing room, Lorena stared at her reflection in the full-length mirror. The gown, of pale pink silk and lace, was exquisite. The veil, which trailed behind her, was as light and airy as a spider's web. Not only did she look like the lady of the manor, she thought with a smile, but she felt like one.

"You are pleased?" Miss Tomlinson asked when Lorena emerged from the dressing room.

"Yes, thank you so much. It's beautiful."

The modiste wrapped the gown in tissue paper and carefully laid it in a box. "I hope you will express your pleasure to Lord Demetri."

"I will," Lorena assured her. "Good day."

Demetri was standing beside the buggy when she left the shop. He took the box from her and placed it under the seat, then handed her up.

"Are you happy with it?" Demetri asked as he leaped agilely up beside her.

"Oh, Demetri! Wait until you see it!" She laughed softly. "Miss Tomlinson asked me to be sure and let you know I was pleased."

He grinned as he took up the reins and clucked to the mare. The dressmaker had a lot to lose should Lorena decide to take her business elsewhere.

They made several more stops before returning home.

Men and women came and went all through the day. Demetri had hired people to come in to polish the floors. A florist arranged pots of greenery and baskets of flowers on the porch, in the front parlor and the dining room. He had also hired two maids, not only to serve their guests, prepare the food, and clean up the house afterward, but stay on as full-time employees.

Late that afternoon, he headed down to his lair to rest.

It was near five o'clock when Lorena's family arrived.

"Where's Demetri?" Anna asked, glancing around.

"He had business to attend to," Lorena said. "Papa, please make yourself at home in the back parlor. There's food and drink in the kitchen."

Her father grunted softly, apparently not the least bit disappointed at Demetri's absence. No doubt he was glad of it, she thought, and wondered if her father and her husband would ever be friends.

The girls chattered excitedly as they climbed the stairs to Lorena's bedroom. The florist had also worked his magic here. A large crystal vase of red roses stood on the dresser. A folded note sat beside it. Curious, Lorena opened it.

To my bride on her wedding day
more lovely than any rose
more precious than life itself

"Lorena, you are so lucky," Emma said, her voice tinged with envy as she glanced around the room. "I hope I find a rich man to marry."

"Money isn't everything," Grace Halliday chided. "I would rather see you married to a poor man who treats you with love and respect rather than a rich man who mistreats you."

"I'll marry a nice rich man," Emma said with a grin.

"Is Demetri nice to you?" Anna asked.

"Yes, indeed," Lorena replied as she lifted her wedding gown from the box and laid it out on the bed. "Very nice."

"Oh, sister," Clara murmured, "that's the most beautiful dress I've ever seen."

"Maybe one day you'll wear it," Lorena said as she began to undress.

"Why did you choose pink?" Alice asked. "Blue was always your favorite color."

"Don't you remember the old rhyme? Marry in white, chosen right, marry in blue, love will be true, marry in yellow, ashamed of her fellow, marry in red, wish herself dead, marry in black, wish herself back, marry in gray, travel far away, marry in pink, of you he'll always think. And I want Demetri to think of me always."

The girls sat on the bed, whispering back and forth as Lorena slipped the gown over her head, then sat at the new dressing table Demetri had bought her while her mother arranged her hair and set her veil in place.

Grace sighed as she stepped away. "You look beautiful, daughter."

"Like a princess in a fairy tale," Anna said.

"Girls, go wait downstairs," Grace said. "We'll be down directly."

"You're not going to try to talk me out of this again, are you, Mama?" Lorena asked when they were alone.

"No. I realize it would be a waste of breath. But if you decide later that you've made a mistake, don't be too proud to come home. You'll always be our daughter, no matter what, and always welcome."

"Thank you, Mama." Rising, Lorena hugged her mother. "I love you, too. Please be happy for me."

"I'm happy that you're happy," Grace said. "Come along now, you don't want to be late."

Lorena followed her mother out the door, assuring herself that she would never be sorry for giving her heart to Demetri.

CHAPTER THIRTY

A hired driver and carriage awaited Lorena and her entourage when they left the house. Demetri and her father had gone ahead to meet them at the church.

Lorena's heart was pounding with excitement as she climbed into the coach. In just a few minutes, she would be Demetri's wife.

The church looked like something out of a fairytale, she thought as the carriage pulled up in front of the stairs. The moonlight cast a silver glow on the white stone.

Exiting the coach, she hurried up the stairs, with the girls and her mother trailing behind.

Her father was waiting for her in the vestibule. Grace and the girls hugged Lorena, then hurried into the chapel to take their seats.

Lorena peered through the door. Baskets of flowers had been arranged in front of the altar, the light from dozens of candles filled the room with a warm rosy glow. Sir Everleigh sat in the second pew on the right, his sister beside him. But she had eyes only for Demetri. He stood beside the priest at the altar, looking resplendent in a wine-colored frock coat, black vest, cravat, and dark gray trousers.

"Are you sure about this, Lorena?" her father asked as he took her arm.

"Yes, Papa, as sure as I am that I love you."

He blinked rapidly as he cleared his throat. "Be happy, daughter."

At a signal from the priest, they started down the aisle.

Demetri smiled inwardly as he watched Lorena walking toward him on her father's arm. Never had she looked more beautiful. A shy smile curved her lips when she met his gaze and he, who hadn't prayed in centuries, sent a prayer of gratitude to heaven for sending her into his life.

Her hand was trembling slightly when he reached for it.

Lorena felt Demetri's love sweep over her as their fingers entwined, saw it in the depths of his midnight-blue eyes as they exchanged their vows to love, honor and cherish each other so long as they lived. And then, his gaze never leaving hers, Demetri placed a ring on her finger, the most beautifully exquisite ring she had ever seen.

"I now pronounce you man and wife," the priest declared, "legally and lawfully wed. Demetri, you have kiss your bride."

Lorena's eyelids fluttered down as Demetri claimed his first kiss as her husband. It was warm and tender, a promise of forever, reinforced by his words as he whispered, "I will love and cherish and protect you all the days of your life."

She hugged him tightly for a moment, and then her family gathered around, her sisters hugging her while Sir Everleigh congratulated Demetri.

"You're all invited to our house for refreshments," Lorena said.

Talking and laughing, they left the church. The Hallidays took Demetri's plush carriage. Lorena and Demetri stepped into the hired one. The driver closed the door behind them. Sir Everleigh and Beatrice followed in their own rig.

"Alone at last," Demetri murmured as he drew her into his arms. "Do you know how much I love you?"

"Not as much as I love you."

"Not as much," he agreed, caressing her cheek. "But much, much more. I have waited centuries for you." Crushing her close, he slanted his mouth over hers.

She leaned into him as the carriage lurched forward, her arms twining around his neck as she crawled into his lap. His kiss deepened, growing more intense as his tongue dueled with hers in a dance both ancient and new. She moaned low in her throat as his hand slid under her skirts to caress her thigh.

When he lifted his head, she murmured, "More," only then realizing the carriage had stopped.

"We're home, love." He kissed her lightly. "But be assured we will resume where we left off when we are again alone."

Lorena scooted onto the seat and straightened her gown and her veil before allowing Demetri to hand her out of the carriage.

She blushed as their guests applauded their arrival. She looked at Demetri, wondering if everyone knew what they'd been doing inside the coach. Laughing softly, he said, "Not to worry, my sweet, it doesn't show."

, Lorena felt like an imposter, letting the maids wait on her. She was accustomed to serving, not being served. She had never hosted a party and she wasn't sure how to behave. Fortunately, everyone seemed to be having a good time. The girls explored the house while Sir Everleigh entertained her parents with stories of his travels to Italy and Scotland.

Demetri sat beside her, faintly amused by her discomfort. He would have to take her out into society more often, let her practice being a lady until it became second nature. In a few years, he would have to move on, before people began to notice that he never changed, never aged. It had been the story of his life for the last three-and-a half centuries, finding a new place to live, settling down, then moving on every twenty years or so. It kept him from getting bored with one place. He frowned. What would Lorena think when he told her they would soon have to find a new city, a new house? Would she object to leaving her family behind?

It was nearing ten o'clock when Sir Everleigh rose to take his leave. "I wish you both every happiness," he said, as he shook Demetri's hand, then kissed Lorena on the cheek. "If you ever need anything, you have only to ask."

"Thank you, my lord," Lorena replied, thinking how lucky Demetri was to have him for a friend.

Her family left a short time later amid numerous hugs and good wishes. When she walked them to the door, her mother took her aside. "Remember what I said, daughter. If ever you're unhappy or he mistreats you, don't be too proud to come home."

Lorena sighed as she closed the door and then leaned back against it. Why couldn't her parents be happy for her? Couldn't they see how much she loved Demetri, how much he cared for her, how lucky she was to have him as her husband?

"Give them time," Demetri said, drawing her into his arms.

"I can't imagine what their reaction would be if they knew what you are."

He laughed softly. "I am confident your father would be here in a heartbeat with a stake in one hand and a flaming torch in the other."

"Demetri!" She shuddered at the grotesque image his words brought to mind. "Don't even think that!"

"He would not be the first," he said with a careless shrug. "Nor the last."

She batted her eyes at him. "Is that all you can think about on our wedding night?"

"Most assuredly not." Taking her by the hand, he led her up the stairs.

"I need to clean up the kitchen," she protested.

"We have maids for that now," he reminded her as he opened the door to his bedchamber and followed her inside.

"I forgot."

He closed and locked the door. Someone had turned down the bed, lit the candles on the dresser. A bottle of wine and a pair of crystal goblets waited on the bedside table.

A sudden warmth engulfed Lorena as his gaze moved over her. They had made love before. Why did she suddenly feel so nervous? So shy?

She shivered as he removed her veil and laid it over the chair in the corner. His eyes were hot as he turned her around and slowly unfastened the long row of buttons down the back of her gown, slid her petticoat down over her hips. He turned her around to face her, then knelt and removed her shoes.

"You are the most beautiful woman I have ever seen," he murmured as she stepped out of her gown. "The kindest, sweetest, most generous woman I have ever known."

"I am pleased that you think so, my lord husband."

Anticipation coiled deep in her belly as he stood and removed the rest of her undergarments. Deciding turnabout was fair play, she began to undress him with fingers that trembled.

When she finished, he took her in his arms and carried her to bed, then stretched out beside her and drew her into his embrace. Her whole body came alive as he began to kiss and caress her, all the while murmuring that he loved her, would always love her.

Caught up in the magic of his touch, she explored his hard-muscled body in a way she never had before, reveling in the feel of his skin against hers, the way his muscles bunched and flexed at her touch, the low groan of pleasure that erupted from his lips. They had made love before, she thought again, but tonight was different somehow, more meaningful, more intimate.

When he rose over her, she wrapped her arms around his neck and held him close. When he murmured, "Let me," she acquiesced. He bit her ever so gently, moaned softly as the pleasure she felt grew stronger, deeper, along with the realization that she wasn't just feeling her own climax but his, as well.

Sated and exhausted, she fell asleep in his arms with his name on her lips.

CHAPTER THIRTY-ONE

Oliver Ainsley muttered every oath he had ever heard as he paced the parlor floor. Last night, Lorena had committed the ultimate, unforgiveable sin. She had married the vampire. How long until that creature turned her into the same kind of abhorrent, inhuman monster? How long before she lost her humanity and began to delight in feasting on human blood?

Overcome with rage, he hurled a chair against the wall. It was not to be borne!

He would have married her, given her his name, granted her every wish, her every desire, turned her into a great lady. Instead, she had rejected him in favor of that vile blood drinker!

He stopped pacing when the butler coughed.

"What is it?" Oliver snapped.

"I believe the gentleman you have been expecting has arrived. He would not give me his name."

"Thank you, Moss. Please show him in."

Oliver swallowed his fear as a tall, angular man with a shock of white-gold hair and empty gray eyes strode into the room.

"You sent for me," he said, his voice like the dead of winter.

Oliver cleared his throat. "Yes. Thank you for coming."

"Aren't you going to offer me a drink?"

"Certainly. I have port…"

The vampire raised one brow as his gaze settled on Oliver's throat.

"See here," Oliver began, only to fall silent as the vampire's eyes blazed red.

Frozen with fear, he could only stand there while Serghei grasped his shoulders and sank his fangs into his throat. It was over in an instant, but Oliver knew he would forever relive it in his nightmares.

Serghei lifted his head and licked his lips. "What can I do for you?"

Oliver touched his hand to his neck, felt the warmth of his own blood on his skin. "I…I want a man dead. His name is Demetri."

Recognition flickered in the hunter's eyes. "Master vampires cost more."

"How much more?"

"An additional two thousand pounds. I require half now and half when it's done."

"At that price, I will need some bit of proof that the matter had been dealt with," Oliver said.

"Of course. Will the head be sufficient?"

Oliver nodded. "Please, sit while I collect the funds." It took all of his self-control not to run out of the creature's presence.

In his room, he poured a shot of whiskey and downed it in a single swallow before going to the safe in the wall and withdrawing the necessary funds.

And all the while he wondered if he was making the worst mistake of his life. He had always considered Demetri to be an irredeemable monster. But he had been sadly mistaken.

The real monster was waiting for him downstairs.

CHAPTER THIRTY-TWO

After leaving Ainsley's house, Serghei prowled the town's dark streets, oblivious to the screams of a woman being raped in an alley, the frightened cries of a homeless child, the dead body lying in a ditch on the side of the road. He had no interest in the welfare of humanity. They mattered little, save as a ready supply of the blood he craved. Man, woman, or child, ill or sick, alive or dead, all were the same to him—a food source, nothing more.

He hunted for the sheer pleasure of killing, of pitting his strength against human and vampire alike. He had killed the one who turned him, and too many others to count. A law unto himself, he had no thought for anything other than his own survival, no matter what the cost.

Leaving the town, he strolled toward the home of his intended victim. Demetri lived in a large old manor house in need of a coat of paint and a gardener.

Curious, he climbed the porch stairs and tried the door. It was locked, of course. But it was the inherent power of the threshold that repelled him. It was galling to think that something so simple could keep him out. He had tried everything at his command on other thresholds, other doors and windows, but all withstood his attempts to cross.

Lifting his head, he opened his vampire senses. There were three women in the house. And one vampire. All the women were asleep.

But Demetri was awake. And he was strong, far stronger than any other master vampire Serghei had encountered. He clenched his hands as the vampire's power rolled over him.

This one would not be as easy to take down as the rest.

Serghei grinned into the darkness. At last, a worthy opponent. And when he had taken Demetri's head, he would feast on the woman and then on the maids, one by one.

Whistling softly, he blended into the shadows of the night as he went in search of a place to pass the daylight hours.

CHAPTER THIRTY-THREE

Demetri's first thought when he woke was not of his lovely bride, but of the hunter that Ainsley had hired. He had heard Serghei sniffing around the house that night, sensed his frustration because he had been unable to find a way past the threshold.

Demetri shook his head. How could Ainsley have been fool enough to hire a killer like Serghei? Had he any idea of the kind of soulless monster he was dealing with? Demetri cursed under his breath. Should Serghei succeed in taking his head, the hunter was just as likely to take Ainsley's, as well. Serghei was truly a rogue, a man with no scruples and no conscience. He cared for nothing and no one.

And now he was here.

Demetri stared at the ceiling. There was little in life that frightened him. But the thought that Lorena might be in danger, that scared the hell out of him.

Throwing the covers aside, he dressed and went in search of his bride.

He found her sitting in the back parlor, looking none too happy. "What is it?" he asked. "What has put that frown on your face?"

"The maids."

"They displeased you?"

"I don't want them here."

He looked at her askance.

"It was kind of you to hire them, but I don't want someone waiting on me. I'm not comfortable giving orders. And if they clean the house and do all the chores, what will I do with my days? I can't just sit and do nothing."

He nodded slowly. "I had not thought of that. I will dismiss them immediately."

Lorena stared after him. She felt a twinge of guilt for putting them out of work, but she needed to be busy, to feel useful. Sure, she could take up sewing or tatting but those were hobbies for women who had been born to wealth, who expected to be waited on hand and foot and enjoyed giving orders. She was not one of them.

She looked up when Demetri returned.

"They will be gone shortly. I have given them references and a tidy sum."

"Thank you."

Taking her hands, he pulled her to her feet and into his arms. "What would you like to do today?"

"I don't care, as long as we're together."

He slid his fingers up into the silky hair at her nape and kissed her. "We could spend the day in bed."

She laughed softly. "Then what would we do tonight?"

"A repeat of this afternoon?"

"Husband, you may have the endurance of twenty men, but I don't. Maybe something a little less … um … exhausting?"

"Very well. I know you have been wanting to redecorate the house. How about if we go into town and look for furniture, and maybe stop for a bite to eat? Would you like that better?"

"Not better," she said with a grin. "Nothing could ever be better than being in your arms."

❧ ❧ ❧

The last person Demetri had expected to see in town was Oliver Ainsley. From Ainsley's expression, it was equally obvious he was thinking the same thing.

They came face to face on the cobbles as Ainsley emerged from the tailor shop adjacent to Miss Mavis' Tea Room.

"You!" Ainsley hissed.

"In the flesh."

Lorena glanced at the two men who were glowering at each other, bristling like dogs over a bone.

"I trust I will never see you again," Oliver said with a smirk.

"You should not underestimate me," Demetri warned. "Nor trust the creature you have hired. I bid you good day, sir," he said, his voice filled with disdain.

Face flushed, Oliver crossed the street.

"What was *that* all about?" Lorena asked. "And what did you mean, in the flesh?"

"Not now," he said as he ushered her into the tea room.

Lorena ordered her usual, but she hardly tasted her meal or the custard tart she had for dessert. She couldn't think of anything but the icy exchange between Demetri and Oliver. She had the distinct impression that if she hadn't been there, they might have come to blows. As for Demetri, he was uncharacteristically silent, his thoughts obviously turned inward.

"Let's go home," Lorena said as they left the tea room.

"Do you not wish to look at new furniture?"

"I want to know what's going on with you and Oliver."

A muscle twitched in his jaw. "Very well." He lifted her onto the hackney seat and swung up beside her.

The tension between them was thick on the drive home.

Once inside, Lorena perched on the edge of the sofa, hands clenched in her lap. "Tell me," she said. "Tell me what's going on."

Demetri paced the floor in front of the hearth. "Ainsley hired a vampire hunter who is now a master vampire."

"He's a vampire who hunts vampires?"

"He is a hired killer. Anyone is fair game if the price is right."

"But why would Oliver hire someone when he's a hunter himself?"

"Because he knows he cannot defeat me."

"And he thinks the man he hired can?"

"Yes."

Her voice quivered as she asked, "Can he?"

Demetri stopped pacing and drew her into his arms. "That I do not know. But once again I must ask you not to leave the house unless I am with you. As a master vampire, Serghei can be awake during the day. The only thing he cannot do is enter our home uninvited."

Lorena sat in the kitchen, gazing out the back door. It was mid-afternoon and Demetri had gone to his bedchamber to rest for an hour, as he often did in the heat of the day. She felt numb, unable to think of anything but the new threat hanging over their heads. Would Demetri go out to meet the hunter? Would it be a long, bloody battle, or quickly over? What would she do if Demetri was defeated? It was an outcome she couldn't imagine. But anything was possible. He had admitted to being distracted when Fairfield and

Oliver overpowered him. Yet he had survived. She had to believe he would prevail against this hunter, as well.

But what if he didn't? Bloody images paraded across her mind, each more gruesome than the last. Pressing her hands to her temples, she let out a cry of denial.

In a heartbeat, Demetri was kneeling beside her, his brow furrowed with concern.

With a sob, she threw her arms around his neck and buried her face against his shoulder.

"Shh, my love, do not worry so."

"I can't help it."

"I have defeated other hunters," he said, stroking her hair. "I have defeated other master vampires, one or two older than Serghei. Do not count me out yet."

"You've fought other vampires?" she asked, sniffing back her tears.

"Yes."

"Why do vampires fight each other? Do you not all want the same things?"

"No." Rising, he drew Lorena to her feet and led her into the back parlor. Settling on the sofa, he lifted her onto his lap, his arm circling her waist. "Vampires tend to live solitary lives. We trust no one, not even our own kind. We are also territorial creatures. I have claimed this town as my own and..." He paused.

"Go on."

"I have destroyed others who tried to take it from me."

"Why?"

"I do not feed where I live, nor do I allow anyone else to do so. No one in this town has been killed by a vampire since I came here. It takes only one body drained of blood to rouse the population. The next thing you know, you have frightened men hunting the night with stakes and torches," he said ruefully. "It is not a pretty sight."

"What if this Serghei kills someone?"

"Should he do so, the hunters who live in this town would naturally assume it was me. No doubt they would come after me and rob him of his reward."

It didn't seem like much of a deterrent, she thought.

"Worrying solves nothing," he remarked.

"I can't help it. I'm afraid. What if…?

Wanting to stifle any further questions, he kissed her.

All too aware of what he was trying to do, she started to resist, but as he deepened the kiss, all thought of Serghei fled her mind and there was only Demetri's mouth on hers, his tongue dueling with hers as his hand stroked the length of her body, slid under her skirts to caress her thigh.

She moaned softly, felt her body melting at his assault on her senses. He knew her so well, knew just where to touch to kindle the fire inside her.

He drew her down on the floor, his mouth never leaving hers, his hands working their magic. Her fingers were clumsy in their haste to undress him and then, somehow, their clothing was gone and there was nothing between them but desire as two became one. She murmured his name when he bit her, magnifying the pleasure until she thought she might die of it. She cried out as warmth flowed through her, dug her fingers into his back as he convulsed, carrying them both over the edge. After a moment, he rolled onto his side, taking her with him, her breasts crushed against his chest.

Eyes closed, she basked in the moment as their bodies cooled and their breathing returned to normal. When she opened them again, he was watching her, his expression pensive.

"What are you thinking?" she asked.

"How much I love you. How you have changed my life. How precious you are to me."

Cupping his cheek in her palm, she whispered, "And you to me."

His arms tightened around her and for the first time since she had met him, she saw fear behind his eyes.

Lorena frowned as she watched Demetri dress. "Do you have to go hunting tonight?"

He looked up from fastening his trousers. "Would you have me go hungry?" he asked with a wry grin.

"If I have to stay inside, so should you. After all, it's you he wants, not me."

"Lorena..."

"Can't you miss a day or two?"

He finished fastening his pants and pulled on his shirt. "I can go without for days, perhaps longer, if necessary. But it weakens me."

She had a brief mental image of how he had looked in Fairfield's cellar. "You can drink from me."

"I cannot drink from you every day without doing you harm, my love. While Serghei is in town, I am going to need more from my prey than the little I usually take, which means I will need to feed on more than one." Or kill the one, he thought.

"You will be careful, won't you?"

"I promise." He sat on the sofa beside her and pulled on his boots. "I will not be gone long." He kissed her, hard and quick, and then willed himself into the city.

Lorena sucked in a breath as he vanished from her sight. She told herself there was nothing to worry about. He had existed for hundreds of years. Surely he could survive the night.

Demetri preyed on the first two mortals he found, quickly and efficiently. He was turning for home when he caught a whiff of blood and death on the wind. He followed the smell to the edge of the city where he found the body of a young girl lying in a ditch, her throat savaged.

The unmistakable scent of vampire hung in the air. The same scent that had lingered on the grounds of his house the night before.

Serghei.

Frowning, Demetri regarded the girl for a moment. He should take the body to the police, but he couldn't risk being seen dropping it off at the constable's office. Or the morgue. Lifting the corpse out of the ditch, he quickly dug a shallow grave and lowered her into it. Sooner or later, she would be found.

A thought took him home.

He found Lorena asleep on the sofa wrapped in a blanket, her head pillowed on her hand.

Lifting her, blanket and all, he carried her to his room, undressed her down to her undergarments and tucked her into bed. Shedding his own clothes, he washed his hands and face before crawling in beside her.

"Sweet dreams, my love," he murmured as he brushed a kiss across her lips.

Pulling her close to his side, he wondered if leaving town might be the wisest thing to do, the best way to keep her safe. It would mean finding a new house with a secure lair, claiming a new territory as his own.

Tomorrow, he thought as he closed his eyes. He would discuss it with her tomorrow.

Lorena woke to the sound of someone pounding on the front door. Grabbing Demetri's robe, she slipped it on as she hurried downstairs. A glance at the clock told her it was a little after six.

"Who's there?" she called.

"It's me."

Lorena quickly unlocked and opened the door. "Mama, what's wrong?"

"Your father's been in an accident. I fear he's badly hurt."

"What happened?"

"He was chopping wood and the axe slipped and sliced into his leg."

"Did you summon a doctor?"

"Yes, he's on his way but…" Grace dabbed at the tears in her eyes. "Hurry!"

"Go back home and look after Papa. I'll be there as soon I get dressed."

Clasping Lorena's hands in hers, she whispered, "I love you, daughter."

"I love you, too."

Lorena frowned as she ran up the stairs, troubled by her mother's parting words without knowing why. She roused Demetri and told him what had happened before hurrying into her room to dress.

Twenty minutes later, the horses were saddled and they were on their way.

❧ ❧ ❧

The horizon was turning pink and azure when they neared their destination. Demetri reined the stallion to a halt, all his senses suddenly alert. Something wasn't right. Lorena had said her father had been injured but there was no scent of fresh blood or pain. Only panic and fear.

He reached out with his senses, seeking the source of his unrest, but there was nothing.

"What's wrong?" Lorena asked. "Why did we stop?"

"Something is amiss." His nostrils flared as the coppery scent of freshly spilled blood drifted through the air.

Lorena glanced around, but saw nothing to alarm her until her mother stepped outside, her face pale, her hands covered in blood. With a cry, she slapped the reins against the mare's flanks.

Demetri called, "Lorena, wait!" as he caught other scents wafting out of the house, but it was too late.

As the mare skidded to stop, Serghei materialized, lifted Lorena from the horse's back and darted into the house.

"Coward! Hiding behind a woman's skirts!" Demetri spat the words. "Come out and face me man to man."

"All in good time," Serghei called. "But I have not yet fed."

"Damn you!"

Sergei's laughter fouled the air. "Patience, vampire. This will not take long."

Rage boiled inside Demetri. Vaulting from the back of the stallion, he burst through the front door and came face to face with Serghei. Oliver Ainsley held Lorena in his arms. Lord Dutton held a pistol, the barrel aimed at Lorena's family. The blood trickling from Halliday's neck explained the blood on his wife's hands.

Lord Stanton stepped out from behind the open door and slammed it shut.

"This is how it is going to be," Serghei said. "You will submit to me and I will spare the lives of these people. If you refuse, they will all be shot now. All but the woman known as Lorena."

Demetri's gaze darted to Ainsley, who grinned triumphantly.

"You bloody coward," Demetri hissed.

"Which will it be?" Serghei asked impatiently.

"Let them go now." Demetri clenched his hands to still the impotent rage boiling inside of him. He should have suspected something like this, he thought. Should have known it was a trap.

"I think not."

"How can I trust you to keep your word?"

"My word as a gentleman?" Serghei asked with a smirk.

Demetri snorted. "I would as soon trust a snake."

"I grow weary with waiting."

Demetri glanced at Lorena. She was trembling in Ainsley's grasp, her face pale, her eyes wide and afraid.

Lorena screamed, "No!" as Demetri dropped to his knees.

Serghei stepped forward, a sword suddenly appearing in his hand.

With a tortured cry, Lorena turned in Ainsley's grasp and raked her nails down his cheek.

With a howl of pain, Oliver released her and pressed his hand to his cheek.

Freed from his grasp, Lorena darted across the room.

Demetri lunged to his feet and drove his fist into Serghei's face, then grabbed the sword from his hand.

Lord Dutton turned toward the commotion. Taking advantage of his distraction, Halliday grabbed the fireplace poker and struck the man a vicious blow across the back of the head. When Dutton hit the floor, Halliday grabbed the pistol and shot Stanton between the eyes.

Ainsley cowered in a corner, eyes darting toward Stanton's body, which now blocked the front door.

Ignoring the confusion around them, Serghei and Demetri faced each other.

Lorena stared at the two men, thinking she had never seen anything as frightening in her life as the two vampires sizing each other up, their eyes crimson red, their lips pulled back to reveal their fangs.

They moved in a blur, coming together, fangs slashing, hands like claws as they ripped through cloth and flesh. In seconds, both were splattered with blood. She watched in horrified fascination as wounds that would have killed an ordinary man healed almost immediately. She was vaguely aware of her sisters, crying in each other's arms, of her mother wrapping a cloth around her father's neck. But she never took her gaze from Demetri. He fought with a kind of deadly beauty, his whole being focused on his opponent. They closed and parted and each time, fresh blood spilled from their wounds.

It seemed as though the fight had gone on for hours, though it was only minutes, when Serghei grabbed the fallen fireplace poker and lunged forward, the sharp end driving toward Demetri's heart.

She screamed, certain Demetri would be killed, but at the last moment, he ducked under the weapon and buried his fangs deep in Serghei's throat at the same time he ripped Serghei's heart from his chest.

Lorena turned away, nausea roiling in the pit of her stomach.

Silence hung as still as death over the house.

Lorena wiped her mouth on the hem of her dress as her parents and sisters clustered around her, all talking and crying at once. Looking over their heads, she glanced around, searching for Demetri, but he was gone. And so was Serghei's body.

And so was Oliver.

CHAPTER THIRTY-FOUR

"So, daughter," Morton Halliday said, his voice thick with anger and accusation. "It appears all the rumors were true, after all. Did you know what he was when you married him?"

Lorena nodded, a sense of guilt sweeping through her when she glanced at the thick bandage that covered the dreadful bite on her father's neck. She sat on the sofa, hands clenched in her lap. They had spent the last hour cleaning up the mess. They had thrown the bloody carpet away. Her father had burned the vampire's heart. The bodies had been carried into the barn until they could be taken to town.

"You knew?" Grace exclaimed, her eyes wide with disbelief. "You knew and yet you brought him into our home. You married him. How could you? The man is a monster."

"When you were so sick, he saved your life, Mama. And he saved all of you tonight."

Halliday snorted. "We would not have been in danger if you'd never wed the man."

"You can't blame Demetri for this!" she exclaimed. "Blame Oliver. He hired Serghei to destroy Demetri."

"Oliver Ainsley?" Grace shook her head. "A man of his breeding? I just can't believe it."

"He's the monster," Lorena retorted. "He and Lord Fairfield once kept Demetri locked in a cage in a cellar and denied him…nourishment. They were going to kill him when he'd done nothing to them. Nothing!"

"Good riddance," Halliday said, pacing the floor. "He's left all of us in a hell of a fix. No one's going to believe what happened here. No one. Hell, I can hardly believe it myself. And how are we supposed to explain the deaths of the men who were killed here tonight?"

She had no answer for that. Oliver was of the nobility. Who would believe he was a vampire hunter? No one would take her family's word over his, although what plausible excuse Oliver could come up with for being here was beyond her. Of course, Oliver could simply deny he had been there at all, since they had no way of proving it.

But none of that mattered now. All that mattered was Demetri.

Where had he gone?

Was he coming back?

Demetri transported his grisly burden several miles away from town. A barren stretch of ground in the heart of a grove of trees served as a burial place. He made sure the hole was deep before he dumped Serghei's remains into the grave. It took only a few moments to replace the dirt.

He stood there a short while, his skin tingling from the heat of the sun, his face, hands and clothing splattered with Serghei's blood and his own. No doubt he looked like a grave-robber. Or a ghoul.

Disgusted by his own stink, he willed himself home. After making sure Lorena had not returned, he filled the tub with water and heated it with a glance. Removing his clothing, he bundled them together and tossed them aside. He would burn them later.

Lowering himself into the tub, he closed his eyes. His wounds had all healed, leaving no trace behind. He had lost a good deal of blood during the battle, arousing his need to feed. The scent of Halliday's blood, combined with that of Stanton and Dutton, had been almost overpowering. It had taken all his self-control not to bury his fangs in Halliday's neck.

But, temptation or not, he shouldn't have left Lorena behind to face her family alone.

Stepping out of the tub, he quickly dried off. A thought lit a fire in the hearth and he threw his bloody clothes into the flames.

Minutes later, clad in a clean shirt and trousers, he pulled on his boots, then donned a hat, cloak, and gloves to protect himself from the light of the morning sun. He needed to feed before he did anything else. He entertained a fleeting thought of dining on Ainsley, but the thought was unappealing. As was the thought of leaving the man alive a second longer.

But his first priority was to feed, something much more difficult to accomplish in the light of day.

And then he needed to see Lorena.

Her father answered the door, pistol in hand. "You!" he hissed. "How dare you come back here."

"I wish to see my wife."

"You are no longer welcome in this house."

"May I remind you, sir, that this is *my* house. Now, put that pistol down and get out of my way."

"Demetri!" Lorena threw herself into his arms when he crossed the threshold. Her gaze ran over him, relief evident in her eyes when she saw he was unhurt.

"I have come to take you home, if you want to go."

"Of course, I do."

"How can you go with that creature?" Halliday demanded. "You've seen what he is. What has he done to you, that you would go with him now?"

"I love him, Papa. No matter what."

"You're a fool!"

Crying, "No," Lorena threw herself in front of Demetri as her father fired the pistol.

Lorena stared uncomprehending at the bright red stain that blossomed across the bodice of her dress.

Demetri caught her before she fell.

For a moment, there was silence in the room. Then pandemonium as Grace and the girls burst into tears.

"What have I done?" His face ashen, Halliday stared at the gun in his hand, then tossed it away.

"Help her, please," Grace begged. "She said you healed me when I was ill. Can you not heal her, as well?"

"She is not ill," he said, cradling Lorena to his chest. "She is dying." He had only moments to decide whether to let her go or bestow the dark gift upon her. Aware of the seconds ticking by, he transported the two of them to his bedroom. Sitting on the edge of the bed, he caressed her cheek. Her heart beat was slow and uneven, her face pale. So pale.

For once, the scent of her blood did not tempt him.

How could he make this decision for her? They had discussed it once. He remembered it clearly. He had told her she was very young to be worrying about aging, that she had plenty of time. *When you are older,* he had said, *we can discuss it.*

But unless he turned her in the next few moments, she would never grow older.

Tears stung his eyes. "Forgive me, my love," he whispered as he lowered his head to her neck. "But I cannot let you go."

CHAPTER THIRTY-FIVE

She dreamed of walking through the night, but a night like no other. The sky was crimson-red, the trees were black and twisted, and the air…it smelled of blood. Hot. Fresh. A figure moved through the darkness, a moonlit shadow in a long black cloak. Voices told her to run, that he was a monster. Evil. Inhuman. But he seemed so lonely. She took a step toward him and when she did, he whirled around to face her and all she could see were his eyes—as red as flame. And then another voice, a familiar voice, urging her to drink…to drink and live…

Demetri remained at Lorena's side all through the night. He had never turned anyone before, had been tormented as he wondered what the results would be had he done it wrong. Would she simply slip away? Or transform into something neither vampire nor human, but some grotesque abomination in-between?

He breathed a sigh of relief as the color slowly returned to her cheeks, smiled as the beat of her heart grew stronger. Her skin took on a faint translucence that few mortals would notice. She would sleep through the rest of the night and tomorrow, and wake with the setting of the sun into a whole new world.

Certain she was no longer in any danger from the change, Demetri set new wards around the property and then left the house.

Although it was late, lights still burned in the Halliday's front window. A wave of his hand opened the door. Fear and shock chased themselves across the faces of her parents. The girls cowered back against the sofa, their eyes wide and afraid.

"Look at me, all of you."

Unable to resist his command, they obediently met his gaze, their expressions impassive as his power washed over them. When they were in his thrall, he erased all memory of what had happened from their minds and planted a different memory, one where they had spent a pleasant evening together, one where sparks from the fire had badly singed the rug in front of the hearth to explain its absence. He found Halliday's pistol and tucked it into the waistband of his trousers, checked to make sure there were no telltale traces of blood left on the floor or the walls.

When he was satisfied with the condition of the house, he headed for the barn, hefted a body on each shoulder and carried them into town. He dumped Stanton and Dutton in an alley behind one of the local taverns and quickly relieved them of their cash and valuables.

Satisfied that the town's people would assume the two men had been robbed, he returned to the Hallidays'. Swinging onto the stallion's back, he took up the reins of Lorena's mount and headed for home.

When he returned to the bedroom, he found Lorena as he had left her—looking like a sleeping princess in a fairy tale.

Undressing, he crawled into bed, put his arm around her and surrendered to the dark sleep.

CHAPTER THIRTY-SIX

Oliver Ainsley cowered in his bedroom as the sun peeked through the clouds. He hadn't been able to rest since Serghei's grisly death the night before, hadn't eaten or slept, hadn't been able to think clearly. He had been a hunter for years, but never had he seen anything as gruesome as watching two vampires try to tear each other apart. He had driven stakes into vampire hearts, but he'd never ripped a living one from a man's chest.

He had fled the house in terror but he hadn't gone far. Some morbid sense of curiosity had sent him creeping back. He was sorry now that he had. He had peered through the window just in time to see Lorena throw herself in front of Demetri, taking the bullet meant for the vampire. And now the vampire lived and the woman he had loved—the only woman he had ever loved—was dead. Dutton and Stanton were also dead. Not by his hand and yet guilt festered inside him. They would not have been there at all but for him. What had Demetri done with the bodies? He poured himself another drink. He couldn't contact their families, had to plead ignorance should they contact him for information of their whereabouts.

He downed the whiskey in a single swallow. How soon would Demetri come after him and exact vengeance for causing Lorena's death? He shuddered as he imagined the vampire's hand reaching into his chest and ripping out his beating heart.

Staggering to the wardrobe, he withdrew a lacquered mahogany box from the top shelf. Inside, nestled on a bed of rich red velvet, rested a pair of gleaming dueling pistols.

CHAPTER THIRTY-SEVEN

Demetri woke thirty minutes before sunset, his first thought for Lorena. She hadn't moved since last night. Her breathing was slow, but that was normal. What would she think when she woke? How would she handle the first, unavoidable hunger pain that welcomed every fledgling? Would she fight the urge to feed, thereby making the pain worse? He had no experience with fledglings, only his own memories. His sire had told him what he needed to know to survive and abandoned him a few days later.

A thought lit the lamp beside the bed so that she wouldn't awake in darkness. His nerves were strung tight when she took a deep breath, moaned softly, and opened her eyes.

"Good evening, my love," he murmured.

"Demetri. I had the most unusual dream."

"I am not surprised, after what happened yesterday."

"Yesterday?" She frowned a moment, then bolted upright. "We need to go see my parents, try to explain..."

"There is nothing to explain."

"What do you mean?"

"The bodies have been buried. The memory of Serghei and everything that happened has been erased from their minds."

"Erased?"

He nodded once, curtly.

"But...how?"

"I simply wiped it from their minds and planted another memory."

She blinked at him and then, with a cry, clutched her stomach.

Demetri brushed a lock of hair from her brow. "Relax, my love."

"Something's wrong. Make it stop."

He bit into his wrist and held it in front of her.

She stared at the dark red blood oozing from the shallow wound, her expression one of revulsion, and then she grabbed his arm and sank her fangs into his flesh.

He let her drink until, abruptly, she lifted her head, her eyes wide with fear and confusion. "What's wrong with me?"

"What else do you remember of yesterday?"

She frowned. "You disappeared after the fight was over. And took Serghei's body away, didn't you?"

"Go on."

"My parents were angry. Papa worried about how he was going to explain two dead bodies...When you came back to get me, my father was still furious. He...he threatened you with a pistol..." Her voice trailed off as her frown deepened. "My father..." She pressed her hand to her chest. "My father shot me." She lifted her gaze to his. "He shot me."

"Yes."

"There's no wound. You healed me, didn't you? Like you healed my mother."

"Not quite."

"What do you mean?"

"You were dying..."

"So was my mother."

"She would have lived another day or two. But you were past the point where I could heal you."

"Then how…?" Her eyes widened in disbelief. "You didn't… did you?"

"I could not lose you, love," he said, his voice thick with anguish. "Hate me if you wish, but I could not let you go."

"It wasn't a dream," she murmured. Brow furrowed, she stared at the floor, and then her head jerked up. "I'm a vampire, aren't I?"

"Yes."

She stared at him, then glanced around the room. "Everything looks different. Sounds different. Smells different." She lifted her hands, turned them back and forth. "I'm different."

"Lorena…"

"I want to be alone."

With a nod of assent, he left the room and closed the door behind him.

Lorena ran her fingers over her face, stripped off her undergarments and trailed her hands over her body. Was she still Lorena? She felt the same, yet different. Stronger. More confident.

She would never see the sun again. Never indulge in the custard tarts she loved. Her parents would hate her, the way they hated Demetri. She would have to learn to hunt. Why wasn't the thought more repulsive? She had bitten Demetri and reveled in it. How long before he would let her bite him again?

She should be shocked, horrified, by her thoughts. Why wasn't she?

She knew Demetri was standing outside her door. She could sense his presence, his distress, the guilt he felt for what he'd done. Why did he feel guilty? He had saved her life. Was he sorry?

Was she?

Going to the window, she drew back the heavy drapes and stared out into the darkness, let out a harsh cry of denial when her reflection didn't stare back at her from the window pane. She would never see herself again, never be able to see how she looked in her beautiful cheval mirror.

The door flew open and Demetri rushed inside. He glanced around, then frowned. "Are you in pain?"

Tears dripped down her cheeks as she fell into his arms. "I can't see myself," she wailed. "I don't exist anymore."

"Of course you do, my love," he said, patting her back. "You will get used to it, in time."

"I ... I don't want to."

He held her close while she cried. He knew it wasn't just her lack of a reflection behind her tears, it was the sudden, overwhelming realization of the life she had lost and would never have again. He had experienced the same sense of loss, of grief, although in a vastly different way. He had not wept his anguish. Instead, he had gone on a killing spree that, thankfully, had lasted only one night.

Gradually, her tears slowed, followed by a deep, shuddering breath.

Lifting a corner of the sheet, he dried her eyes, fetched her a glass of wine.

"I'd rather have tea," she remarked, a note of resignation in her voice. But she drained the goblet.

His gaze searched hers. "Lorena, did I make the wrong choice?"

She stared into her empty glass. Would she rather be Nosferatu, or dead? Cold in her grave, or warm in Demetri's embrace? "No. I can't say I'm glad to be a vampire, but I am glad to be alive." She wasn't undead, she thought as she pressed a hand to her heart. It still beat. She still breathed. She could see and hear and feel. Taste the wine, sweet on her tongue. *Vampire.* She had never believed in them, and then she had met Demetri. And now she was like him. It seemed impossible. She wanted to hate him, but how could she? She loved him no matter what he was, no matter what he'd done. True, her old life was gone, but he had given her a new one.

Setting the goblet aside, she cupped his cheek in her palm and kissed him. "Thank you for saving me."

"I feared you would hate me."

"Never. Will my family be able to tell that I've changed?"

"Perhaps."

"Do I look different?"

His gaze moved over her face. "Yes. And no. You look much the same. Your skin is a little paler, your eyes a little brighter, your hair a little more lustrous. If they do not see you for several days, they may not notice." He ran his fingers through the heavy fall of her hair. "How do you feel?"

"Wonderful. As if I could run for miles and miles and never get tired."

He laughed softly. "You can."

"Will you let me drink from you again when I get hungry? Or is it thirsty?"

"If you like."

"It's not really hunger or thirst, is it?" she murmured thoughtfully. "More like a combination of the two."

He smiled, amused by the turn of her thoughts, by her growing acceptance of it all. He had been so afraid she would despise him, hate what she had become. Worried that she might choose to walk into the sun and end her life rather than face her new reality.

"I want to go outside," she said. "Can we?"

"If you wish."

"I do!"

It took only minutes to get ready. When she stepped through the front door, it was like emerging into a brand new world. Always before, things had been dull, colorless, in the dark. Now, she saw everything as though the sun was still shining overhead. Sights and sounds and smells assaulted her senses. The sky had never looked so big, the stars so close, the moon so bright.

Lorena turned in a slow circle. "This is amazing!" she exclaimed. "How could anyone not want this?" She threw her arms around him. Unaccustomed to her new strength, she knocked him backward. Laughing, he wrapped his arms around her and fell back on the ground.

Still holding her tight, he claimed her lips with his. The touch of his mouth on hers sparked a flame deep within her. A kiss wasn't enough. Would never be enough. In seconds, their clothes vanished. The grass was cool and damp against her bare skin, but it didn't matter. Nothing mattered but being in Demetri's arms.

She gasped his name when he tucked her beneath him, his eyes hot with need and desire.

She wanted him, she thought, needed him with a desperation she'd never felt before. Always before, when they made love, he had been gentle, as if she were made of spun glass and might shatter in his arms. But tonight was different. There was no holding back now and she gloried in his possession, the power in his touch, the low growl in his voice as he declared he loved her, would always love her.

And then he was rising over her, and there was no more time for thought.

Later, wrapped in the warmth and security of his arms, Lorena gazed up at the star-studded sky. And then, to her surprise, her mind touched Demetri's. She frowned as she read his thoughts. She had expected him to be thinking of her, of the incredible passion they had just shared. Instead, he was thinking of death. Oliver Ainsley's death.

"You said you wouldn't kill Oliver," she reminded him.

"It is no longer a subject open to discussion. He dies. Tonight."

"But…"

"I warned him to leave me alone. He is to blame for everything that's happened. Had Serghei defeated me, your family would be dead now and you…you would be in Ainsley's house. I will not allow him the opportunity to try again."

"But…everything turned out all right."

"Stanton and Dutton are dead," Demetri reminded her. "That, too, is Ainsley's fault." Not that he cared. They had both been hunters. But they had died needlessly, leaving behind grieving widows and children.

Rising, he took Lorena's hands in his and pulled her to her feet. Side by side, they gathered their clothing and returned to the house.

"I'm going to take a bath," Lorena said with a come-hither smile. "Will you wash my back?"

"Whatever my lady wants," he said, flashing her a wicked grin.

He waited until she stepped into the bedroom, then pulled on his trousers, shirt, and boots and left the house.

Moments later, Demetri materialized on the porch in front of Ainsley's manor house. To his surprise, the door opened silently. Odd, he thought. He would have expected Ainsley to have set guards around the perimeter, and to have revoked his invitation.

Demetri paused inside the door. The house was eerily silent. And empty of life.

He found Ainsley sprawled on the floor of his bedroom, the side of his head a bloody pulp. A dueling pistol lay near his hand.

"Coward to the last," Demetri murmured.

Lorena smiled when Demetri materialized beside the bath tub. "Will you teach me how to do that?"

"And much more." Kneeling beside the tub, he took the lavender-scented soap from her hand.

Noticing his serious expression, her smile faded "You killed him, didn't you?"

"Sadly, no. He took his own life."

"I hope it was quick."

"Quicker than I would have hoped."

Lorena bit down on her lip as he washed her back. And her front. At any other time, it would have been a pleasurable experience, a time for laughter and teasing. But not tonight. It wasn't her that Demetri was thinking about as his hands moved over her, but Oliver. Was he sorry his enemy was dead? Or only sorry that he hadn't been the one responsible for taking his life? A little voice in the back of her mind warned her not to ask.

He rose and left the room when she stepped out of the tub.

Lorena dried off, pulled on her nightgown and robe and went in search of her husband.

She found him in the back parlor. He stood in front of the fireplace, staring into the hearth, a glass of wine in his hand. His dark eyes were hooded when he turned to look at her.

"Do you want to be alone?" she asked.

"No, my love. I have been alone most of my life until you." Setting the crystal goblet on the mantel, he opened his arms.

She went to him gladly, sighed as he folded her into his embrace.

"You have a lot to learn," he said quietly. "How to defend yourself, how to recognize hunters, how to call prey to you, and erase your memory from their minds. So many things."

"Good thing I have all the time in the world to learn, isn't it?" She might live for centuries, impossible as that seemed. The very idea was going to take some getting used to.

"Indeed." His gaze burned into hers, hot and hungry. "I have many other things to teach you, my love. Far more pleasant things," he said as he caressed her cheek. "But I must warn you, some of them will make you blush."

"I look forward to your instruction, my lord husband. Perhaps we should start tonight?"

"A splendid suggestion," he said, as he swung her into his arms and carried her swiftly up the stairs to his room. "Maybe we should."

~*finis*~

Surrender the Dawn
By Amanda Ashley

Angelina Rossi has always been fascinated with vampires. She loves the movies, the TV shows, the books. After reading a love story between a woman and a vampire, she finds herself yearning for a love like that. What if vampires really do exist?

Determined to find out, Angie searches every Goth club in the city, ending up at a nightclub called Nick's Nightmare. The attraction between Angie and Declan Nicolae, the club's owner, is instant and undeniable.

Declan is an ancient vampire who, having once tasted Angie's blood, is determined to never let her go. For a time, romance blooms and all is well, until Samantha, Angie's best friend, becomes one of the Undead and Angie learns vampires do exist...and that the man she loves is one of them.

Surrender the Dawn
Chapter One

*A*nd *so he bestowed on her the vampire's kiss, sweeping her into a world of love and a life that would never end.*

With a heartfelt sigh, Angelina Rossi closed the book. If only she could find a love as lasting and fulfilling as the one portrayed in the novel. A love that was stronger, deeper, and more enduring than mere mortal attraction.

If only vampires truly existed. Not that she really wanted to meet one, but what if they *were* real? They had always fascinated her, ever since she saw her first *Dracula* movie at the tender age of eight. Instead of being frightened or rooting for the hero, she had been enchanted by the monster. She had even shed a tear when the hero drove a stake into the vampire's heart. To this day, in books, movies, or plays, she felt sympathy for the poor Undead creatures.

Setting the book aside, Angie padded to the front window, drew back the curtain, and peered out into the darkness. What if vampires were real? Was that really so far-fetched? After all, stories and legends of the Undead went back thousands of years and were cited in every nation and country on earth. If such creatures were only myth, why had the tales of their existence lasted so long? Bookstores and libraries had entire sections devoted to vampires and the supernatural.

Why waste all that shelf space on something that never existed? People believed in witches. Why not vampires?

Even as the thought crossed her mind, she knew it wasn't a valid argument. After all, there were tons of books about Bigfoot and the Loch Ness monster and space aliens, too. There was no hard evidence to back up the existence of any of those creatures, either. Of course, lots of people said they had seen Bigfoot and Nessie. Some folks claimed to have pictures, although all the ones she had seen looked photoshopped. She had never heard of anyone who claimed to have seen a vampire. Then again, maybe those who saw one didn't live long enough to tell anyone.

A sobering thought.

Wishing real life was more like the romance novels she loved, Angie turned away from the window. And then she grinned. Maybe she should put an ad in the paper.

Wanted: Tall, dark. handsome stranger who prefers the night. Objective…

Angie frowned. She had no objective, just an over-active imagination. But she couldn't help wondering if tall, dark, handsome, creatures of the night did exist, and if so, were they as romantic as the ones she read about? Or scary, blood-sucking monsters like the ones portrayed in the movies?

With a shake of her head, Angie turned off the lights and went to bed. Maybe she needed to see a shrink, she mused as she pulled the covers up to her chin. After all, who in their right mind would *want* to come face-to-face with one of the children of the night?

In the morning, Angie carried a cup of coffee into her home office and settled down in front of her computer. She had been working as a freelance columnist for a local magazine for the last three years. It wasn't the best paying job in the world, but it was something she could do at home in her PJs, which was a big plus as far as she was concerned. Not only that, but her editor, Jennifer Martin, had given her *carte blanche* to pick and choose her own topics.

She worked steadily, taking a fifteen-minute break to stand and stretch every hour or so. As always when she was writing, the time flew by. She broke for lunch at one.

In the kitchen, while preparing a ham and cheese sandwich, she found herself thinking about vampires again. What if they *were* real, she mused while she ate. Did they really sleep in coffins? Were they truly dead to the world when the sun was up? Why would they be repelled by garlic? Or crosses? Or silver? What happened if they didn't like blood? Were they really immortal? If vampires didn't have a soul, and they weren't really alive, were they just animated corpses, like zombies? She shuddered. How disgusting would that be?

Maybe she needed to stop reading paranormal romances and start reading cozy mysteries instead.

And maybe not.

Back at her desk, she stared, unseeing at her computer screen. If someone wanted to find a vampire, where would they look?

Google, of course! She would go online as soon as she finished her work for the day.

Angie stood in front of the mirror in the bathroom, carefully applying her make-up. She had spent hours online looking for vampires, and while she hadn't found any links to the real thing, she had found numerous books and movies on the subject, as well as half a dozen web sites advertising Goth clubs that claimed to be hangouts for creatures of the night. Curious to see what they were all about, she had jotted down the addresses of the five closest to home.

Hoping "creatures of the night" applied only to the Undead and not werewolves, zombies, demons, or trolls, Angie stepped into her heels, grabbed her handbag and keys, and left the house.

Drac's Den was the first tavern on her list. Angie shook her head when she stepped through the door. The walls were black, the floor tiled in bright red. No doubt so the blood wouldn't show, she thought with a grimace as she made her way toward the long, curved bar in the back.

The bartender, clad in a white shirt and long, black cape, leered at her as he took her order. It was all she could do not to laugh in his face when he flashed his obviously fake plastic fangs at her.

She carried her drink to a small table where she could people-watch. Men and women alike wore nothing but black. The men sported suits, some looking new while others looked like they had been bought from second-hand stores. The women all wore long dresses. Black lipstick and eye shadow made their faces look pale in the dim light. Most of them also had long, straight, black hair, real or fake.

With a shake of her head, Angie finished her drink and left the tavern. Maybe she would have better luck tomorrow night.

Angie went to a different nightclub every Saturday night for the next four weeks—Nick's Nightmare, the Devil's Tavern, Mel's Hell, and The Pit.

She was amazed to discover that so many people spent their weekends pretending to be creatures of the night. In her search for a genuine vampire, she had seen some truly bizarre things, like the man who had filed his teeth to sharp points, a woman who carried a flask rumored to be filled with real blood, and the man who led his girlfriend around on a slender gold chain. Angie had learned that some wanna-be vampires actually indulged in drinking from each other, which she found beyond gross.

At home that night, she tossed her handbag on the sofa, kicked off her shoes, and decided she had wasted enough time looking for the Undead. No more vampire haunts for her. The Pit had been the last stop. Goth clubs—and the people who frequented them—were just too weird.

Despite her good intentions, she found herself back at Nick's Nightmare the following Saturday night. Of all the places she had visited, this one seemed to be the most "normal." Sort of like Halloween every night, with men and women in bizarre costumes but behaving—mostly—like regular people with a peculiar penchant for the macabre. The décor was dark but not grim, the music low and sensual, the lighting subdued.

Angie had been sitting at the bar nursing a drink for about ten minutes when a man sat down next to her. He was of medium height and not bad looking, but the way he leered at her creeped her out.

"Hello, gorgeous," he drawled. "Can I buy you a drink?"

"No, thank you."

He rested one hand on her knee. "How about a dance?"

"No," she said, her voice frigid as she pushed his hand away. "Thank you."

"Come on, honey, don't play hard to get."

She was debating what to do next when a deep, male voice said, "Take a hike, Mulgrew."

The man stood and left without a word.

Angie glanced over her shoulder to see a tall, broad-shouldered man with dark hair and compelling green eyes looming over her. Like every other man in the place, he was dressed all in black, but on him, it looked fabulous. She recalled seeing him in a couple of the other nightclubs, always in the company of one pretty woman or another.

Tonight, he was alone.

He gestured at the stool beside her. "May I?"

"It's a free country."

"I've seen you in here before." He made a vague gesture with his hand, encompassing the room behind them. "You don't seem like the type to frequent places like this."

"Oh? Why is that?"

"Well, for starters, you're dressed all wrong."

Angie stared at her white slacks and navy-blue sweater and shrugged. "I left my Halloween costume at home."

His laugh was deep and sensual and the sound of it did funny things in the pit of her stomach. "The Goth crowd." His voice slid over her like silk over velvet. "They always look like they're in mourning, don't they?"

She lifted one brow. "So do you."

"*Touché*, my lady. I've seen you in some of the other nightclubs," he remarked. "Are you looking for something special?"

"Excuse me?"

Brow furrowed, he studied her a moment, and then he grinned. "Sorry."

Wondering what he was apologizing for, she said, "I've seen you in those other places, too. Were *you* looking for—how did you put it? Something special?"

"I was." His gaze moved over her.

The intensity of it made Angie's toes curl even as it sent a shaft of unexpected desire spiraling through her. She licked her lips, feeling as if she had suddenly strayed into unknown territory. "And now?" she asked, tremulously.

"I think maybe I've found it."

Suddenly frightened without knowing why, Angie grabbed her handbag, muttered, "It was nice meeting you. Good night," and practically ran out the door.

Back at home, safe inside her own house, with the front door double-locked behind her, she felt suddenly foolish. What on earth was wrong with her? Sure, it had been a long time since a handsome man flirted with her but that was no reason to behave like some silly schoolgirl.

With a sigh, she tossed her handbag on the sofa, kicked off her shoes and headed for her bedroom.

Muttering, "The next time some sexy guy makes a pass at you, try to act like a grown-up," she undressed and crawled into bed, only to lie there, wide-awake and restless, the memory of his deep, silky smooth voice echoing in her mind.

ABOUT THE AUTHOR

Amanda Ashley started writing for the fun of it. Her first book, a historical romance written as Madeline Baker, was published in 1985. Since then, she has published numerous historical and paranormal romances and novellas, many of which have appeared on various bestseller lists, including the *New York Times* Bestseller List and *USA Today*.

Amanda makes her home in Southern California, where she and her husband share their house with a Pomeranian named Lady, a cat named Kitty, and a tortoise named Buddy.

For more information on her books, please visit her websites at

www.amandaashley.net

and

www.madelinebaker.net

Email: darkwritr@aol.com

About the Publisher

This book is published on behalf of the author by the Ethan Ellenberg Literary Agency.
https://ethanellenberg.com
Email: agent@ethanellenberg.com

Manufactured by Amazon.ca
Bolton, ON

39826914R00175